PRAISE FOR MEL.

"With her wonderful characters and resonating emotions, Melissa Foster is a must-read author!"

—*New York Times* bestseller Julie Kenner

"Melissa Foster is synonymous with sexy, swoony, heartfelt romance!"

—*New York Times* bestseller Lauren Blakely

"You can always rely on Melissa Foster to deliver a story that's fresh, emotional, and entertaining."

—*New York Times* bestseller Brenda Novak

"Melissa Foster writes worlds that draw you in, with strong heroes and brave heroines surrounded by a community that makes you want to crawl right on through the page and live there."

—*New York Times* bestseller Julia Kent

"When it comes to contemporary romances with realistic characters, an emotional love story, and smokin'-hot sex, author Melissa Foster always delivers!"

—*The Romance Reviews*

"Foster writes characters that are complex and loyal, and each new story brings further depth and development to a redefined concept of family."

—*RT Book Reviews*

"Melissa Foster definitely knows how to spin a tale and keep you flipping the pages."

—*Book Loving Fairy*

LOVE
like
OURS

MORE BOOKS BY MELISSA FOSTER

LOVE IN BLOOM ROMANCE SERIES

SNOW SISTERS

Sisters in Love
Sisters in Bloom
Sisters in White

THE BRADENS

Lovers at Heart
Destined for Love
Friendship on Fire
Sea of Love
Bursting with Love
Hearts at Play
Taken by Love
Fated for Love
Romancing My Love
Flirting with Love
Dreaming of Love
Crashing into Love
Healed by Love
Surrender My Love
River of Love
Crushing on Love
Whisper of Love
Thrill of Love

THE BRADENS & MONTGOMERYS

Embracing Her Heart
Anything for Love
Trails of Love

BRADEN NOVELLAS

Promise My Love
Our New Love
Daring Her Love
Story of Love
Love at Last

THE REMINGTONS

Game of Love
Stroke of Love
Flames of Love
Slope of Love
Read, Write, Love
Touched by Love

SEASIDE SUMMERS

Seaside Dreams
Seaside Hearts
Seaside Sunsets
Seaside Secrets
Seaside Nights
Seaside Embrace
Seaside Lovers
Seaside Whispers

BAYSIDE SUMMERS

Bayside Desires
Bayside Passions
Bayside Heat
Bayside Escape

THE RYDERS

Seized by Love
Claimed by Love
Chased by Love
Rescued by Love
Swept into Love

SUGAR LAKE

The Real Thing
Only for You

SEXY STAND-ALONE ROMANCE

Tru Blue
Truly, Madly, Whiskey

Driving Whiskey Wild
Wicked Whiskey Love

BILLIONAIRES AFTER DARK SERIES

Wild Boys After Dark

Logan
Heath
Jackson
Cooper

Bad Boys After Dark

Mick
Dylan
Carson
Brett

HARBORSIDE NIGHTS SERIES

Includes characters from the Love in Bloom Series

Catching Cassidy
Discovering Delilah
Tempting Tristan

STAND-ALONE NOVELS

Chasing Amanda (mystery/suspense)
Come Back to Me (mystery/suspense)
Have No Shame (historical fiction/romance)
Love, Lies & Mystery (three-book bundle)
Megan's Way (literary fiction)
Traces of Kara (psychological thriller)
Where Petals Fall (suspense)

LOVE
like
OURS

MELISSA
FOSTER

Montlake
Romance

Published by Montlake Romance, Seattle

www.apub.com

Amazon, the Amazon logo, and Montlake Romance are trademarks of Amazon.com, Inc., or its affiliates.

ISBN-13: 9781503905450
ISBN-10: 1503905454

Cover design by Letitia Hasser

Cover photography by Wander Aguiar

Printed in the United States of America

For families and caregivers struggling to navigate life with Alzheimer's.

CHAPTER ONE

"YOU NEED A reset. A total overhaul," Piper insisted. "If you were a house, I'd tear out a few of the walls and open them up, redecorate—"

"She's not a *house*," Bridgette said. "And she doesn't need to redecorate. She's gorgeous."

"Well, she needs to unlock that chastity belt, or I'll cut the damn thing off," Piper threatened.

"Stop!" Talia Dalton snapped at her younger sisters over Bluetooth as she drove through the quaint town of Harmony Pointe, toward Beckwith University, the small private college where she taught. Balancing her coffee and the steering wheel, she tried to whip her head to the side to move a wayward lock of hair that had flown into her eyes. As if her family's pestering wasn't enough, she had to drive with her window cracked when it was snowing out because her car had developed a weird odor overnight. If only she could start the day over. She'd have turned her phone *off*.

"This is why I didn't come by to have breakfast with you guys," Talia said. She and her family often stopped in at their sister Willow's bakery to touch base before their days got crazy. "I do not need a total anything. I'm perfectly . . . *content*."

"Content isn't *happy*," Willow said. She had recently wed actor-turned-screenplay-screenwriter Zane Walker, and they were joyously, blissfully in love.

Talia would give *just about anything* to have even a moment of what they had. Well, anything except having her sisters direct her love life. She and her sisters were in the midst of planning a wedding for Bridgette and her fiancé, Bodhi, and unfortunately, her sisters had decided to take on the task of finding Talia a man, too. They'd driven her bonkers over the last few weeks, pushing her to put herself *out there* more often. Talia had a busy life and little patience for dating games. Not that she knew much about them, having dated very little over the past few *years*. She winced at that reality. But men were not the most trustworthy creatures on the planet. A fact she'd learned the hard way. Bridgette and Willow had gotten lucky, which meant there probably weren't many guys left around Sweetwater, their small hometown, who could be trusted the way Zane, Bodhi, and Talia's brother, Ben, could. If only Ben were on the phone with them. He'd help her calm the Dalton chaos, but he was out of town for a business meeting and wouldn't be back until tomorrow.

"You should take a cooking class," Willow said. "You might learn to love cooking, and you might find a great guy there. A chef!"

If she looked like Willow—blond, curvy, and totally unaware of how gorgeous she was—maybe men would flock to her. But Talia took after her father; she was tall, dark, lean, and, above all else, hyperaware of every vibe she put out, verbal or otherwise.

"Chefs don't need classes, Wills," their mother corrected. "But Talia, you could take a sailing lesson or go on one of those singles' cruises."

"You could go to one of Benny's friend Treat Braden's resorts! I hear they're gorgeous."

"Aurelia? You're jumping on the pestering-Talia bandwagon, too?" Talia asked. Aurelia Stark had grown up with them and had recently moved back to Sweetwater. She was helping Willow in the bakery while they figured out the best plan of attack to purchase the bookstore Aurelia's grandmother had once owned and combine it with the bakery.

"It's not a bandwagon," Aurelia said. "It's a . . . sisterhood!"

Someone shoot me now, please?

"Oh! I know! Go to a rave!" Bridgette suggested. "Or hit a bar or go on a bar *crawl!* How fun would that be? All kinds of people go to bars. Heck, Bodhi and I could go with you, although I'd have to ugly up my sexy beast. Either that or learn to fight off skanky hos who try to pick him up."

They all laughed, even Talia, because Bodhi Booker only had eyes for Bridgette and loved her and Louie, her adorable five-year-old son, fiercely.

"There's an idea. We can tramp up Talia for a night," Piper suggested. "Just one night of wildness could pop her cork! What about Fletch? You're taking care of him like he's your man, so . . ."

Talia gritted her teeth and nearly crushed her coffee cup as she white-knuckled the steering wheel with one hand and turned on to the college campus. Ryan "Fletch" Fletcher was Talia's good friend and colleague. His appendix had ruptured, and he'd ended up in the hospital for a week with peritonitis. He was now home recovering, which was why Talia was teaching his classes and walking his adorable Bernese mountain dog, Molly. She was not about to let Piper turn their friendship into a sham.

"Can we please just stop this nonsense? Fletch and I are colleagues and friends, and that is all we will ever be. Some of us, *Piper,* are able to have male friends we don't want to sleep with. I'm a professor, not a playgirl. I can't just go into a bar and throw myself at a man. Not to mention that I would never do that. Trustworthy men don't hang out in bars. And I'm not going to do any of the other things you suggested. This is a journey of the heart, not a mission." She didn't mean to raise her voice, but she was too annoyed to rein herself in. "Men don't just *fall* into people's laps. You *all* know that. If you want to meet the right guy, you have to be in the appropriate place at the perfect time. Life changes don't come easily. I'm not going to wake up tomorrow and suddenly be a mix of each of you!"

"Fine!" Piper relented. Talia pictured her waiflike, and toughest, sister's arms crossed, eyes narrowed, and that construction-booted foot of hers tapping anxiously. "If you want to grow up to be a spinster English literature professor with five cats and a furry pus—"

"Piper!" their mother hollered. "Language, please! Sheesh, you girls go about things the hard way sometimes. How do you feel today, Talia?"

"Annoyed and hungry. Not that I could eat with this stench in my car." She turned in to the parking lot and trolled for a parking spot. "It's like someone dumped perfume in here."

A long stretch of silence followed her comment.

"Oh shit. Mom?" Piper said with a warning tone.

Talia spotted a car pulling out and whipped into the next row.

"Mom . . . ?" The amusement in Willow's voice did not go unnoticed. "Please tell me you didn't."

Talia's ears perked up, but some jackass took her parking space, and she sped to the next aisle. She gulped her coffee, trying to finish before she had to start her class.

"What? It was just a little love potion," their mother said.

Talia spit out her coffee, drenching her shirt. She tried to shove her cup into the holder, ignoring her sister's questions—"What happened? What was that? Talia?"

"Damn it, Mom! Enough with your love potions!" she snapped as she shot a glance at the passenger seat and stretched to snag a tissue from her purse. Her gaze flicked up just as a man darted out in front of the car. Talia slammed on her brakes and screamed.

Shit, shit, shit! She threw her car into park, meeting the angry eyes of the long-haired, scruffy-looking guy she'd almost killed. Two of the largest hands she'd ever seen were pressed flat on the hood. Phone call forgotten, she hurried out of her car, shivering against the frigid winter air.

"Are you okay? I'm so sorry!"

He turned so slowly, she was sure she'd actually hit him. She did a quick visual inspection. Her gaze caught on frayed holes in the tight denim stretched over his thick thighs. She lingered a moment too long there, but *wow*, they were nice-looking. She forced herself to look lower. *No blood. No broken knees. Thank God.*

"Way to keep your eyes on the road," he said in a low, gravelly voice that sounded irritated.

"Sorry!" she snapped, her teeth chattering from cold. She lifted her gaze to meet piercing blue eyes—so shockingly vibrant her breath caught in her throat, making her even more nervous and agitated. "What were you thinking, running out in front of my car like that?" *Holy crap!* She hadn't meant to say that! Now he'd think she was an awful driver *and* a bitch.

He arched a brow so lazily, it grated on her last nerve. His hair was tousled, like he'd rolled out of bed, shoved his feet into boots, and thrown on a parka. *Probably in his eighth year of college, without a single degree. Floating through life without any direction or ambition.*

"Well, you're still standing. That's good." She tried to calm her racing heart. But he was staring at her with the most serious—*and tired?*—expression, like he was either waiting for her to say more or was exhausted from a night of partying and couldn't put together a sentence. What did he want her to do, get down on her knees and apologize? She breathed deeply, forcing a softer tone. "I'm really sorry. I'm usually a much more careful driver. Did I hurt you?"

"No." He ran his large hand over what had to be at least a week's worth of scruff. "You're shaking. Are you sure *you're* okay?"

"I almost killed you. How do you think I am?" *Darn it!* "I'm sorry. I'm just shaken up. But I'm glad you're okay."

He hiked a thumb over his shoulder, and the sun caught on a gold ring on his pinkie. "I've got a class to get to." His lips quirked up and he said, "Eyes on the road next time."

She climbed into her car and cranked the heat, watching him in the distance. Her purse and phone had slid to the floor, and she remembered the call she'd been on when she'd almost killed the guy. She pulled carefully into a parking spot and cut the engine. She retrieved her phone and saw at least a dozen missed calls from her sisters and mother. If she hadn't been so worked up and distracted this wouldn't have happened. She pressed her hand to her chest, breathing deeply in an effort to calm down. Her clothes were wet, and she was shaking, but as she gazed out the windshield, it was those deep-set blue eyes she saw.

"Good Lord," she said. "I almost killed him, all because my family is on a manhunt." She picked up the phone and called Willow.

"Oh my God, are you okay?" Willow asked breathlessly. "We were about to call the police."

"I'm fine, but everyone's crazy scheming stops *now*."

"Are we still on for Friday night?" Derek asked as he pulled his phone from his pocket and checked the time. He had to be at work in an hour, giving him just enough time to pick up his father's meds and grab something to eat.

"Absolutely. My place, around eight. Bring something Mediterranean." India pulled her sunglasses from the top of her mass of corkscrew curls as they left class. "Need me to hold your hand across the parking lot so you don't get hit?"

"Very funny. What I need is for people to watch where they're going." Although he'd been so wiped out this morning, he was practically sleepwalking. He slipped his phone back into his pocket and said, "I thought you had a study group today."

Her brown eyes widened. "Oh shit! I gotta boogie." She kissed his cheek. "Thanks!"

He shook his head, smiling. It struck him that forgetfulness could be funny *or* heartbreaking, as it was with his father, who was suffering from Alzheimer's. His momentary smile faded fast.

As he made his way toward the exit, he passed an open door, and a woman's voice sent a streak of awareness through him. He stopped walking, took a few steps backward, and peered into the room. Sure enough, the *Parking Lot Plower* stood at the front of the class, looking hot as fuck in her body-hugging white blouse, which was speckled with whatever she'd spilled on it this morning, and a beige skirt. She was tall and slim, with full breasts and legs that went on forever. Her hair was like chocolate silk, hanging loose over her shoulders, framing high cheekbones, a slim, perky nose, and serious eyes. She looked completely in control, confident with an air of refinement that reminded him of classic actresses, the very opposite of how rattled she'd appeared that morning. He'd wondered if she was really okay. And hadn't stopped thinking about her since.

He stepped into the doorway to hear her more clearly, wondering how many guys in the class were actually paying attention and not filling their mental spank banks with images for later. She was either oblivious to the sensual vibes she naturally emitted, or excellent at ignoring that vixenish side of herself as she held her chin up high and stood ramrod straight. The epitome of a professional.

"Over the past twenty years," she said as she paced, "changing geopolitical and socioeconomic conditions have shifted society's constructs of American manhood."

Holy shit. What was she lecturing about?

Her gaze swept over the crowd—over *him*—to the other side of the room, then quickly darted back to him.

Hello, beautiful. Remember me? The man you almost killed?

Her eyes widened, and she stumbled for words. He slipped off his parka and settled into a seat, no longer hungry. At least not for food.

CHAPTER TWO

MONDAY EVENING TALIA worked late and stopped by Fletch's house with chicken soup she'd picked up from the diner in Harmony Pointe. She drained the noodles and chicken, to avoid irritating his sensitive stomach, and poured the broth into a bowl. Then she filled Molly's bowl with dog food and brought the soup to Fletch.

She set the bowl on the coffee table. "Your girlfriend stopped by your class today. She seemed more than disappointed to see me rather than you." She was referring to Dina Manco, or as Fletch referred to her, Dina Man-Eater Manco. "She peered into the classroom, gave me a dirty look, and then took off. Are you sure you never hooked up with her?"

Fletch gave her a deadpan look. "Don't demean me like that. I have no idea how the woman got tenured. The woman hits on men like it's her job. More importantly, when are you going to let me set you up with one of my buddies?"

Molly lumbered over and sniffed around Fletch's soup bowl.

"Go finish your dinner, Mol." Talia set her hands on her hips, glaring at him. "You look and feel like hell and you're asking me *that*? Didn't we have a conversation about topics that were off-limits when we first became friends?"

Fletch managed a semi-smile as he pushed up to a sitting position. "We did, but that was eight years ago." He tapped his temple. "I tend to forget things."

"Uh-huh." She plunked herself down beside him on the couch, took off her heels, and tucked one leg beneath her, taking a moment to look him over. His blond hair was matted from sleep, his face had lost its color, and he had gray circles beneath his eyes. He looked like a washed-out version of himself, and beyond exhausted. Fletch was like a brother to her. When they were together, neither one had ulterior motives or hoped for a romantic relationship with the other, which made their relationship easy and comfortable. She reached over and touched his forehead. At least he had no fever. "Can you just get better already? Are you feeling any better?"

"Slowly. I swear it's like this thing zapped two years' worth of my energy," he said, shifting a little on the cushion. "Falling asleep is a nightmare with the pain in my stomach. But don't think you'll thwart my question with your caring nature."

She sighed. "Who got to you? My mother or one of my sisters?"

"A gentleman never tells."

"I'm going to kill them *all*. I almost ran over a man in the parking lot this morning because my sisters and mother were harassing me on the phone. And now my car smells like God knows what from one of my mother's love potions."

He laughed, which turned into coughing, grabbed his chest, and sank back against the cushions with a groan. "Sorry. Good old Roxie."

"Watch out, or I'll sic her on you." Fletch was divorced, and everyone knew better than to try to hook him up with anyone. His ex-wife had cheated on him, leaving him with the same lack of trust in the opposite sex that Talia had, which was probably why they were such good friends. Well, that and the fact that they had many things in common, like how seriously they took their careers and their love of academics.

She nodded toward the soup. "Eat. You need your nourishment. The guy I nearly killed is one of your students. He showed up late to class, ogled me for the longest time without ever cracking a notebook, and then he left early. I get so sick of students who aren't serious. They're just wasting money."

"Half the kids in our classes have never had to earn a penny in their life. They have no idea how valuable the education is that they're wasting. But as far as being ogled goes, you just described the habits of just about every girl I've ever taught. Only they usually show up wearing slinky outfits. What does the guy look like?"

"I don't know. He had blue eyes." Blue eyes that she couldn't *stop* seeing, and broad shoulders. *Really* broad shoulders and powerful thighs . . . "And long hair," she said to distract herself from going any further off the deep end. "I want to drag his butt to a barber."

And now that she was thinking about it, that butt of his was pretty darn nice, too.

Oh God . . . Now I'm thinking like Piper.

"Again, that describes way too many guys, Tal. Take it as a compliment. Every student's got a dirty-professor fantasy. Don't pretend half your students don't fantasize about you."

"I wouldn't know. I see them as *students* not *guys.*"

"Mm-hm. Then why's the guy you nailed in the parking lot sitting between us on the couch?" He arched a brow and ate a spoonful of broth.

"He is *not!*"

Fletch chuckled, then grabbed his stomach, moaning with pain. Talia reached for the bowl and set it on the coffee table. "Lie back and put your feet up. I'll get you some water."

She pushed to her feet, and he grabbed her hand. "It wasn't your mother or sisters. I care about you, and hot girls aren't supposed to spend their evenings playing nursemaid and walking their friend's dog."

She didn't think of herself as *hot*, but they'd been through that argument before and she wasn't about to get into it again.

Molly lumbered over with her leash in her mouth and whined.

Talia loved her up. "I love your dog. But if you keep talking about setting me up with your friends, you'll have to find someone else to bring you soup. It'll be just me and Molly, right, girl? Your daddy can wither away to bones for all we care if he doesn't stop the setup talk."

Molly licked Talia's cheek.

"I think she agrees." Talia filled a glass with water.

After Fletch was situated, Talia bundled up in her long red coat, thick wool scarf, and gloves and headed outside with Molly. Molly loved to walk through town and greeted everyone they passed. Every few steps she bit at the snow piled up beside the sidewalk. It was a game to her, catching snow, and Talia was sure it was the dog's way of reminding her that she'd like to catch a few snowballs.

Their breath clouded in the frigid air. Talia didn't mind the cold when she was dressed for it, unlike this morning, when she hadn't had her coat on and her top had been wet with coffee. Her mind drifted back to her encounter with Mr. Blue Eyes. She conjured his face, and her body heated up. He wasn't even her type. And she *definitely* had a type, which did not include long hair, torn jeans, or disrespectfully attending classes late and leaving early.

She slowed as a couple stopped to pet Molly.

"He's beautiful," the woman said.

"He's a she," Talia said, glad for the distraction from her thoughts. "*Molly*, and thank you. She belongs to a friend."

The man hugged the woman and kissed her cheek. "If you want one, we can get one."

"Maybe after the baby's born." The woman touched her belly, which was hidden behind a puffy coat. They thanked her and went on their way.

A pang of longing washed through Talia, and she huffed out a breath. She hadn't thought of her single status very often until Willow had fallen in love with Zane and then Bridgette and Bodhi had found each other. She was thrilled for her sisters, truly she was. But it was like their happiness had flicked a switch inside her, creating some sort of alert system she had no control over.

Now she had inescapable, and *annoying*, pangs nearly every time she saw a happy couple.

"Come on, Mol," she said, and led her to the corner to cross the street toward the park. Throwing snowballs seemed a much better option than dodging *pangs*.

When the light changed and the line of cars came to a halt, Talia and Molly headed into the street. As they approached the center of the road, a Subaru that had been stopped at the crosswalk inched forward. Talia stopped, gripping Molly's leash tighter, and waited for the car to stop again.

"Come on, girl," Talia said, taking a step forward and watching the Subaru like a hawk.

The car inched forward again. She stopped and glared at the driver's tinted window. It opened, revealing Mr. Blue Eyes, a smile lifting his incredibly full lips. Talia had never been struck dumb, but in that moment, those eyes and those *kissable* lips did her in, rendering her unable to process a single thought past *Holy fudge*.

"How does it feel to be in the target zone?" He raised his brows.

Molly barked and ran toward the car, jerking Talia from her ridiculous reverie. "Molly!"

"Hello, beautiful girl," he said to the dog with a hefty dose of knee-weakening sweetness as Molly went paws-up on the door. Blue Eyes reached out with both hands to love up Molly, revealing several beaded bracelets around his wrist, as he allowed the happy dog to lick his scruffy, gorgeous face.

Someone honked, and those wicked blue eyes drifted up to Talia's, setting off all sorts of fireworks in her belly. She yanked on Molly's leash, her pulse racing faster than it had when she'd nearly run him over.

"I'm heading in to work," he said. "You should stop by and let me buy you a drink."

"I'm not a big drinker." *And I don't meet men I don't know in strange places.*

"No drinks. We'll just talk."

The cars behind him honked again, but he didn't seem to care. His gaze remained locked on hers like metal to magnet. "I'm bartending at Decadence. It's off Main Street." He winked and said, "Hope to see ya around, *Teach*."

Over the next hour, as Talia walked Molly and returned her to Fletch, she thought of at least fifty reasons she should not go to Decadence and only two reasons she should. She was pretty sure that showing her sisters she wasn't a shut-in and getting one last glimpse of Mr. Blue Eyes weren't the best motives. But as she stood staring at the entrance of what was obviously some type of upscale nightclub, panic bloomed inside her so hard. Just then her phone vibrated with a text from Piper.

Maybe you can track down hot almost-roadkill guy and give him my number!

She read her sister's text for the third time. Her gut twisted at the thought of Piper's hands on the man she couldn't stop thinking about. She shoved her phone into her coat pocket and pulled open the door to the club out of spite . . . or maybe lust.

A group of people came up behind her, and a very large man reached over her head and held the door. "Go on, sweetheart. I've got the door."

The three women and two guys who were with him ushered her into the crowded, dimly lit club. She had no choice but to move with them toward the long wooden bar flanking the right side of the room. Music blared as she weaved around tables and dancing couples. When she neared the bar, she spotted Mr. Blue Eyes serving a drink to a gorgeous blonde. He and a burly, darkly handsome man with short black hair moved swiftly between filling orders and chatting over the bar with what seemed like at least a dozen men and women. Her stomach turned. What was she thinking? She wasn't about to become a groupie for some slacker student, no matter how magnetic his eyes were.

The object of her lust looked over, and their eyes caught and *held*. Electric currents ignited between them, rooting her in place. The other bartender leaned toward her and said, "Hey, babe. What's your pleasure?"

Mr. Blue Eyes placed one hand on the burly guy's shoulder and yanked him back. "Dude, that's my future wife you're talking to. Back off."

Future wife?

The women and men gathered at that end of the bar turned to check her out. The other bartender eyed them. Talia's stomach knotted up. She wanted to run out of there, but she was afraid a single step on her wobbly legs would send her to her knees.

Mr. Blue Eyes lifted his chin, a confident and all-too-sexy smile on his lips as he leaned over the bar, ignoring the two women eyeing him, and said, "Hey, Teach. What can I get you?"

Oh shit. She couldn't do this. She didn't want a drink. She didn't want to be there. Only . . . she didn't want to look away from *him*, either.

"Don't worry. I've got you covered, brown-eyed girl," he said in a soothing, protective voice that rattled her to her core.

Her insides swirled at the endearment, and she reminded herself that calling her *brown-eyed girl* or *Teach* negated the need for him to remember her name. Wasn't he sly? Her phone vibrated again, and she thought of Piper giving her grief for being a wimp. Or worse, coming there on her own to pick up the man who had finished making her a drink and was now watching her so intently she practically felt his big hands moving over her skin. Even as another employee tapped him on the shoulder, his gaze never wavered. She thought about the exit, contemplating making a break for it, but Blue Eyes was on the move, a few steps from where she stood, lifting that strong, scruff-covered chin again and holding up a drink. He flicked his chin, sending his hair away from his face, and holy moly, what a gorgeous face that was. The way he held her gaze made her feel like the only woman in the bar. She reached for the glass despite everything inside her telling her to leave. Her sisters would never believe this. *She* didn't believe it.

"I've got to cover a friend's shift," he said in a belly-twisting bedroom voice that awakened her girly parts. "Hang around. We can chat after I'm done."

She watched him walk away, trying not to stare at the worn denim hugging his incredible, strong-looking ass. She didn't know how long she stood there, watching the doors he'd walked through, but at some point the bar went nearly pitch-black and the music changed to a fast, staccato beat. People cheered and shouted as the crowd moved toward a stage she hadn't noticed at the back of the room. Neon blue lights flashed as curtains parted, and a man's silhouette became visible, tall and broad, chin down. Talia held her breath as his hips began gyrating and he danced out of the shadows and into billowing smoke rising from the stage. As if in slow motion, the smoke cleared, revealing the hip-thrusting, muscular-armed, thick-legged, blue-eyed bartender wearing dark slacks and an open button-down shirt, showing just enough skin to make her mouth go dry.

She. Couldn't. Breathe.

Clutching the glass, she downed her drink in one fell swoop and absently set it down on the bar. It tumbled onto its side as she registered what she'd drank. *A Shirley Temple.* She looked up at the man parading around onstage like the heartthrob he was. He had actually listened when she'd said she didn't drink. Why did that touch her so deeply?

She had to get out of there. His hotness was clearly making her lose her mind.

She started working her way through the crowd, heading for the exit. But he was like a hot and hectic train wreck, and she had to look again. He grabbed his shirt, those sexy hips moving so fast and furious she could feel them against her own as he tore his shirt off and tossed it into the crowd. She pushed through the cheering mob, needing to get away. The music peaked.

She *had* to look, and—*ohmygod!*—he ripped his slacks off. Tore them from front to back, and they fell to the stage in a heap. Her jaw dropped open, her heart slamming faster than the frantic music as a woman tried to climb onto the stage and a big, bearded man stopped her. Piercing blue eyes met Talia's, captivating her as he dropped to the ground, moving with grace and power like a fucking caterpillar on steroids. With his eyes locked on Talia, his ass shot up and drilled down in wild pulses, and his strong arms dragged him toward the edge of the stage. Talia's insides clenched and heated, desire pooling low in her belly. Women threw money, men cheered him on, and he mouthed the words to the song as if he were singing directly to *her*.

Talia's phone vibrated, awakening her sex-starved brain. She thrust her hand into her pocket, needing to be grounded by something real. Something familiar. *Something without a G-string or a formidable package nestled between its thick, powerful thighs.* She took one last long, lascivious look at the man she had no business watching, and then she hightailed it out of there.

She was shaking when she reached her car, images of him writhing before her seared into her brain. She drove away knowing she could never go back there. She could never look that man in the eyes again.

Except maybe in her dreams when she was alone, in the dark of night, with only herself to answer to.

CHAPTER THREE

THERE WAS ABSOLUTELY no good reason for Derek to be sitting in what he now knew was a class called Millennial Masculinities, when he should be catching up on the sleep he didn't get last night, triple-checking his thesis, or any number of important things. But it had been a long damn time since a woman had intrigued him as much as the Parking Lot Plower, aka Professor Fletcher, had, which was why he'd given up on his Wednesday afternoon to-do list and sat like the rest of her students, watching the hottest teacher on the planet stroll across the floor as she talked about the shredding of masculinity in America.

"How about societal expectations?" she asked the class. She was wearing glasses today, giving her an even hotter, more studious look. "Men have gone through major physical changes, from Neanderthals to metrosexuals. Most men these days do a fair amount of manscaping. Does that emasculate them? Or does it make them appear confident in their own skin?"

As the students raised their hands and called out opinions, Derek wondered what she'd thought of his hairy chest when she'd been watching him dance. He hadn't expected her to show up, and when she had, everything and everyone had seemed dull in comparison. Listening to her thoughts on masculinity intrigued him even more, especially since he'd experienced being asked to conform to societal expectations firsthand. When the owner of Decadence had asked him to fill in as a male dancer, they'd also asked him to wax *everything*. They'd even gone so far as to say that most men who had hair on their bodies these days were seen as "bears"—heavyset, hairy gay or bisexual men. The Parking Lot Plower was asking all the right questions. Derek hadn't given in to the pressure to wax, and as a result, he earned more money dancing than he had at his full-time accounting job, and the extra income came in handy to help pay for his ailing father's medical care.

The impeccably polished professor handled each response eloquently, showing appreciation for class participation and also posing more thought-provoking questions. Derek watched the other students, particularly the guys, and he realized that while they were definitely looking at her as a hot woman, they seemed to also be drawn in to her intellectual prowess—*the most alluring quality of all*—like he was.

After class, he waited for most of the students to clear out before approaching her. He hooked his finger in the collar of his bomber jacket and slung it over his shoulder as he descended the stairs of the lecture hall.

She stood at the side of a long table, gathering papers and putting them in a big leather bag. Without a word, she turned to face him. Her cheeks flushed, despite the rigid, and obviously purposeful, set of her jaw. She righted her glasses on the bridge of her nose, standing up a little straighter in the process. Then she crossed her arms over her chest, but not before he noticed her nipples rising to greet him against her sheer blue blouse. Damn, she was adorable.

"Yes?" she asked, lifting her dark brows.

"I really enjoyed that discussion," he said honestly.

She turned away and reached for a pretty red coat. He moved behind her and lifted the collar and sleeve, helping her on with it. A look he couldn't read washed over her face. Worry? Confusion? He couldn't be sure, but it was something a little uncomfortable with a hint of surprise.

She slung her bag over her shoulder and flashed a tight smile. "Thank you. If you came to class on time, you might gain more from it."

Touché. "Probably so, but my life is a little complicated. I feel lucky to have caught any of it." *Not to mention that I'm not really in this class.*

"Everyone's lives are complicated," she said, heading for the door.

He fell into step beside her. "Yes, that's truer than you might think. I was wondering if you had a few minutes to further discuss today's topics?" He held the door open for her to pass through.

She looked at him for a long moment and said, "Thank you."

"Great," he said, feeling a tinge of something he hadn't felt for a very long time. The thrill of attraction.

"I meant thank you for holding the door open. I haven't eaten all day and have just enough time for a quick cup of coffee and a salad at the cafeteria before my next class."

"Great. We can chat over coffee."

Her stride slowed, and she glanced at him out of the corner of her eye, clearly assessing the situation. She stopped and faced him head-on, and it *finally* dawned on him why she was hesitant.

"Look, I'm not a weirdo or a stalker. It was a fluke when I saw you in the crosswalk. I was on my way to work and thought I'd tease you about almost hitting me." He held his hands up in surrender. "I'm sorry if that was in bad taste." He pushed a hand through his hair, a nervous habit he'd never been able to break, and said, "I really did enjoy your class. All I'm asking for is a little intellectual stimulation." As the words left his lips, he realized how true they were and how much he'd missed having meaningful conversations with people about something other than his father's medical care.

She pursed her lips and continued walking toward the exit. "I don't think that's a good idea."

"Why? It's a *conversation.* I'm not asking you to sleep with me."

Her cheeks heated, and her expression turned stern. "I wouldn't want anyone to get the wrong idea."

He scrubbed a hand over his jaw, realizing he'd completely misunderstood. "I'm an idiot. I thought you were under the impression I was hitting on you. But this is about my dancing, isn't it?"

She raised her brows in answer as they left the building.

"That's *what I do*, not *who I am*." He took a step back and said, "I misjudged you. I thought you saw beyond societal expectations and generalizations. I guess I was wrong."

She stopped cold. Her pretty brows knitted as she worried her lower lip between her teeth. "I . . . I'm sorry. That was unfair and unprofessional of me."

"I wouldn't go that far. There are a lot of guys who dance who probably aren't worth your time. I'm not one of them." He'd never been keen on dancing or stripping down to a G-string for bar dwellers, but he earned nearly five times as much in a few hours as he did in two weeks as a bartender. It wasn't hard to do the math. He'd earned six figures each of the past few years, which went a long way in caring for his father and enabled him to save a nice little nest egg to use toward his real goal—opening an adult day-care facility.

When she began walking again, he kept pace with her. "I'm Derek, by the way. Derek Grant. I assume I should call you Professor Fletcher?"

"Not unless you want to call me by the wrong name. I'm filling in for a sick friend and teaching his class." Her lips curved up in the most devastating smile, easing the professional mask she wore so well. "I'm Professor Dalton."

"It's a pleasure to meet you, Professor Dalton." That smile. Damn . . . It was radiant.

As they walked across campus to the cafeteria, making small talk, he couldn't stop stealing glances, loving the way her smile lit up her face. He had a feeling she didn't just wear that professional mask, but she hid behind it—and he couldn't wait to strip it away and get to know the woman behind the armor.

Talia wanted to take a picture of herself having coffee with Mr. Blue Eyes Male Dancer and text it to her sisters and mother with the caption, *Now will you leave me alone? This is me stepping so far out of my comfort zone I might get lost!*

Derek surprised her by helping her off with her coat and pulling out her chair, making her even more curious about him. Last night her curiosity had been fed by their brief interaction and the episode of *Magic Mike* she'd accidentally stumbled upon. Or more specifically, by his mesmerizing blue eyes and the sensual moves she'd seen in her dreams. Now she wondered about his manners, which seemed to have risen to the surface overnight. She wondered who had raised him to listen when a woman spoke, help her with her coat, and pull out her chair. With most of the men she'd gone out with, she was lucky they remembered to click the button on the key fob to unlock her door.

The man wearing worn-out jeans, leather boots, and a black sweater, all of which had seen better days, definitely piqued her interest.

And she was nervous.

Super nervous.

So nervous she forgot to get a salad and would be existing on only caffeine for the next few hours.

"Didn't you want to grab a salad?" he asked.

Was he a mind reader? She couldn't believe he'd remembered when she'd forgotten. "Yes, but I'm fine."

"I can grab one for you real quick. I wouldn't want you to starve because I'm sucking up all your time." He hiked a thumb over his shoulder as he'd done the other day in the parking lot, flashing his ring and colorful bracelets.

She usually hated jewelry on men, but they made him seem exotic. She couldn't help wondering if they were emotionally significant to him, or if he was a Johnny Depp wannabe.

"It's okay. I'm fine, really." It was a total lie, but she wasn't used to not being in control of her emotions, which seemed to be taking jaunts in ten different directions, because now she was thinking about Derek *sucking* . . . and not her *time*, which was crazy. She was his teacher, not his *fantasy*.

Yikes. That wasn't helpful.

She sipped her coffee and did what she did best, sat up a little straighter and slipped into professor mode. "You wanted to talk about the class?"

"Yes. I guess I haven't broken out of my Neanderthal stage." He tugged down the collar of his sweater, revealing a patch of dark chest hair, and his lips curved up in a sexy smile.

She swallowed hard, because holy cow, did she *love* chest hair. Her dark dreams had been so real last night, she'd felt that dusting of hair on her fingers and palms, his leg hair on her thighs . . .

"You posed a lot of questions about the physicality of men and how it translated to their alpha status. I was curious about *your* thoughts on that."

"I . . ."

He tugged his collar down again. "Do you think this makes me more masculine than Chris Evans in *Captain America* because he shaved his chest?"

She laughed at the reference. "To be honest, *no*. He was really ripped in that movie, and he *acted* manly, so it wouldn't have made a difference if he had chest hair or not. In class, I was really focusing on changing gender roles and societal expectations and how they have an effect on masculinity, but personally, I don't think generalizing is fair."

"Interesting, considering that's where your mind went when you learned I was a dancer." Before she could respond, he said, "Generalizations happen, accidentally or not. It's how we handle things after we've acknowledged them that matters. I think we're made to be different. Some men are more masculine than others, and some women are more feminine."

He leaned closer, bringing a wave of potent maleness so strong it felt tangible, like it moved around her, against her, and, oh boy, she had no idea what to do with *that*. He pointed to a woman across the cafeteria who was wearing a black miniskirt, black tights, high-heeled boots, and a tight white sweater. "That woman, for example, doesn't look feminine to me. She looks hard, while you"—his blue eyes moved slowly and purposefully from her eyes all the way down her body, then back up again, creating a flurry of heat in her belly—"appear to be extremely feminine."

He sat back, and the air rushed from her lungs.

Who did he see when he looked at her? She'd had her heart broken in college, and her ex had said she wasn't feminine enough, wasn't outgoing enough, wasn't . . . *enough*, period. It seemed odd now, as she thought about it, how she'd reacted, but ever since, she'd tried to be even *less* feminine, focusing on her academics and hiding behind schoolbooks and her more natural studious persona, heightening it to keep men at bay. She was adept at protecting her heart, but being feminine? She wasn't even sure how to feel that way anymore.

"But that's all visual, so really, it's meaningless," he added. "Just as meaningless as whether a man is a caretaker or a lumberjack. What a person does, or what they look like, is not necessarily representative of who they are inside—masculine or feminine." He watched her with a shimmer of something in his eyes. "Here's an example. You're a professor. That's what you do for a living, but it's not *who* you are. Is the person you are feminine, like your attire and mannerisms convey?"

"That's a very personal question," she said, trying to avoid answering.

"Exactly!" His eyes sparked with excitement. "Who you are is not necessarily who you want everyone to *think* you are."

She took another sip of her coffee, mentally cataloging how different Derek was from what she'd expected. He'd come across as a strange mix of gruff and aloof when she'd nearly run him over, and she'd had him pegged as unambitious. When she'd seen him dancing, she'd added *player* to that assumption. But there was obviously much more to this intelligent man than met the eye. It was time to figure him out.

"You *strip*, bartend, come to class late and leave early," she said, the tease in her voice clear as day. "Is that what you do? Who *you* are?"

"I'm a dancer, technically *not* a stripper, since I don't take everything off. It's like wearing a bathing suit."

Maybe on a European beach, but I don't know any guys who wear G-string bathing suits around here.

His expression turned serious, and he held her gaze as he said, "For the past few years, I've taken care of my father, who was diagnosed with early-onset Alzheimer's, and yes, I work part-time at a bar, bartending and occasionally dancing. The first is definitely who I am. The latter, not so much, but it offers the flexible hours I need and pays the bills." He cocked his head and said, "Tag. You're it."

Her heart broke for him, and she gave herself a virtual slap upside her head for making assumptions about the type of person he was. But still, she couldn't stop seeing him up on that stage, baring himself for all to see. "I'm sorry about your father. That must be terribly hard to deal with."

"Yeah," he said in a slightly scratchy voice, as if his emotions were clogging his throat. "It's been hard to see him deteriorate so quickly. But you know, people's lives are *complicated*." He picked up his coffee and took another drink, watching her over the rim.

"I'm sorry. I didn't mean to come across as judgmental."

"No one ever does." A smile softened his rough edges, but it was a sad smile. One that said his mind was on his father, not her assumptions.

"It's the teacher in me," she said apologetically. "I see too many students throwing away their educations, and I completely misjudged you. I can't imagine how difficult it must be to watch your parent slip away like that."

"It's okay."

"No, it's really not. You asked me if being a teacher is who I am, and I avoided answering." Thinking of her sisters, she said, "I've been asked that a lot lately. I guess I'm trying to figure out the answer."

His eyes swept assessingly over her face. "And how's that going for you?"

"I'm not very good at stepping out of my comfort zone." She surprised herself with her honesty, but Derek was being forthright, and the truth came easily.

"Like having coffee with a guy you almost ran over?"

She laughed softly. "Yes. I'm sorry about that, too. I'm really a very good driver, but my family was on Bluetooth doing their best to drive me crazy."

"Don't sweat it. My day needed a little livening up. I would do just about anything to have a crazy family around."

"It's just you and your father?"

He nodded and twisted the ring on his pinkie. "*Team Grant*. Since I was fourteen, when we lost my mother."

"Oh, Derek. I'm so sorry. I seem to be saying that a lot to you."

"You can stop," he said with a low laugh. "I appreciate the sentiment, but this is part of life. I'm thankful I can be here for my dad. I've traveled all over the world, and I've seen too many orphans who never had a chance to know their parents. I'm pretty blessed."

She was drawn in by his incredible outlook, and suddenly the things she and her sisters worried about felt silly, when he was dealing with so much. He seemed to have a solid grasp on life and what was important, and she wanted to know more about him. How did he stay so positive even after losing his mother, and now dealing with his father slipping away from an awful disease?

They talked about what it was like to care for his father and how he'd felt when he'd left his job and started bartending, and later, dancing.

"But doesn't it bother you?" she asked carefully. "Objectifying yourself like that?"

"You never know what you'll do until you're forced into situations that push you out of your comfort zone," he said with a spark of *this hits home* in his eyes. "You're at the beginning of your journey, dabbling with stepping outside your comfort zone. I was thrust into mine without any thought or warning. I went from being a guy with a full-time accounting job to being a caretaker who needed a job that would allow me to change plans at the drop of a hat but offered a high enough income to create a life, and a future, for me and my father."

He paused long enough for his harsh realities to sink in even deeper.

"I won't apologize, or feel bad about myself, for getting up on that stage and earning the money I need," he said earnestly. "As I said, it's what I do, not who I am, and anyone who can't see past that is too shortsighted to be around a guy like me anyway. I have a life that requires calmness, a focus on schedules and details. There are enough hard times on the road ahead of me. I don't need to add feeling like shit about myself to them."

"I understand." And she did, which led to a host of conflicting emotions inside her.

The alarm on her phone sounded, indicating she had ten minutes to get to her next class. For the first time in forever, she wished she had more time to spend with a man, which startled her, because on the surface, Derek set off every warning bell she'd ever constructed.

"Duty calls," she said more lightly than she felt. She reminded herself that in addition to being a male dancer, he was her *student*, but that did little to quell the desire she had to get to know him better. She rose to her feet and reached for her coat.

"Let me get that." He helped her on with it. "Thank you for talking with me. I really enjoyed it."

As she shouldered her bag, he put on his coat and slung his backpack over his shoulder.

"So did I. Good luck with your dad."

"Thanks. I'm not trying to get an in with the teacher or anything, but since you're trying to step outside your comfort zone, I wonder if you'd like a friend to come along when you walk your pooch tonight? I love animals, and I don't get to spend much time with them."

She should probably turn him down, if not for his dancing, then because of the student-teacher relationship. But he wasn't asking her on a date, and she really enjoyed talking with him. Wasn't this the perfect opportunity to take another step outside her comfort zone?

"She's not my dog, but sure. I'd like that."

He leaned closer, speaking in a low, sexy voice. "Ah, the plot of who Professor Dalton really is thickens. A dog walker? A secret pet stealer?"

She laughed as they headed for the door. "I'm helping my friend. Fletch is the professor for the class I teach on Monday and Wednesday afternoons, and Molly is his dog. Fletch's appendix burst, and he ended up with peritonitis, which is why I'm teaching his class and walking Molly."

"So you're a caretaker, too?" He held the door open and put a hand on her back as she passed through, leaning in as he said, "See? We're already finding out more about who *you* are, Professor Dalton."

She stopped walking and he quickly dropped his hand, as if he realized he'd overstepped his bounds—which he had, but she wasn't so sure she minded. "You can call me Talia, but please, not in class."

"Talia. A feminine name for a beautiful woman."

She felt her cheeks flush. It had been a long time since a man had called her beautiful, and it felt like more than a come-on. He was looking at her the same way he had the other night, making her feel like she was all he saw. They made plans to meet at the park at eight, and even though she knew she was treading a fine line, she told herself she could handle being friends with a student.

As she headed for her class, Derek called out to her, "You should call your family."

"Why would I do that?"

"Tell them you stepped outside your comfort zone, you made a friend's day, *and* you're still alive."

CHAPTER FOUR

"GO, *MIJO*. HE will be fine." Maria Gonzales ushered Derek toward the front door of his house Wednesday evening. She had been their neighbor since before Derek was born, and she loved his parents as much as Derek did. A nurse by profession, and a trusted friend, Maria had cared for his mother until the very end of her life, and now, when Derek was in school or at work, she cared for his father.

"Maybe I should just run over and tell her I need to cancel." His father was particularly agitated this evening, and Derek hated leaving him when he was like that. He should have gotten Talia's phone number, but he'd been so caught up in her agreeing to see him again, he'd forgotten to ask for it.

Maria narrowed her dark eyes and pointed at him in the way only mothers could pull off. "You have given up enough already. I can sing to him. I can calm him down. What I can't do"—she patted her hand over his heart—"is fill this up the way the woman who lights up your eyes can."

"Okay," he said, still warring with guilt over leaving. "But I'll make it an early night. And if he doesn't settle down, please call me. Promise?"

"Of course. Now, you promise me something." She grabbed his black beanie and handed it to him, then lifted his coat from the rack by the door and held it open for him to push his arms through. He was a solid foot taller than Maria, and he had to bend his knees to shrug on the coat. "Promise me you will stop worrying for ten minutes and enjoy yourself. Your papa would want that."

"Yeah, I know he would," he relented, and pulled on his knit hat. "Thanks, Maria."

He hugged her and drew in a deep breath. He'd been living on deep breaths for the past few years, and he wondered if he'd ever get used to it.

"Don't forget your backpack." She picked it up, and they both heard the unfamiliar *clink* of metal on metal. She peered inside, and her eyes lit up. "Ah, your delicious tuxedo mochas?"

He shrugged. "Don't make a big deal out of it. It's a cold night."

"Mm-hm." She patted his cheek and said, "So that's why you asked if you could use two of my thermoses. Go, *mijo*. Go warm up your new *friend*."

The park was only a few minutes from his neighborhood, made quicker because he jogged the short distance. As he neared the entrance, snowflakes melted against his cheeks. His gaze swept over the park where he'd spent his youth chasing balls and having picnics with his family. Not for the first time, he was struck by the simplicity of nature. In such a complicated world, it seemed almost a gift to witness fresh snow kissing empty benches and decorating the peaked roof of the gazebo. He spotted Talia walking Molly by a big tree he used to climb when he was a kid. Her long dark hair fell over her shoulders from beneath a red knit hat. She'd changed out of her skirt and wore a pair of jeans tucked into fur-trimmed boots. She looked up as he approached, lifting her hand in a tentative wave.

Her big brown eyes captivated him, the way they were wary and confident at once. He'd noticed it over coffee. Every time she started to open up, she quickly tightened the reins. But she had shown up at the bar, she'd confronted him about his dancing, and she was here now, all of which told him just how confident she really was. He couldn't suppress a smile as he closed the distance between them. How long had it been since his heart beat this hard because of a woman? He had the overwhelming urge to greet her with a kiss. The impulse was so strong, he didn't trust himself not to, so he petted Molly instead.

"How does it feel to step outside your comfort zone two times in one day?" he asked jovially.

She lowered her gaze, snowflakes dotting her long lashes. "It feels a little like when I was younger and snuck out of the house at night with my girlfriends. I got away with it, but the next morning over breakfast I confessed everything."

He stepped closer, wanting to soak in her innocence, her honesty, and anything else she'd let him. "How'd that go over?"

"My mother told me that sometimes it was good to be bad. My father wanted to ground me, but my younger sister Piper, who never thinks before she speaks, told him that I shouldn't be grounded because I came clean, and if he grounded me he was sending a message to her and my other younger siblings that they should never tell the truth."

He laughed. "Sounds like Piper is a pistol."

"You have no idea," she said as they walked along the path that ran through the park. "But my father bought it, and I didn't get grounded. To this day, Piper has never let me forget that she's the one who saved me from the punishment."

"How many siblings do you have?"

"I have three sisters and one brother. I'm the oldest. Then comes Ben. He's a venture capitalist, and in a lot of ways, he's the sibling I'm closest to. Piper is next in line. She works with my father as a contractor."

"As in a *builder*?"

"Yeah. She's only about as big as a twig, but she's tough as nails and seriously talented."

"That's cool." He playfully nudged her arm and said, "Almost as cool as being a professor."

She laughed. "Trust me, all of my siblings are *much* cooler than me. You should meet Willow. Talk about cool? She's fearless. She owns a bakery in Sweetwater, where we live, and she recently married Zane Walker, who is Ben's best friend."

"The actor?" he asked.

"Yes, well, former actor, really. He's written a screenplay and he's working on getting it made into a movie. Willow is as outgoing as Piper, without the chip on her shoulder, and she's *beyond* beautiful, but she doesn't like Hollywood very much, so they spend most of their time here."

"I don't blame her for that. Why do I get the feeling you think she's more beautiful than you are?"

"Because she *is*," she said frankly. "My sisters are gorgeous, each in their own way. Willow's a buxom blonde with a warm personality that everyone adores. Piper's like a pixie doll, as beautiful as she is fierce. And Bridgette, the youngest, has hair about a million shades of brown and blond. She was always the riskiest of us, which makes her even more attractive. She ran away and married a musician when she was in college. Unfortunately, she lost him to an accident right after their son, Louie, was born. But she's amazing, the way she handled raising Louie alone these last few years."

"That must have been very difficult for her."

"It was, but she never complained, and she's always managed to keep a piece of Louie's father alive in his life. Louie collects baseball cards, like his dad did. And now Bridgette's wildly in love with Bodhi Booker, who is an incredible man. We're in the midst of planning their wedding."

Her eyes lit up when she spoke about her family, and he wanted to keep her talking, to experience that passionate side of her. "You really love your family, don't you?"

"I do, even though they drive me bonkers sometimes."

Molly stopped to sniff a bush, and Derek stepped closer to Talia, loving the caution and heat battling in her eyes. "And tell me, *Parking Lot Plower*, what makes you think you're not more beautiful than all of them put together?"

She laughed, and the playful, unrestrained sound wound through the air like a song. "*Parking Lot Plower?* Seriously?"

"Well, you're more of a *princess* than a *plower*, but *Princess Hit and Run* doesn't really work since you didn't drive away."

She covered her face, and Molly rubbed against her leg, panting up at her. "I can't believe you called me that! I'm a great driver. The best in my family. I was just distracted, and I'm sure you weren't watching where you were going, or you would have seen me approaching, right? Maybe I should call you . . ." She scrunched her nose, looking freaking adorable, and said, "Oh, heck! I've got nothing!"

"Nothing? Well, what am I doing hanging out with a woman who's got nothing to offer?"

"*Hey*, I've got things to offer." She was smiling again, breathtakingly radiant. "I'm just not snarky enough to figure out what to call you. I don't even know you well enough to pretend to figure something out."

He couldn't resist reaching up and brushing a snowflake from her cheek. The light in her eyes heated, burning up the space between them. "You've got a hell of a lot to offer, Talia Dalton. I don't know your sisters, but I've met a lot of women in my travels, and I have yet to meet any who are as pretty, or as interesting, as you."

She worried her tempting lower lip. He stood so close, all he'd have to do was lean in to worry it *for* her. Their breath mingled, and *man*, did he want to *mingle* with her. But the caution in her eyes had him stepping back, struggling to regain control of his runaway desires.

"I, um . . ." She looked down at Molly, then out at the street, and finally, back at him. "Thank you?"

Now he was the one laughing. "You have no idea how attractive you are, do you? Or how refreshing and intriguing it is to talk to a woman who isn't afraid to go deeper than clothes or makeup."

"Oh boy," she said on a long exhalation.

"I'll shut up now, for fear of you taking better aim in the parking lot next time." He nodded to Molly, who was digging her nose in the snow. "Is she allowed off leash?"

"Sure. Why?"

"Oh, you are cautious, aren't you?" He picked up a handful of snow and made a snowball. "I thought I'd toss it for her."

"How did you know she loves that?"

"Most dogs do."

She unhooked Molly's chain, and they spent the next little while throwing snowballs for the pup and talking. Talia told him about her parents. Her mother made soaps and fragrances and sold them in shops in Sweetwater, and her father had been a professor before he'd retired and opened the contracting company he and Piper now ran.

"You said you traveled," she said. "I've never been any place interesting. Was your dad in the military?" She threw a snowball for Molly, smiling as the dog caught it in her mouth.

"No. I grew up right here in Harmony Pointe, in the house where my father and I live." He tossed another snowball and said, "My father was a chef. When I was a kid, I'd hang out at the restaurant where he worked. I didn't travel until I was out of high school. My father had done the same thing, traveled before going to college. I wanted to be just like him, you know? I backpacked for almost two years internationally, staying in hostels, kibbutzim, on communal farms when I could, and then I came back and went to college. My father insisted that I get a degree before going to culinary school, and I was good with numbers. I got that from my mother. I worked as an accountant for a while, saved a little money toward culinary school. Then my dad lost his job, and I've been taking care of him ever since."

"Did he lose his job because of his illness?" she asked thoughtfully and crossed her arms, tucking her hands beneath to ward off the cold.

Molly ran a little too far for his comfort, and he whistled, calling her back.

"It was before he received his diagnosis, but yeah. He made all sorts of errors and had trouble problem solving. They tried to work with him, but we didn't know what was going on. And my dad was stubborn. He had a thing about not going to doctors. Now medical appointments are a normal part of his life."

"That makes me sad, but he's lucky to have you to care for him. It's an honorable thing, to give up so much of your life for your father."

"*Family.* They've got to come first, you know?"

She dug into the snow and made a snowball. "Team Grant all the way."

"Yeah. All the way and then some." Unexpected emotions bubbled up inside him, and when she threw the snowball at him, it was exactly what he needed to break through them. He dropped his backpack and said, "You're in for it now!"

She shrieked and ran across the snow. He darted after her, but she dashed through the gazebo, scooped up a handful of snow, and tossed it at him. It hit him square in the face, and she gasped.

"Sorry!"

He teasingly growled and made a huge snowball, lightly packed so as not to hurt her, and stalked toward her.

She stumbled backward, waving her hands. "No, please!" she said between laughs.

Her killer smile was almost enough to stop him in his tracks. "Oh *yes*, Parking Lot Princess. You are *mine!*"

She grabbed another handful of snow and lobbed it at him, missing by a mile. Then she sprinted away. He took off after her and she turned, tripping over her own feet. He lunged, catching her in his arms, but their momentum sent them both to the snow. She landed on top of him, both of them laughing. Molly whined and licked their faces.

Her teeth chattered. "Sorry!"

"Hell, Talia. I'm not."

Her eyes widened, then brimmed with heat again, dark and alluring as they skimmed over his face and lingered on his lips. Her body sank exquisitely into his. Even separated by coats and clothing, she felt incredible. Molly lay in the snow, watching them as if she felt the unbelievable moment, too. When Talia's eyes found his again, they were like windows to her soul. Every sexy thought was right there on the surface, so tempting he was about to lean up and take a kiss, when she suddenly schooled her expression, as if she'd just realized she'd shown her true emotions, and rolled off him.

She lay on her back beside him, staring up at the sky, breathing heavily.

He leaned over her and gazed deeply into her troubled, beautiful eyes. Whatever this was between them was magnificent and stronger than anything he'd ever felt, but the caution in her eyes won again. "I'm sorry. I didn't mean to cross a line. It's been a long time since I've"—*wanted to kiss a woman*—"felt whatever this is between us."

She pressed her lips together, and as he backed off, she grabbed his sleeve and said, "Me too. It's been a long time."

Man, she was so close, her desire evident in her tight grasp on his sleeve and the longing look in her eyes, but the tentativeness was still there, brimming before him. He swallowed his desires and went for levity.

"Do you have an ailing family member you're caring for, too?"

She shook her head. "I have fear of the unknown, trust issues, and a full life."

"Is that all?" He helped her to her feet, both of them smiling with his tease.

Molly got up, wagging her tail.

Talia's teeth were still chattering. He put his hands on her arms and rubbed them, itching to pull her against him and heat her up with a scorching-hot kiss. Instead he took her hand and said, "I've got something to warm you up."

"Um . . . ?" Her cheeks pinked up again.

He chuckled. "Yeah, *that*, but since we've already tabled the good stuff . . ." With Molly in tow, he led her to where his backpack lay in the snow. He dug out the thermoses he'd brought and handed her one. "It's not as fun, but this should do the trick."

She pulled her hat a little lower on her ears. "What is it?"

"Tuxedo mocha. Have you ever had one?"

She shook her head, wrapping both hands around the warm thermos. "Thank you for not making me an alcoholic drink the other night, by the way. That was really nice of you to remember."

"You're hard to forget, Talia." He loved the sultry look that earned him and had to distract himself before he made the mistake of *tasting* that look. "I shouldn't have waited so long to give this to you. The whipped cream and chocolate curls are probably melted."

"You had me at whipped cream." She took a sip and closed her eyes, moaning appreciatively. "Holy cow," she said breathlessly. "This is heaven in a cup."

He clenched his jaw as his mind chased that moan down an X-rated path. "It'll be even better next time, when I make it fresh for you."

"Next time?" she asked, and took another sip.

The tip of her tongue swept over her lips, seriously testing his ability to hold *his* tongue. He shouldered his backpack and took Molly's leash from where it dangled out of Talia's pocket. As he hooked it onto Molly's collar, he said, "How can I help you step out of your comfort zone and get over *all* your hurdles if we don't see each other again?"

Speaking of hurdles, he realized he'd been so caught up in her, he hadn't told her the truth about having stumbled into her classroom. As he opened his mouth to do so, his phone rang. His gut pitched as he dug it out of his pocket and saw Maria's number. "I'm sorry. I need to take this."

Talia was flirting with a thin and dangerous line. Technically speaking, Derek was her student, at least until Fletch was better, and personally speaking, she was already *way* outside her comfort zone. Sure, she surrounded herself with new and different people on a near-daily basis, but she didn't meet them for walks or nearly *kiss* them. And boy, did she want to kiss Derek! It had taken every ounce of restraint not to lean up and taste his full lips, to feel the emotions of a man who had given up everything for his father. She *wanted* to see him again, to get to know even more about him, and there was no denying she wanted much more than a kiss, which floored her.

Maybe Piper was wearing off on her.

She watched him talking on the phone, not wanting their evening to end, but as worry fell over his face like a curtain, she had a feeling it was about to.

He tucked his phone in his pocket, and those gorgeous blue eyes held a hint of sorrow. "That was Maria. She takes care of my father. He's having a hard night, and sometimes I'm the only one who can calm him down." He stepped closer. "I really didn't want tonight to end so soon."

"Me, either." She was usually much more careful about sharing her feelings, but Derek was testing all the things she thought she knew about herself. "I'm sorry he's having a hard time. Of course you have to go. What will you do to help calm him?"

He pulled off his beanie—which was also crazy sexy. She loved beanies—and raked a hand through his hair, pulling it away from his face. His long hair had been one of the first things she'd noticed, along with his intense blue eyes, and embarrassingly, she'd let his holey jeans and long hair sway her impression of him. Now she wanted to run her fingers through his hair and get to know him better. Everything she'd seen in him since their first encounter made him even more attractive—his love and loyalty toward his father, his kindness, his sense of humor and intelligence. She wondered how she could have mistaken him for anything less than the man he was, and she couldn't deny that she'd never seen a more beautiful man. *Which is probably the same way the women who watch him dance feel.*

That reality hit her like a kick to the stomach.

"When he gets like this," Derek said, bringing her back to their conversation, "all it usually takes is playing my guitar and singing to him. One song and he'll be out like a light. He taught me to play when I was a kid." He paused for a moment, then said, "You know, you could come with me. I know it's a little strange as an extension of our night, but . . ." He took her hand in his again, and his gaze turned tender, softening her resolve. "I'd really like to spend more time with you."

The image of him playing his guitar for his father pushed away the cold reality of his dancing. Her thoughts raced. She glanced at Molly to try to sort them, but all she heard was *Go!* There wasn't much else to sort through. Apparently, her cautious brain had taken a hiatus for the night, because she said, "I have to bring Molly home first."

Ten minutes later she was rushing into Fletch's house, talking a mile a minute as she wiped Molly's paws and hung up the leash. "I don't know what's wrong with me. I'm never like this! I'm going with a guy I barely know, and almost *ran over*, to see his father? What am I doing?"

She paced, and Fletch sat on the couch, chuckling.

"*Why* are you laughing?" She looked in the mirror on the wall and said, "I half expected to see Piper looking back at me. I almost *kissed* him, Fletch. When have I ever done that the first time I've gone out with someone? And this *wasn't* a date! *And* he's a stripper. Well, he says he's a *dancer*, but . . . *yeah*, there's that little golden nugget."

"A *stripper*? Tal, I'm afraid you're going to have to explain this one to me."

"He works at Decadence, which I thought was an upscale pub." She paced his living room.

"Upscale *club*, sure."

"You know it? You've been there?" Maybe that should surprise her, but it didn't. She assumed most people went to clubs like that and she was just the odd girl out. She'd heard Piper talk about male dancers like they were no big deal.

Her stomach clenched. *What if Piper has seen him dance?*

"Decadence features male and female dancers," Fletch explained. "But I wouldn't call it a strip club. It's classier than those."

"Do not tell me about your trips to *those*, please." She glared at him. "What is wrong with me? He *strips* to a G-string, does pelvic thrusts that could make a girl's toes curl, *and* he's my student! Well, he's your student, which means he's temporarily my student, and I can't kiss him."

Fletch patted the cushion beside him, and she sank down to it with a groan.

"You can't kiss your student."

"I *know*!" She threw her hands up. "This is a bad idea. I shouldn't go to his house."

"But you *can* be friends with him, and honestly, babe, I've never seen you this caught up in anyone. *Ever.* Maybe it's good for you. Maybe you needed a friend who's more cutting-edge than boring old me. We both know *I'm* not going to push your boundaries. But no, you can't kiss him."

"*Ugh!* So what should I do? I shouldn't go, right? I should just text him and say thanks but no thanks." She leaned back and closed her eyes, trying to ignore the pain slicing through her at the idea of doing that.

"You know you probably shouldn't go."

She opened her eyes and gave him a deadpan look. "Thanks."

"At least not while he's your student. The whole dancing thing, well, that's another issue. I mean, what kind of guy is he? You should have Ben check him out."

"My brother is *not* doing a background check on him! He gave up his job to care for his father, who has Alzheimer's. He seems like a really good guy, Fletch. The kind of guy that if he didn't dance and wasn't my student, I would like to . . ."

"Go out with? Get to know better? I get it. And it's obvious that you want to go to his place right now. But, Tal, this is how professors get themselves in trouble. They tell themselves they can handle the girls in the short skirts or guys wanting to ball them, but they can't. Plus, a *dancer?* I can't even see you going into a club like that."

She looked away.

"Holy shit! You went to see him dance? What has gotten into you?"

"I don't know! I didn't know I was going to see him dance. It just happened." She buried her face in her hands, and when she looked up again, she stared straight ahead, visualizing Derek's face, the way his eyes went from playful to sensual in the space of a second and then turned deep and thoughtful as he spoke of his father. "I think it's his eyes. They're riveting. I got sucked in."

"You don't get *sucked in*, especially over eyes, which means this guy must have a lot more than just a hot bod and a pretty face going on. But still, that doesn't change the fact that as far as the school's concerned, you're in a power position over him right now. We both know carnal desires can be a lot stronger than rational thoughts."

She sighed. "You're right. You're absolutely one hundred percent right." She pushed to her feet and said, "Thank you for reminding me that at the very core of ourselves, we're all animals. I'll text him on my way out and tell him I'm not coming over."

"You must be really wild about this guy, because you didn't even notice I showered."

Her gaze swept over his damp, finger-combed hair, and she caught the scent of soap. "You still look like hell, only cleaner. And I'm not going to hug you, because you just turned me away from the first guy who has made me hot and bothered in years."

"You still love me," he called after her. "Or at least you will when you're not getting fired because of having hot sex with a student."

She stopped by the front door and glanced back at him. "Now it's not just *balling* him, but I'm missing out on *hot* sex? You are very cruel, Professor Fletcher. I sure hope you're well soon, because now every time I take Molly for a walk I'm going to see his mesmerizing blue eyes gazing up at me."

"*Up?* Wait! Were you lying on top of him?"

She arched a brow and spoke as snootily as she could. "Hm. You'll never know now, will you? Sleep well, libido killer."

"That's only until he's no longer *your* student," he yelled as she opened the front door. "Once you no longer have power over him, you're free to satisfy your every desire with Mr. G-String."

She glared at him, even though she knew she was doing the right thing by not going to see Derek. But she wasn't ready to let him go just yet. "How fast can you be well enough to teach?"

CHAPTER FIVE

BRIDGETTE FLEW THROUGH the back door of Willow's bakery Friday morning and said, "Where were you hiding yesterday?" She shrugged off her coat and tossed it on a counter.

Talia *had* spent her day off hiding, but more to keep herself from doing something stupid than to avoid seeing her sisters. After sending a quick text to Derek Wednesday night saying she couldn't make it to meet his father after all, she'd spent the rest of the night thinking about their *almost* kiss, reliving the feel of him against her and the weight of his stare boring into her. She'd woken up Thursday morning hot, bothered, and beyond flustered. It didn't help that Derek had texted her twice yesterday, once asking if she wanted to hang out at lunch and the other apologizing for crossing a line with their almost kiss. She'd been *this close* to responding with something sexier than *Don't worry about it. We didn't cross any lines. Sorry I can't meet you for lunch. I'm swamped,* but she had to wrap her head around his dancing—*or not*—and she was afraid to see too much of him before Fletch took over his class again.

She took a bite of her chocolate-cream doughnut and glanced at Willow, who was pulling a tray of muffins from one of the ovens.

"You know she's not talking about me," Willow said as she set the tray on the counter. "Where's the little man, Bridge?"

"Today is bring-your-pet-to-school day. Bodhi's taking Louie in and bringing Dahlia." Dahlia was their Great Dane. Bridgette leaned her hip against the counter in her pretty blue dress and stared at Talia, who had a mouthful of doughnut.

"Her second," Willow said as Piper came through the back door.

Piper tugged off her coat and tossed it on a chair. "Whose second what?"

"Tal's second doughnut," Bridgette said. "Plus, she dodged most of my texts yesterday."

"Yeah? Mine too." Piper grabbed a muffin and sat on the counter beside where Talia was leaning against it. Her construction boots swung as she bit into her breakfast.

Piper's torn work jeans sent Talia's mind racing back to Derek and his sexy butt as he'd walked away from her at the bar in those formfitting jeans, which led her to him taking off his clothes, dancing like he was sex personified . . . She took another big bite of her doughnut.

"It doesn't work, you know," Piper said.

Talia arched a brow, her mouth full of sweets.

Piper grinned. "Substituting sugar for sex."

She choked on the doughnut, which sent her into a coughing fit.

Piper smirked, Bridgette laughed, and Willow handed her a glass of water.

Talia chugged it down. "Who says I'm doing that?" She shoved the rest of her doughnut in her mouth. Sure, she looked like a chipmunk, but she didn't care. Because that sugar was going to have to hold her over or she was in trouble.

Willow took Talia's plate. "You're cut off, and if you're not substituting, then you lost your job or something equally bad has happened, because you never eat like this or hide from us."

"I didn't *hide* from any of you. I returned your texts." Talia wiped her mouth as all three sisters glared at her. "What?"

"You sent me a text that said, 'I'm not dead,'" Bridgette reminded her.

"You asked if I was still alive." Talia rolled her eyes. "I spent the day with Fletch. Is that such a big deal?"

"Not unless you finally gave in and took my advice about that fine piece of professorial ass," Piper said. "If you didn't bang him, you were definitely hiding."

"*Fine!*" Talia relented. "I *was* hiding from you guys and keeping myself safe. Fletch kept me in check. You guys would have thrown me to the wolves. Or rather, one very fine, very *off-limits*, long-haired, blue-eyed, insanely sexy and loyal wolf." *Great.* Now she was thinking about his eyes and that body moving like a sex machine. She shook her head to try to clear the heat from her veins and noticed her sisters gaping at her. There was no way she'd tell them about his G-string-flaunting job. Nope. Piper would drive right to the bar and sit there until she got a good look at him, and she had no idea what her other sisters would do or say, but more than likely, they'd be just as conflicted as she was.

"Long hair? Blue eyes?" Piper said. "Do tell, dear sister. Does he have tats, too? Because you can throw that beefcake my way. I know just what to do with a guy like that."

"God, Pipe! Where is your *off* button? There's not much to tell," Talia lied.

"Oh yes there is if it's about you and a long-haired guy," Bridgette said. "I can't even imagine you looking at a man who isn't completely clean-cut."

"Yeah, that makes two of us," Talia mumbled. "Apparently my normal brain has decided to jump ship. It's a wonder I can still teach."

Willow waved another doughnut in front of her. "If you tell us, I'll give you this."

Talia snagged it. She needed all the help she could get. "I'm always the sister who has nothing new and exciting to talk about, and suddenly I've skipped right over new and exciting and gone straight to *losing my mind over a student.*"

"What?" her sisters said at once.

"A student?" Bridgette blinked several times. "Like . . . a *kid*? How old is he?"

"No! Like an adult! Geez, Bridge. Who do you think I am?" Talia paced as she ate the doughnut. "I don't know exactly how old he is, probably around my age. He's the guy I almost hit in the parking lot."

"Well, you sure took my advice about nailing a hot guy." Piper slid off the counter, laughing at Talia, who was glowering at her. "That explains the tight sweaterdress and fuck-me boots."

"These are not fuck-me boots!" Talia snapped.

Her sisters exchanged a look that told her they knew she was full of shit.

"Yeah, you're right," Piper said. "Knee-high suede and three-inch heels definitely don't scream *take me*."

"No, not at all," Bridgette said with a soft laugh. "Neither does the dress that shows your incredible figure."

Talia rolled her eyes.

"What's the big deal?" Piper asked. "You *finally* have a sex drive! Just do him and move on. It's not like he'll tell on you."

"Ohmygod. Piper!" Bridgette chided her. "She cannot *do* a student. And she's never like this, which means *something*."

"Yeah, it means I'm going to weigh three hundred pounds by the time Fletch is ready to teach his class, which is when I'll be free to see the one and only, mysteriously intriguing Derek G-String Grant."

"Hold the flipping phone!" Piper snapped. "G-string? How would you know this if you didn't bang him?"

Talia met each of their expectant faces, realizing what she'd accidentally let slip. "I was kidding. He looks like he wears a G-string, that's all. His name is Derek Grant."

"*Derek Grant.*" Willow looked up from where she was frosting doughnuts. Her braided hair lay in a thick plait down her back, a few wispy locks framing her face. In her jeans and Sweetie Pie Bakery T-shirt, she could pass for closer to twenty than thirty. "I like that name, and so what if you have to wait a little while? Just be friends until Fletch takes over and you won't lose your job by dating him. Friends is nice. It builds a solid foundation."

"Says the girl who gets sex every night of the week," Piper said. "While Talia's coochie hasn't been tickled by a man in God only knows how long."

"We're *not* talking about my sex life," Talia said. "I never should have said anything to you about him, but . . ." She crossed her arms, uncrossed them, and reached for her glasses, which were not on her nose because she was wearing contacts today. And yes, she'd worn a particularly curve-hugging outfit because *come on, it feels good to have Derek's interest, even if he is off-limits.*

Her phone vibrated, and her sisters crowded around her as she dug it out of her purse. "God, you're like flies to honey."

"We're all here, so unless it's Ben . . ." Willow said, peering over Talia's shoulder.

"Or Mom or Dad," Bridgette said. "Or Aurelia."

"Aurelia's with Ben. We needed supplies from the city, and Ben was heading there for a meeting, so they went together," Willow said, then squealed when Talia unlocked her phone screen and Derek's message popped up. "Nope! It's *him!*"

"Do you mind?" Talia leaned away as she opened the text. Her sisters leaned with her.

"He wants you to meet him after class," Piper said. "At least we know he's not a wimp."

"How can you possibly know that from a text?" Talia asked.

"He's going after what he wants. That's a *man*, not a pushover." Piper grabbed another muffin. "My vote is that you meet him after class. I have to get to a job site, but I want details. Including all the juicy stuff you pretend not to want, because I can tell by your doughnut-eating face that this guy's got you thinking about every single one of them." She headed for the door, snagged her coat, and said, "And if you blow me off, I'll show up at that class you're teaching for Fletch one day and embarrass the hell out of you."

Talia groaned.

"Love you, sis." Piper disappeared out the door, then poked her head back in and pointed at Willow. "You, me, Aurelia. Next weekend. We need to firm up renovation dates for the bakery and bookstore merger. Got it?"

"Shoot. I forgot to tell you that Aurelia is still working out her finances. We're going to need some time," Willow said. "But we'll keep you in the loop."

"Okay, and we're on for bridal gown shopping Saturday? Do *not* reschedule, or you'll have *me* to deal with. I turned down a really hot date for this." On that threat, Piper slipped away.

Talia grabbed her coat. "I need to get to work, too. Did you guys get Mom a birthday gift yet? I can't decide what to buy her." Their mother's birthday dinner was next week.

"Nope," her sisters said in unison.

"What about a weekend away for her and Dad?" Talia suggested. "Maybe something they can use in the spring or summer?"

"I'd pitch in for that," Willow said. "I think we should pay for the weekend but let them plan the dates."

"Me too. Can you pick a place, Tal?" Bridgette asked. "I'm swamped." She pulled out her phone and began texting. "I'm asking Ben and Piper if they want to pitch in."

"Sure. I'll get on it." Talia made a mental note to start looking into romantic getaways, which sent her mind straight back to Mr. Blue Eyes. "I'd better get going."

"Piper and Ben are both in," Bridgette said.

"Wait!" Willow went around the kitchen putting cannoli and other treats in a box. "Take these in case you decide to meet Derek. You're one hot tamale. Chances are he's having just as rough a time as you are." She winked and said, "A little sugar goes a long way."

"What makes you think they'll make it all the way to Harmony Pointe?" Talia asked, wondering how many pastries she could eat before she exploded. She put on her coat, grabbed her purse, and picked up the box.

"Because she knows how you hate to keep presents from the people they're meant for," Bridgette said as she headed for the door that led from the kitchen into the bakery. Her flower shop was attached to Willow's bakery by an arched opening. "Now you have an excuse to see Derek instead of an excuse not to."

Damn it. They knew her too well. "Would one of you please tell Piper I decided *not* to see him? Or tell her I decided *to* see him. I don't care what you say, as long as you stop her from showing up and embarrassing me."

"On it!" Willow promised. "And Tal?" she said softly as Bridgette left the kitchen.

"Hm?"

"You look even more beautiful with that sparkle in your eye. At least think about seeing him, okay? One more baby step out of your comfort zone? For me? You don't have to do anything inappropriate, but he obviously has had an effect on you. A good one."

"As if I *can* stop thinking about him."

As much as her sister's words comforted her, she wondered if Willow would be as supportive if she knew about his dancing.

Talia's class was even more interesting than the others Derek had attended, and not just because Professor Dalton had seared herself into his mind over the last few days, stroking his darkest thoughts and becoming the headliner in his late-night fantasies. Maybe more surprising was that as hot as those thoughts were, he wanted to talk to her more, to get to know everything about her. She brought up concepts and posed questions in class that made him think about things in new ways, which he liked—even if it was hard as hell trying to concentrate with her strutting around in a skintight sweaterdress he wanted to rip off her and fuck-me boots he wanted to leave *on*. He hadn't been surprised when she'd backed out of meeting his father. It wasn't exactly the most alluring offer. *Hey, come meet my dad who may or may not remember who I am.* But they'd connected. He'd felt it as strongly then as he did now, and when she hadn't taken him up on getting together for lunch yesterday, it had only made him more determined to change her mind.

He strode toward her after class, drinking in her lush curves, when their gazes collided. The air sizzled and pulsed between them as the other students milled about. A blush on her cheeks deepened with his every step. *Oh yeah, beautiful. You might have run scared the other night, but there's no way you're getting off that easy.* The closer he came, the harder she breathed. He loved knowing she was as into him as he was into her.

"How's it going, *Teach*?"

She swallowed hard, crossing and uncrossing her arms, looking even more adorably nervous than she had the other day. He wanted to take her in his arms and kiss her until she couldn't remember why she'd been rattled in the first place.

"I got your text," he said, stepping closer. Not near enough for the other students to notice, but enough to make Talia's eyes darken and his pulse spike. It had been so long since he'd felt that way, he welcomed the strange fluttering sensation in his chest. "You said you had something for me? I'm hoping it's something you *can't* give me here."

"Derek."

The whispered warning landed loud and clear.

He held up his hands, unable to stop teasing. "Hey, I just figured I overstepped my bounds Wednesday night and you might want me to stand in front of your car so you could aim better this time."

That earned a smile. One he wanted to see a hell of a lot more of. "I could pin a target on my chest." He ran his hand over his chest.

"Stop!" She touched his arm and then quickly withdrew, her gaze darting around them.

He didn't want to make her uncomfortable around her students, so he said, "Feel like getting out from under the microscope and going for a walk?"

"Um . . ." She lowered her gaze, her face turning serious.

He held up her coat, and her face blanched. Her pretty eyes darted around them again.

"Sorry. I wasn't thinking." He handed her the coat.

"No. It's sweet of you. I'm just . . . I can't . . . Let's take a walk and talk."

It was freezing outside, and Derek struggled to keep from pulling Talia closer as she shivered beside him. "Listen, Talia, about the other night. I know it was a weird offer to come and hang out at the house while my dad was having a hard time."

"No. It wasn't weird. It was nice, and I wanted to go, but . . ."

The sincerity in her eyes told him she was being honest. When she didn't elaborate, he said, "I'm meeting some friends for a potluck dinner tonight. We try to get together every week or two, nothing too crazy. I'd love it if you'd come with me."

She stopped walking and huffed out a breath. "Derek, I really like you, and I had a great time the other night, but I can't go out with you. I'm your teacher."

"Yeah, about that . . ." He looked out at the parking lot, pushed the hair from his eyes, and met her gaze again, feeling a little like he'd been caught skipping school. "You're not *really* my teacher."

"Well, *substitute*, but still. As far as the school's concerned, it's called being in a power position," she explained.

He mentally ran through about a dozen positions of power in which he'd like to be tangled up with her. She must have read his dirty thoughts, because she said, "Not *that* type of power position," in a hushed and shocked tone. "Geez! What is wrong with everyone today? They have sex on the brain."

He laughed. Then he realized what she'd said, and a spark of jealousy silenced his laughter. "*Wait.* Do you have students *propositioning* you?"

"No. My sisters are just wicked, that's all."

He breathed a sigh of relief. "Wicked can be fun," he said, earning an eye roll and another sexy blush. "You're pretty good at holding your ground, so unless there's a student pushing you past your comfort zone . . ."

"Well, there is this *one* student . . ."

"Good-looking long-haired guy? Likes to hang out around your car bumper?"

"I see you know him?" She pointed to her car. "I actually have something for you in my car."

"I don't know, *Teach.* Is this like when adults offer kids candy to take a ride in their van? I'm smart. You've got to show me the candy first."

She grabbed his arm and dragged him toward her car. "Shut up before I change my mind and keep it all for myself."

"I do like it when you're bossy and *handsy.*"

She dropped his arm.

"Listen, Talia, you misunderstood what I meant before. I'm not registered for that class."

"What do you mean?" She dug her keys from her purse. "You're in it."

"I mean, I was walking by the other day and heard your voice. I peeked into the room, saw you teaching, and I was . . ." He shrugged. "I was taken by you, so I sat down to listen. The material was incredibly interesting, but I'd be lying if I said that was the only reason I came back for the next class and the next."

She blinked several times. "So . . . ?"

"I'm sorry. I should have told you sooner, but when we had coffee I wasn't thinking about that, and honestly, it was the most fun I'd had in a long time. I don't often have a chance to meet interesting, beautiful women."

"You work at a *bar*. You take your clothes off and *dance* at a bar. You must meet women all the time," she said sharply.

"That's really bugging you, isn't it?"

She didn't answer, but she held his gaze.

"Like I said, it's what I do and what I will continue to do for as long as I have to. And yes, I meet plenty of women. But they're not interesting, and many are less than stable or looking for a quick fuck, not exactly the kind of women I'd want to spend time with. I'm not a typical twenty-nine-year-old bachelor who's out partying on the weekends or looking to get laid. I've got the weight of the world on my shoulders, and sometimes it feels like I'm climbing toward fifty instead of thirty. I was going to tell you about not being registered for the class the other night, but Maria called before I could. And I thought I'd tell you when you came over. But then . . ."

"I blew you off," she said softly. "I didn't want to, but I didn't trust myself, and I thought you were my student. And yes, I am wrestling with your dancing, which is totally unfair. It's my own hang-up. But I've never been in this position before where I really liked someone and had to deal with anything like this."

"Funny, I think most women would have a harder time with the fact that I can't just go out whenever I want to, or that my father's illness means my life will revolve around him, more than around them, for a very long time."

"I told you I have trust issues," she said confidently. *Impressively.* "But I'm not so insecure that I need your full-time attention. I understand what you're going through."

"And I wouldn't be pursuing you if I thought I'd cause them to worsen. I know myself. You just have to be willing to give yourself a chance to get to know me better."

She sighed, confusion rising in her eyes. "Now I don't know if I should be flattered or annoyed about the class."

He looked up at the sky. "Please go with flattered." Going for levity, he waggled his brows and said, "Maybe you should *thank* me. Now you don't have to trust yourself."

Her cheeks pinked up, but her eyes heated again. How did she manage to look so sexy and innocent at once?

"Nobody's ever done anything like that for me before, so this might seem weird, but I have to ask. Have *you* done something like this before? Pretended to be involved in something to get a woman's attention?"

"Hell no. I was as shocked as you are. But I'm thinking about registering for the class anyway, because I'm pretty sure it's not fair for me to enjoy it so much without paying for it."

"Do you need the credit?"

He shook his head. "I'm finishing my last class for my master's in health administration."

"Wow, did I ever have you pegged wrong. It's too late to register for the class, but you can still come and enjoy it. Besides, Fletch and I have different teaching styles. You might enjoy it more—or less—when he teaches it." She opened her car door and handed him a box from Sweetie Pie Bakery. "My sister Willow, the baker, sent these for you."

As he took the box, he placed his fingers over hers. "Does this mean you're going with *flattery* and you'll come with me tonight?"

She inhaled deeply and nodded. "I *am* flattered, and I guess kind of relieved, too. I'd love to go with you, but if it's potluck, you don't want me cooking. I pretty much suck at it, but I can ask Willow to make dessert and bring that."

"Awesome. There's a Mediterranean theme. I'm sure Willow knows a dozen desserts that will work, and if not, bring anything. Or nothing.

It doesn't matter. I'm just glad you'll be there." He nearly hauled her in for a kiss, but stopped himself. "I'm not sure why your sister is sending me treats, but let's see what Willow has brought to the table." He opened the box, and his mouth watered at the sight of creamy cannoli, doughnuts, and other pastries.

"Since you came clean, I think I should, too," Talia said sweetly. "She gave those to you as a way to get me to see you again."

"Seriously? You weren't going to? And here I thought we had a connection."

"We did! That's the problem. I probably wouldn't have seen you again, at least until Fletch took over his class. What can I say? I'm a rule follower."

"You're freaking adorable is what you are. With my father's current state, I'm used to living by rules, and I have a great deal of respect for those who can adhere to them." He held up the box. "Do you want one?"

"No, thanks. I ate three doughnuts this morning in an attempt to substitute sugar for sex." Her eyes widened, and she slapped her hand over her mouth. "I can't believe I said that!"

He laughed, closed the distance between them, and placed his hand on her hip, because he couldn't stand not touching her for a minute longer. "For what it's worth, been there, done that. But my substitute of choice is a hard workout. Since I can't exactly go for a run at the moment, I think we can both use a cannoli." He opened the box and handed her one. "Just don't eat it around me."

"Why?"

"Your sexy mouth on *that*?" He shook his head. "No workout could ever erase that image."

CHAPTER SIX

DEREK BUTTONED HIS white linen shirt, put on his beige vest, and grabbed his gray tweed sport coat on the way out of his bedroom. He tugged it on as he went to say good night to his father. There was a time when Jonah Grant had seemed larger-than-life. Whether he was playing his guitar, cooking, or helping Derek with homework, he'd had an authoritative presence about him. Upbeat yet stern. As Derek breezed into the living room, he took in his father's scruffy cheeks—Jonah had developed a hatred for shaving lately—and the blue baseball cap that had become part of his daily attire. The disease had claimed so much of him that he often thought he was a young man again. Derek was hit with a familiar wave of conflicting emotions. He considered every day he had with his father a blessing, even though some days were beyond difficult to get through.

He crouched beside his chair, covering his father's hand with his own. "Pop?" He waited for his father to look over. "I'll be home later, okay? It's potluck night with my friends. Sunday you and I will go to the museum."

His father's blue eyes drifted down Derek's chest. "You look nice, Archie."

Derek's heart sank.

Maria looked up from where she was reading on the couch with an empathetic expression on her face. She knew the feeling of holding her breath to see which man they were speaking to—the lucid father, the disoriented patient, or the guy who had jumped back in time, suddenly fifteen or twenty years old again.

"Thanks, Pop." *It's me, Derek, your son.* Stifling the futile reminder had become as rote as checking his father's meds and adhering to a daily schedule. His father's lucid moments came and went. Derek had long ago accepted that part of the unfair disease. It was the mention of his father's brother, Archie, that bothered him most. Archie and his father had been close as kids, but Archie was an artist and lived overseas. He had been adopted and hadn't inherited the genes for this awful disease, which Derek was grateful for. But he wished his uncle lived closer, as he visited only once a year. Early-onset Alzheimer's progressed quicker than other forms of the disease, and the more his father disappeared, the more it hurt knowing he probably had only a handful of visits left with his brother.

"I haven't seen you wear those pants for a while," Maria said with a twinkle of delight in her eyes. "It must be a very special potluck dinner. I should iron those for you, *mijo*. Oy, and that shirt, too. You're rumpled. Your mama would shake her head at you."

"No time." Derek had filled in for half of a coworker's shift at the bar this afternoon and had barely had time to shower and dress after getting home. He patted his father's hand, kissed his cheek, and whispered, "Love you."

Maria pointed to her cheek, and Derek pressed a kiss to it. "Thanks again for staying later tonight. I'm not sure how long we'll be, but I'm only a phone call away. We're going to India's."

"Take your time. I'll sleep in the guest room if you're too late. We're having a good night so far." Derek often had to work until past midnight, and on those nights Maria sometimes stayed in the guest room. "You go, have fun. I'll call if we need you."

Derek grabbed the cooler with the dish he'd prepared, and twenty minutes later he stood at Talia's front door, trying to calm his nerves.

He was used to stepping outside his comfort zone. Hell, the past few years had kicked him in the ass. There was nothing comfortable about dancing at the bar, watching his father deteriorate before his eyes, relying on Maria as a son should never have to, and giving up most of his autonomy. But picking up Talia for their first date brought a new feeling. Where his father's illness sometimes made him feel weak for not being able to protect him, picking up Talia brought a rush of adrenaline, of strength and vitality, topped off with red-hot desire.

Derek had heard of Sugar Lake, though he'd never been to Sweetwater. From what he'd seen on his drive in, it was a charming town with cobblestone streets and old-fashioned storefronts. Talia's two-story town house was located just beyond the marina, overlooking Sugar Lake, which was half-frozen. He knocked on the door, and seconds later he was staring at the most gorgeous woman he'd ever seen. Cascades of dark hair tumbled over her sleek, bare shoulders. Hints of olive-colored lace peeked out beneath an off-the-shoulder beige sweater. Tight jeans hugged her mile-long legs, tucked into knee-high, olive-colored suede boots. Her lusciously plump lips and the expressive brown eyes that had first reeled him in smiled back at him.

"Wow," slipped out before he could form a more refined greeting. "You look gorgeous." He leaned in and kissed her cheek. "Mm. And you smell like Tuscany in the summertime. Fresh, citrusy, and utterly alluring."

"Thank you," she said with an air of disbelief. She blinked several times, her eyes roaming over his face and hair, then slowly down the length of him.

He ran his hand down his rumpled vest and shirt. "I didn't have time to iron."

"Who needs an iron?" she said a little breathlessly. "You look incredible. I never knew I had a thing for guys with long hair, but for lack of a better word, *wow* yourself. I *love* your hair up and kind of down like that. Don't get me wrong; I really like it down, too."

He absently touched his hair. He'd pinned it back, but strands always broke free. He'd never thought about it much until now, and he was glad he'd pinned it up.

"And your outfit is perfect, like you walked out of a *Casual Male* fashion magazine or something. Maybe I should change?" She took a step back into the foyer, and he touched her hand.

"Don't change a thing. We're perfectly matched. Two *wows.*"

She laughed softly and tucked her hair behind her ear. "Come in while I get my coat."

He stepped inside and felt Talia all around him, from the pretty peach walls with white accents to the demure gray couch with colorful throw pillows in the living room to the left of the foyer. A ceramic bowl holding a set of keys and a pen sat on a table by the front door, along with a small notebook, a box from Sweetie Pie Bakery, and a flyer for a cooking class. He remembered Talia's derogatory comment about her cooking skills and brightened at the thought of her taking a class. It seemed a very *Talia* thing to do.

He glanced at a group of photographs on a table at the base of the stairs. The resemblance between Talia and her family was too strong to deny. She had her father's eyes, her mother's nose, and she was *much* prettier than any of her sisters. Her brother stood protectively between the girls, with two on either side, his arms around them all. He was glad she had him looking after her. But his favorite picture was of a little brown-haired, brown-eyed Talia and three tiny blondes, all wearing polka-dot bikinis with oranges stuffed in the tops like boobs. They were arm in arm, beaming at the camera with gap-toothed grins. Behind the girls, a lanky boy stood with his arms out, showing off his biceps.

That single picture told him everything he needed to know about Talia, her happy childhood, and her close-knit family.

"I like your place," he said as she retrieved her coat from the foyer closet.

"Thanks. I've rented here for several years. I like the view of the lake, and I can walk to town."

When she turned, his eyes were drawn to a speck of something brown beside her lower lip. "Come here, beautiful. You've got something . . ." He reached up and wiped it off.

She covered her mouth with her hand, and her gaze shifted to a bakery box. Embarrassment shimmered in her eyes.

He chuckled. "How many doughnuts did you devour before our date?"

"It's chocolate baklava." She lowered her hand and said, "How hard did *you* work out before our date?"

"I actually didn't have time to work out." He stepped closer, his gaze lingering on her mouth as she licked her lips. "Can I assume this is chocolate?" He held up his finger, and she answered with a smile. He sucked the sweetness from his finger, and her eyes flamed. "Tell me, Talia, did the sugar do the trick?"

"No," came out in a lustful rush of minty air.

"Good." He pushed both hands into her hair, framing her face between his palms, and gazed deeply into her eyes. "I'm going to kiss you now, so if you don't want me to, you have about three seconds to say 'Please don't.'"

Neither one of them blinked as he mentally struggled through two of the longest seconds of his life. She shot up on her toes, grabbed his jacket, and pulled him into the kiss he was already taking. He sank into her sweet, hot mouth, pulling her closer as he intensified his efforts. Her arms circled his neck, and he swept one arm around her, holding her so tight he could feel her heart beating against his chest. He'd thought about kissing her so many times, wondered if she'd kiss like she did everything else, confidently, with a measure of caution, but as he kissed her harder, more demanding, taking everything she had to give, she was right there with him, her tongue searching, probing, her body shifting and arching, igniting an inferno inside him. He couldn't resist tangling his fingers into her soft, silky hair, earning the most seductive sound he'd ever heard. It wound through him like liquid fire, stoking his most primal urges.

Their kisses were endless, her mouth was magnificent, and if he didn't break their connection soon, he might never stop. He'd promised her a date, and as much as he wanted to continue kissing her—to carry her up to her bedroom, strip her bare, and devour every luscious inch of her—he forced himself to put on the brakes, easing to a series of languid, intoxicating kisses. When they finally parted, he couldn't stand it, and pressed his lips to hers once more.

They came away breathless, and he touched his forehead to hers, holding her trembling body against him. He couldn't remember a single kiss, a single connection, as powerful as this one.

"Wow," they said in unison.

He pressed his lips to hers again. "Sorry. I just had to get that over with or I might have burst."

"Me too," she said softly, running shaky fingers over her lips as if they still tingled like his did.

Her eyes fluttered open, and he was captivated by the raw emotions looking back at him.

"That was supposed to take the edge off before we met my friends."

"Oh . . ."

"I don't think it did," he said with a grin.

"Then you're doing better than me. I *know* it didn't."

The both looked at the bakery box and said, "Sugar!"

On the way to meet his friends, Derek filled Talia in on what they were like. She tried to concentrate on their descriptions, but she was too busy reveling in the aftermath of their incredible kisses. She could still feel the scratch of his scruff, the hard press of his lips. Her ability to focus ebbed, but she'd heard enough that when they arrived, she found they were just as quirky, friendly, and wonderful as he'd described.

India Cosgrove, a vibrant woman who looked to be around Piper's age and size, was hosting the get-together. She had skin the color of honey and the most gorgeous corkscrew curls billowing around her pretty face. She greeted Talia with a tight hug.

"So, you're the woman who nearly ran over our boy," India said with a twinkle in her eyes.

"No, I—" Before Talia could get her response out, Eli Winslow, a dead ringer for Adam Driver, complete with lanky body, angular nose, jet-black hair, and a brown fedora, put his arm around her and pulled her against his side.

"Don't mind India," Eli said as he dragged Talia toward the colorful kitchen. "She's always looking for ways to meet guys."

Talia looked over her shoulder and saw Derek talking with India, but he was watching her and Eli.

In the kitchen, a woman with wavy shoulder-length salt-and-pepper hair and kind eyes set down the dish she'd taken from the oven, pulled off her oven mitts and placed them on the counter, and said, "You must be Talia. I'm Phyllis. It's a pleasure to meet you."

"Hi. Derek's said such nice things about you."

"He's lying again?" Eli teased.

Derek set the cooler he'd brought on the table and then pried Eli's hand from Talia's shoulder, and the two exchanged a manly embrace.

"Good to see you, man. I missed you last week."

"Yeah . . ." Eli shook his head. "Mom had a rough one."

"I'm sorry." Derek stepped behind Talia and leaned in close. His breath slid over her cheek as he pressed a kiss beside her ear and said, "Can I take your coat?" He helped her off with it and laid it over a chair in the corner of the room with the others.

The house smelled spicy and delicious, and it was filled with plants—hanging and potted. Music played in the living room, giving the gathering a festive feel as they set dishes on the table. Derek hummed to the music as he lit candles. He and Phyllis danced around the room, swinging their hips and shoulders. He looked happy. They all did. India whipped from one end of the kitchen to the other, setting out napkins and condiments and directing Talia so she was kept busy, too. Talia had been so nervous when she was getting ready for their date, she'd changed her clothes several times while fielding texts from her sisters, each suggesting a different outfit. His friends were so easygoing, she didn't know what she'd been nervous about.

"I'm envious of your green thumb," she said to India as they carried wineglasses to the table.

India looked around the dining room at the tall palms, hanging ferns, and other plants and said, "They represent life and make me feel like I can breathe, no matter what else is going on."

"Well, they're lovely."

"Why don't we sit down and eat? I have Eli's sangria!" Phyllis set a pitcher on the table, among the veritable feast of falafel, cilantro and lime chicken, paella, and several dishes that hadn't yet been explained but looked delicious.

Derek pulled out Talia's chair. "I know you don't drink, so don't feel pressure to taste the sangria."

"I don't drink much, but I'd like to try it."

He took the seat beside her and filled her glass, then proceeded to pour some for each of the others. Then he took Talia's hand and lifted it to his lips, pressing a kiss to the back of it. "I'm glad you're here."

"Me too. Outside of family and Fletch, I don't get together with people very often. Thank you for inviting me. And thank you," she said to the others, "for letting me join you."

Eli lifted his glass. "To new friends and lovers!"

"Eli." Derek gave him a narrow-eyed warning.

"What?" Eli clinked glasses with India and winked at Talia. "He's a good guy. Don't hold us weirdos against him."

Derek touched his glass to hers. His blue eyes coasted slowly over her, lingering like she was the only thing he saw. His lips curved up in a smile that reached his eyes and filled her heart. Why was she so drawn to him? *Um, maybe because I finally met a guy who has his priorities straight and is interesting and as tasty as hot fudge.* A nest of butterflies swarmed in her belly, and she realized Eli was still looking at her as if he were expecting a response.

"I don't want to hold anything against Derek but *me*." She had no idea where she'd gotten the courage to say that, since she'd never before been that bold. But Derek and his friends made her feel like they were already a couple, and it was the truth. She didn't want him holding another woman.

Eli whipped out his phone and took a few pictures. When he turned the camera on her and Derek, Derek kissed her.

"Nice," Eli said. "My turn!" He grabbed India's shirt as she came around the edge of the table and pushed his lips out like a fish.

India twisted out of his reach, laughing. "Eli! We've been over this."

Eli scoffed. "One day you'll give in."

"Or not." India set a tray of baked brie with figs, walnuts, and pistachios on the table. She sat down and said, "So, Talia. Who do you take care of?"

Talia looked at Derek. "Um . . . ? Take care of?"

"I forgot to mention we're all caring for our parents," Derek explained. "India and her sister take care of their father, who had a stroke last year. Eli's mother had him late in life, and she's struggling with memory problems and severe arthritis."

"She's stubborn as a bull, too," Eli said.

"My parents are elderly, but they're not ill," Phyllis said. "They need help navigating more and more lately."

Talia's heart opened even more to Derek and his friends. "I don't have anyone that I'm taking care of like that, but I can appreciate how hard that must be. How did you guys meet?"

"We met through a support group Eli runs," India explained.

"It's hard," Phyllis agreed. "You can't hold down a full-time job unless you can afford a caregiver. Most friendships go by the wayside. Not many people understand that you have to plan things way ahead of time, often need to be home early, and you might have to cancel at the last minute because your relative is having a hard time." She looked thoughtfully at the others and said, "Then you find a few special people who get it. And they become your new friends. Your new family."

"But not everyone is as understanding," Eli said. "It's tough, taking care of aging parents, and there are plenty of people who feel stuck with the responsibility. Hell, sometimes we all do, and we help each other through those times. We get along so well because we're *not* holding grudges against our parents for something they can't help."

"They raised us," India said. "It seems only fair that we give them the same love and attention they gave us when we needed it most."

"That's beautiful," Talia said. Some days she thought taking care of herself was more than she could handle, and they were giving up huge parts of their lives to take care of their parents. "They're lucky to have you. I'd like to think that if or when the time comes, my siblings and I would share in the caretaking. I guess it really makes you think about your future, and maybe having to put some of your dreams on hold. Each of you must be doing that to some extent."

"Have you told her about Our Friends' House?" India asked.

Derek shook his head. "I didn't want to send her running for the hills just yet."

"Our Friends' House?" Talia asked.

"You mentioned putting our dreams on hold. We've all done that. I once dreamed of running my own restaurant. Father and son, you know? *Team Grant.* But taking care of my father has opened my eyes to what really matters, and I developed a new dream. That's why I went back to school. I want to open an adult day-care center for families like ours whose loved ones aren't ready for a nursing home but need full-time care."

"And we all want in on it," India said. "My sister Sahara is a doctor, and she's going to help part-time. Phyllis is a physical therapist. Derek cooks, entertains, and knows a heck of a lot about running a facility because he's a research nut, and Eli is a therapist."

"*Was,*" Eli corrected her. "I'm more of a part-time counselor now. And India is . . . *India.*"

"Hey!" India scowled at him. "I spent three years working in a doctor's office, handling billing and reception. I'll be taking care of the administrative end as well as just *being me*, and keeping everyone happy."

"Which she does really well," Phyllis added.

"This is brilliant." Talia was unable to hide her astonishment. "This could help so many families. I've heard of adult day-care facilities. But isn't it expensive to put something like this together? Where will you do it?"

"I've spent two years researching and putting together a business profile outlining budgets, staffing, the whole deal. I've also had a few meetings with the administrators of the senior center here in town to pick their brains. They've been really helpful in fielding my questions and giving guidance." Derek spoke passionately, his eyes glimmering with excitement. "And as for where, my father and I live in a massive old farmhouse that needs work, but it's on a quiet street, and I've already obtained preliminary approval to make it into a day-care facility, assuming we get through renovations and meet all the criteria. I've got a nice nest egg from dancing, but I've got another year or so before I'll have enough saved to begin the process, and then I hope to pay off the renovations within two years after that so there aren't any loans hanging over my head."

The image of people throwing money at him when he danced came rushing back. The pieces of his life, and his adamancy about continuing to dance, started to make sense.

"Even with us all chipping in, we're still short a good bit of capital," India explained.

Talia's mind raced in a hundred directions. She wished Ben were there. He might be able to give them some advice. "I wish I knew more about raising capital. This is really impressive."

"We're not doing it to be impressive," Derek said with a serious look in his eyes.

"I understand, but that doesn't lessen how remarkable it is that you all came together and are developing a business that should be available to families around here. This will touch the lives of so many people. It's inspiring. You're *all* inspiring, giving so much of yourselves. Derek, you're lucky that you can afford to work part-time and still make enough to care for your father, while saving money toward the center, but how many people can afford to give up their full-time jobs? I think people will be breaking down your doors to get in."

"We want to keep it small and personable," Phyllis said. "At least at first, until we find our footing."

"This will never be about money," Derek said gently. "This is about people. We always say that what we do for a living isn't who we are, but this endeavor? This *is* about who we are."

The more Talia learned about him, the harder she fell for the man he was and all that he stood for.

Dinner was delicious, and the banter was entertaining. Derek and his friends treated one another like siblings. They had deep discussions about life and lightheartedly pondered how their dreams had changed over the years. They teased and joked and weren't afraid to show their real emotions. Talia couldn't remember the last time she'd enjoyed an evening as much as she enjoyed tonight. Derek and his friends also seemed genuinely interested in hearing about her and the classes she taught. It was easy to see why Derek had bonded with them, and even easier to see that these were more than friends. She imagined gatherings like tonight were rejuvenating for all of them. *Including me.*

They danced around the kitchen as they cleared the table to prepare for dessert, though she was so full from their pre-dinner sugarfest and the delicious meal, she wasn't sure she could eat another bite.

"Talia's sister made chocolate baklava," Derek said, then dipped his head and kissed her shoulder as he walked past.

She felt like she was in a scene from *The Big Chill*—and loved every second of it. Outside of her family, she'd never had friends like these, who were so open and fun, but also serious about family and life. And never in a million years would she have imagined herself dancing around someone else's kitchen with people she'd just met. She gazed across the room at Derek, and her heart stumbled. *Oh yes, Mr. Blue Eyes, you are definitely turning my world upside down, and I never thought I'd like that, either.*

"My favorite!" India said. "You should bring her sometime. Anyone who makes chocolate baklava deserves to feast with us."

"Willow would *love* this. She was very intrigued by my guy and his request for a Mediterranean dessert."

The room went silent, save for the music as Derek's friends exchanged approving glances. Derek took her hand and pulled her against him, and she realized what she'd said.

"Your *guy*?" he asked.

"It just came out," she said quickly, but for the first time since college, she felt—*truly felt*—excited about, and interested in, a man. She didn't want to tiptoe around it or pretend it wasn't the most amazing feeling, so she said, "But I kind of hope it's true. I mean, if you—"

Her words were silenced by the press of his lips. His friends hooted and cheered, making her blush a red streak.

"I'm your guy, beautiful," he said against her lips, and began a sensual dance.

This wasn't a stage dance meant to impress. His body swayed fluidly and somehow also powerfully, moving with her, not *for* her, as he gazed deeply into her eyes. She felt herself letting go, lifting more of her barriers, wanting to be even closer to him. In the next second, images of him up onstage, dancing in front of all those other women, came at her, stealing a little of her joy. She felt herself stiffen, and confusion rose in his eyes. He began singing along with the stereo in a low, seductive voice about taking his arm and walking down the street.

His gaze turned pleading, as if he'd read her mind and understood her struggle. He pressed his cheek to hers, still singing, though this was no song she'd ever heard before. This was meant for her ears only.

"Let it go, sweet Talia. It's not who I am; you know it's true. Be with me. Let me show you." He drew back, never missing a beat. His hands splayed across her back possessively, honesty welling in the depths of his eyes as he said, "You can trust me to be careful with your heart."

All it took was one look for him to understand what was going on in her head and, more importantly, for him to want to make her comfortable. She was safe with him and somehow knew she could trust him not to hurt her. His words soothed her, his body beckoned her, and the tension faded away. She melted against him as he sang to her, and the lingering weight of her worries lifted. It was an amazing and frightening feeling to trust someone that much. They danced through several songs, his friends singing and swaying around them, and soon, to her surprise, it all felt natural—dancing, trusting, the safety of Derek and this group of friends. It didn't matter that she hadn't known any of them long or that there were aspects of Derek's job she struggled with, because those aspects enabled him to give more of himself to his father and, if he realized his dreams, to also help many more families. The way he focused on her, cared about her comfort, made it easy to feel like she belonged. Like *they* belonged *together*. She gave herself permission not to overthink or overanalyze, but to enjoy another romantic evening with the man who made her heart happy.

When the song ended, Derek continued holding her, dancing, as he whispered, "Are you looking for the nearest exit so you can sprint back to your comfort zone yet?"

He'd held her hand all evening and shared his dinner, offering tastes of different dishes and explaining who'd made what. He laughed at her jokes and paid complete attention when she spoke, making it easy to forget this was their first real date. And as she gazed into the bottomless blue eyes of the man who had appeared unexpectedly in her life and was surprising her at every turn, running away was the last thing on her mind.

"I'm actually hoping tonight never ends."

On the drive home, Talia was a hot mess. Her hormones were in overdrive, taking full advantage of their venture out of their comfort zone and making her a nervous wreck. This was worse than finals week when she was in college. Worse than when she lost her virginity, because at least then she'd had enough alcohol in her system to dull her nerves. This was knee-knocking, stomach-tumbling nervousness. *Wanting Derek* had become *all* she could think about. He was as tender and thoughtful as he was manly, and every time those blue eyes locked on her, she got the feeling he looked deeper and saw more of the *real* her than anyone ever had. *Oh*, how she wanted to feel all his tenderness and his virility when he touched her, those big hands wandering all over her naked body. Heat shivered down her spine as he parked by her house and came around to her side of the car to help her out.

"Shall we?" He reached for her hand.

At five nine, Talia was the tallest of her sisters, and she had relatively large hands. Derek's hand *engulfed* hers, sparking more dirty thoughts about what she'd like him to do with them. She usually turned into a motormouth when she was nervous, but as he walked her to her door, she wasn't sure she could even form a coherent *good night* without attacking him.

On the porch, she fidgeted with her keys. Should she invite him in? She wanted to, but would that make her seem easy? She wasn't *easy*, and she had a feeling he already knew that, but right that second, after so many steamy kisses and such a wonderful night, every beat of her heart pushed her to *be* easy with him.

"I can't remember the last time I've had so much fun. Thank you for coming with me tonight." He gathered her in his arms and slid his hand possessively to the nape of her neck. "You're shaking. Cold?"

"Nervous. *So* nervous." *Oh my gosh. I'm so lame . . .*

Flames rose in his eyes. He brushed his lips over her cheek and said, "Let me help you with that."

His lips covered hers, soft and sweet, like the first step outside on a summer day, warm and inviting. *Exhilarating.* His fingers tightened in her hair, and a moan of appreciation crawled from his lungs, vibrating into their kiss. That sound unleashed hours—days? years?—of pent-up desire, and she went a little wild. Kissing him ravenously, she shoved her fingers into his hair, causing it to break free from its tether and tumble over her wrists. Why did that turn her on even more? Her world was spinning, and her body was on a mission, pressing against his hard frame, feeling every inch of his desire, urging him to *take* more. Her hands moved along his broad shoulders, his muscles flexing against her palms as her hands glided down his back. Blood rushed in her ears as she fought the urge to go lower. She wanted to feel more of him so badly, just the thought of touching his ass made her go damp. She craved taking what she wanted, but she'd never been a taker. He intensified their kisses, and every stroke of his tongue chipped away at her good-girl resolve. When he moaned, the greedy sound shattered her last shred of restraint. She lowered her hands to his firm butt, and her emotions skidded and whirled, drawing a long, surrendering moan from her lungs. His hips ground against her, setting off fireworks behind her closed eyelids, and her back met the door, shocking her back to reality.

They were making out like horny teenagers on her front porch!

She reluctantly tore her mouth from his, instantly mourning the loss, and panted out, "We should go inside."

He framed her face with his hands as he'd done earlier, his eyes storming with passion. "If I come in, there's a chance I'll get called away in the middle . . ."

Her entire body clenched in anticipation.

"I don't want to do that to you," he said. "I won't do that to you. In an hour I won't want to leave you even more than I don't want to right now. But make no mistake about this. I *want* you, Talia, only you. I want you like I've never wanted a woman in my life. I want to be closer to you, to feel your naked body against mine. To become one with you in every sense."

Yes . . . God, yes.

Her body shook with desire. She couldn't speak, could barely think.

"My life is complicated, but I want to see you again and again and again," he said. "Even if only for a few stolen minutes, an hour, whatever we can get. Maria is taking care of my father for a few hours tomorrow morning so I can run a few errands. Can I see you then?"

"I promised to go dress shopping with my sisters." Her words came fast and breathless. "What about at night?"

"I have to work. Sunday? I'm taking my father to a museum. Come with us?"

She stifled the urge to accept right away, her brain slowly awakening. "Are you sure you don't want that time alone with him?"

"Talia. My sweet, careful Talia," he said softly. "I want you there. My life is always going to be complicated, and I know it's another strange date request, so I'll understand if you'd rather not—"

"No," she said quickly. "I *want* to go. I just didn't want to intrude."

"Don't worry, my careful girl," he said sweetly. "You're no intrusion. Are you ready for another great date starter? Would it be too much to ask you to meet us at my place? The museum is about half an hour from there, and the fewer changes to my father's routine, the better."

"I don't mind at all." She loved that he wasn't embarrassed to ask for what he needed in order for his father to be comfortable. "Is there anything I should know before meeting him?"

Something akin to gratitude washed over him. "Sometimes he calls me Archie, when he thinks I'm his brother, and he might get agitated when we're out. I never know when something will set him off, so we try to keep to a routine, but even that might not help. And he has moments of lucidity that are like glimpses into who he used to be. They're gifts, and I treasure every single one of them." He opened his hand and looked at it, his fingers curling slowly. "Those moments, they're like sand slipping through my fingers. I try to hold on to them, and . . ." He shrugged, but the longing in his eyes told of his anguish. "What you really need to know is that he was a supportive father who fed my love of music and art and my passion for life. He was a loving husband to my mother and a hardworking man. The person you'll meet is a shell of the man he once was."

"If he did all those things for you, that part of him isn't gone. It lives on inside you, and it'll be an honor to meet him."

He touched his lips to hers in another tummy-tumbling kiss. "Remind me to thank your family for distracting you enough to almost run me over." He kissed her again, softer this time, as if he was weaning them off deeper kisses. "If you haven't yet figured out that I'm not a charmed prince, you will soon."

She couldn't resist running her fingers through his hair. "Princes are given everything in life. I prefer a man who gives as much as he gets."

CHAPTER SEVEN

SATURDAY SUCKED. DEREK ended up working two shifts, one as a bartender and one to cover a dancer who called out sick. Although he'd made a slew of tips dancing, there had been a group of drunk women celebrating their friend's twenty-first birthday, and a handful of them had hung around the parking lot after he closed for the night. He was used to being propositioned—and turning them down—but it never failed to surprise him how far some women went to be noticed. He'd been flashed, offered blow jobs, hand jobs, sex with multiple partners, and just about everything else under the sun. It had always been easy to walk away, especially now, since the only person he wanted to be propositioned by was a certain professor with cautious eyes and a hungry heart.

Sunday afternoon, as he waited for Talia to arrive, he remembered what she'd said about his father's goodness living on in him. Her comment had given him an enormous sense of pride. He looked up from his drawing, taking in his father's profile as he gazed out the window. Missing the man his father had been was a never-ending, bone-deep ache inside him. This disease was cruel not only to the person it lived in, but to those lives that person touched. He'd never regretted anything he had to do to make sure his father had everything he needed, and he knew if his father were lucid, he'd want him to do whatever it took to help other families who were in the same situation. He could only hope that one day Talia would be okay with his dancing, because he needed that income and flexibility to make it all happen.

He set his hand on his father's leg, catching his attention, and said, "Pop, you remember we're going to the museum soon, and my friend Talia is coming along?" Derek knew his father wouldn't remember their plans for the outing, but he always posed questions as if he might, just in case he got lucky. They'd had a nice morning, and his chest constricted as he waited for his father to respond, hoping this wouldn't agitate him.

"Okay," his father said, then went back to looking out the window.

He sighed with relief. Another hurdle avoided. *At least for now.* He went back to drawing, and a few minutes later he heard Talia's car out front. Adrenaline pushed him to his feet, and he watched her through the front window as she parked. "I'll be right back, Pop."

He raked his hands through his hair, taking a moment to settle himself down. He didn't want to seem overly anxious even though he was. He opened the door just as she climbed the porch steps, looking gorgeous bundled up in her red coat and flashing her heart-melting smile. The day they'd spent apart felt like a year. How was it possible that he'd missed her so much in such a short time? Drawn to her like a bee to a flower, he stepped outside and gathered her in his arms. His entire body exhaled. This was so right. She belonged in his arms.

"Hey there, *Teach.* It should be illegal to look as good as you do every day of the week."

Her arms circled his neck, happiness twinkling in her eyes. It was the greatest sight he'd ever seen. Well, other than the lustful looks she'd given him the other night.

"I'm no longer your teacher, and you need to kiss me quick, before I die of anticipation."

"Sweet Jesus, you are the most precious thing."

He lowered his lips to hers, going for a tender kiss, but his first taste of her sent bolts of heat coursing through him, and when she pushed her hands into his hair, making sensual sounds, tenderness was a lost cause. He deepened the kiss, and they stumbled with the force of it, crashing against the wall beside the front door. In his T-shirt, his arms took the brunt of the brick, and those abrasions only made their make-out session that much hotter. She fisted her fingers in his hair, holding on so tight the sting shot to his cock, sending his hips bucking forward.

"Mm," she moaned, and tugged on his hair again.

"Fuck, Talia," he ground out.

He wedged himself between her legs, grinding against her. Their kisses turned rougher, more urgent, as if these few seconds might be all they ever got. And hell if that didn't rattle Derek to his core. Thinking of his father alone in the house, he reluctantly broke away. Her lips glistened, pink and alluring. Fire and ice battled inside him with the realization that he needed to get inside. But he wasn't ready, not yet. He *had* to have more.

He laced his fingers with hers and took her in another cock-throbbing kiss. She arched against him, wanting and needy. *Fuuuck.*

"I can't stop kissing you," he said between bouts of devouring her. "But I have to."

"I know." She went up on her toes, allowing him to consume more of her.

When they finally parted, they were both breathless. He pinned their joined hands above her head, because if she touched his hair again, he was going to lose it. Her eyes said *take me*, her writhing body pleaded *now*, but she was worrying her lower lip in the way that made his insides go soft. He released her hands and gathered her in his arms. "Was that a giant leap outside your comfort zone?"

"You have no idea how giant."

He met her smiling eyes and kissed her softly. "I *do* know, Talia. I see so much that you try to keep hidden."

"Everything with you is outside my comfort zone," she said with a more serious expression. "But I've decided my family is right. It's time I step outside that familiar circle, and I want to do it with you."

Her gaze moved over his face, slowing at his mouth so long, his body rocked into her again, earning a sensual sigh.

"Maybe I'm part of your new comfort zone." He kissed her again, slow and sweet, before finally putting space between them for the last time. He straightened her coat, tucked her hair behind her ear, touching her anywhere he could without ramping up their arousal, because not touching her wasn't an option.

She inhaled deeply and blew it out slowly. "I was nervous about meeting your dad. You got rid of that anxiety, but now there's *this* between us, and I'm going to be hot and bothered all day."

"Want to go back to your car and start over?" he teased.

She shook her head. "It wouldn't matter if we never touched. This heat between us is inescapable. Your eyes do me in every time."

"Man, do I love knowing that."

He kissed her quickly, aware of the minutes ticking by. "Before you meet my father, I just want to remind you again that sometimes he gets agitated, and—"

She quieted him with a hand to his chest. "You don't have to warn me. I read about Alzheimer's last night. From what I understand, with mild dementia, people can go through their normal days, but little things get missed. Maybe their shirt is on backward, or they might go searching for something and can't remember what it was, or tear apart a cabinet and forget they were looking for something altogether and even deny they made the mess if asked. And in moderate dementia, the person lives more moment to moment, needing routine. Even simple things—like a stranger showing up," she said with a compassionate glance, "can throw the person off. There was so much information. I don't remember all of it, but I know some sensory aspects are difficult. A shower can feel like a hailstorm; discomfort can come from spaces feeling confined or cold or any number of things, which can cause the person's world to feel out of control and confusing." She swallowed hard, and hurt rose in her eyes. "Not to mention, they're losing words, and things become hard to process. The language they'd always known, their surroundings, and the people they love are suddenly foreign to them."

She pressed a kiss to the center of his chest and said, "It's such a terrible disease. I don't want to make anything harder for either of you, so if at any point my being around is too much, I won't be hurt if you ask me to leave. And on the flip side, I would really like to get to know the man who raised you, in any form possible."

Derek's throat thickened with emotions. He felt splayed open, with all the heartache he'd experienced exposed. At the same time, he was filled with gratitude and wonder for the woman he'd only just gotten to know who had taken it upon herself to try to at least understand his father and his situation.

Talia wasn't afraid of many things, but when she was researching Alzheimer's, fear and compassion swelled inside her, and she'd ended up in tears. The thought of losing a loved one to such a horrible disease frightened her, but that wasn't the worst of it. She'd learned that early- or younger-onset Alzheimer's was caused by a gene mutation and there was a high probability of it being passed down to children. Derek was not only caring for his father without any familial support, but surely he knew what she'd only just discovered, and that tore her heart out and told her just how strong a man he really was.

Derek slipped her coat from her shoulders and hung it on a hook in the foyer, giving her a moment to take in her surroundings. From the outside, the farmhouse had a welcoming, lived-in feel, though it was in need of a little TLC, with missing shingles and a faded red metal roof over an expansive front porch, which she'd noticed was missing a few balusters. She wondered if Piper or her father could replace them for him. The interior was clean and well loved. Hardwood floors had faded paths from one room to the next, ingrained with the history of family life. A small kitchen was tucked to the left of the front door, the spacious, high-ceilinged living room to the right. The foyer opened to a wide hallway feeding two rooms behind closed doors and another open living area. It was easy to imagine Derek as a boy racing through the house in sock feet.

He took her hand. "Ready?"

She felt tension in the tightness of his grip as he led her into his living room to meet his father. Flaxen-colored walls with off-white trim, earth-toned sofas, and upholstered end chairs made the room feel homey. Bookshelves packed tight ran along a half wall separating the living room from the foyer, and a fireplace flanked with tall windows made Talia want to cuddle up with Derek and hunker down for the evening by a roaring fire. The mantel was decorated with pictures of Derek and, she assumed, his parents, since the man in them appeared to be a younger version of the gentleman currently sitting in a leather recliner, looking through a journal.

Derek squeezed her hand and then released it as he crouched beside his father's chair and touched his hand, drawing his attention. Talia's thoughts skidded at the deep-set, radiant blue eyes gazing up at Derek. Only while Derek's were strikingly aware of everything, his father's eyes had the softness of a man looking at the surface, but not actively participating in his surroundings, which tugged at her heartstrings. She saw so much of Derek in his father's features, the dark brows that arched up at the edges, a square jaw covered with a few days' whiskers, and large hands. Did Derek see himself in his father, too? If so, did that scare him?

"Pop, this is my friend Talia. She's coming with us to the museum today," Derek explained.

His father's eyes moved slowly over her face, and a smile lifted his cheeks. "Eva, you love the museum."

Derek glanced at her, and then he looked at his father and said, "Talia does look a lot like Mom."

She put her hand on Derek's shoulder, recalling what she'd read about helping Alzheimer's patients feel good about themselves. She knew not to try to convince his father she wasn't his late wife. "I'm going to take that as a compliment," she said gently. "I do love museums."

The gratitude in Derek's eyes warmed her to her toes.

"This must be Dusty." His father pointed to a drawing in the leather journal on his lap. "But this is wrong. Dusty was smaller. I'll have to fix that."

Talia glanced at the cartoonish drawing as Derek took the journal from his father's lap.

"Dusty was my father's dog when he was young," Derek explained. "Let's put this down for now so we can go to the museum."

"Eva loves the museum," his father said as he rose to his feet.

They went to the foyer, and as Derek helped his father into his coat, his father's brows knitted and he stared at Talia for a long moment. She could see something changing. Despite having researched the disease, she was struck by how clouds seemed to lift from his father's mind and the way his gaze became clearer, more active.

"Hello," his father said. "Derek, aren't you going to introduce me to your friend?"

"I am." Derek put his arm around Talia, relief evident in the cadence of his voice. "Pop, this is Talia Dalton."

A haunted smile appeared on his father's face. It was the smile of someone who knew they were slipping away. He took Talia's hand between the two of his and said, "How'd my son swindle a pretty girl like you into coming over?"

Derek chuckled. "Talia, *this* is my father, Jonah Grant."

CHAPTER EIGHT

THE HALOWELL HOUSE was a small arts museum located in an old brick Colonial in the historic section of Harmony Pointe. The wide-planked hardwood floors creaked, the walls were chipped, and Norma, the petite, wire-haired woman who ran the place, had to be eighty years old—and one of the kindest women Talia had ever met. Derek hadn't clued her in to the fact that the museum was normally closed on Sundays, but Norma opened it just for Derek and Jonah and had been doing so for the past few years, whenever they wanted to visit.

As his father looked over the artwork hanging on the walls, Derek explained that overstimulation often caused confusion and agitation for his father. He didn't want to give up taking him to the places that Jonah had always enjoyed, so he'd made arrangements with Norma.

"I spent so much time in this museum with my parents when I was growing up that being here brings back good memories. I hope it sparks some for him, too."

She'd been wondering about his mother, but she didn't want to get into a heavy discussion that might sadden him, so she simply asked, "What was your mother like?"

He glanced at his father with a nostalgic expression. "She was everything my father isn't or wasn't. She was an accountant—organized, efficient, and methodical in everything she did. She was careful, like you. My father used to say she was the ink to his pen." His gaze softened.

"Almost every memory I have of my father includes a notebook or drawing pad in his hand or pocket. If he wasn't coming up with recipes or taking notes on life, he was drawing. He was an incredible cartoonist. Still is sometimes."

"Was that his drawing of Dusty?"

He shook his head. "It wasn't Dusty. That was one of mine. But when we get back I'll show you his drawings."

"And yours?" she asked, excited to see another side of him.

He slipped an arm around her waist, eyeing his father. "And mine." Pulling her closer, he said, "I hope you're not too bored."

"Not even a little," she said. "I've never been here, and experiencing it with you and your dad makes it even more special."

After a quick kiss, they joined his father, who seemed to appreciate meandering through the museum. Derek answered his questions and didn't rush him or get irritated when he had to repeat answers several times. Talia added *patience* to the growing list of things about Derek she admired. The brief lucid moments his father experienced throughout the day were as heartbreaking as they were incredible, giving Talia a peek into the depth of their relationship. Those short-lived moments brought new life to Derek's eyes, only to be stolen away far too quickly. She ached at the emotional battering he and his father were going through.

"This is my favorite part of the visit," Derek whispered to her. He put a hand on his father's back and said, "Let's go see what's in the local artist section."

"They have local artists? How nice," his father said as Derek guided him into the next room.

The room was smaller than the others, with only a handful of drawings hanging on the walls. Talia admired the pen-and-ink cartoons, each one signed in the lower-right corner by Jonah. Shocked by the realization, she couldn't help but stare at Jonah, trying to put the pieces of an artist, chef, and father together with the man before her. He was inspecting a drawing, and she tried to see it through his eyes. Did he know it was his? The first cartoon was of a couple sitting on a blanket in the grass. A bottle of wine lay on its side next to a basket overflowing with food. A short-haired woman with wide, happy eyes lay on her stomach, bare feet in the air, her chin propped up in her palms as she watched a man with longish hair drawing in a notebook. The man's expression was serious. He had scruff on his cheeks, his mouth twisted in concentration as he drew a portrait of the woman. The only color in the drawing was the dusty pink on the woman's lips.

"Eva," his father said as he ran his finger over the image of the woman. His eyes filled with pride. "I drew this."

"It's beautiful." Emotions bubbled up inside her, and she looked at Derek, who was a little misty-eyed. "*She's* beautiful."

They moved to the next drawing, this one done in pencil. Eva stood in a field of wildflowers, her arms crossed over her pregnant belly. Her hair was a little longer, blowing away from her face, her eyes half-closed, a small smile on her lips. The wind blew her dress and cardigan, both varying shades of blue, against her, accentuating her belly.

Jonah blinked several times, and Talia wondered if he knew his wife was gone, or if he was reliving the moment he'd drawn that picture.

"I'm *talented*," he said with awe.

"Very talented," she agreed. "These are wonderful." When his father moved on to another picture, she whispered to Derek, "I thought your father was a chef? I didn't know he was also a well-known artist."

Derek squeezed her hand. "Let's just say this is another favor Norma was kind enough to carry out for me."

"You're amazing, arranging all this for your father, letting him relive his glory."

"Maybe I'm allowing us both to relive it."

After leaving the museum, they stopped at Fresh Eats, a small family-owned market, where the owner greeted Derek and his father by name and had their groceries waiting to be paid for. Derek explained that although he'd been raised to do things for himself, when he'd realized errands posed issues for his father, and with the constraints on his time, he'd had to rethink his stance on asking for special favors.

When they arrived back at Derek's house, his father settled in to watch television, and Talia and Derek unloaded the groceries. Talia hadn't known how she'd actually feel, spending the day with Derek and his father, although she'd wanted to enjoy it. As she and Derek put away the groceries, she realized that not only had she thoroughly enjoyed their time together, but Derek had opened up the most intimate part of his life to her.

"I'm not sure if there's anyone around to tell you this," she said, "but you're *really* good with your father."

"Thanks. I don't need anyone to tell me, but I appreciate hearing it from you."

"Everyone needs a pat on the back sometimes."

"Maybe, but this disease strips the ego from everyone it touches—patients, family members, caretakers . . ." Derek said as he put a head of lettuce in the fridge.

"Because you need to ask for special favors?" she asked as he drew her into his arms, smiling as if he hadn't a care in the world, though she knew better. It made her appreciate his happiness even more.

He pressed his lips to hers, soft and warm. "When the person who raised you, who you knew to be smart, funny, and sharp as a tack, doesn't recognize you, or gets angry and says hurtful things, you learn to let go of everything you were taught about standing up for yourself or expecting appreciation. Because that's the disease taking over, and that man in there? He doesn't need to feel any worse than he already does about what's happening to him. Better that I accept being wrong, take a verbal lashing that I know is not from his heart, or even become invisible when need be, and he remain in a peaceful place for as long as he can."

"I was thinking too narrowly, and I take it back. You aren't 'really good with him'; you're amazing all around."

"No, I'm not, babe. I'm just a regular guy taking care of his father the best way he can." He kissed her again. "I'd really like it if you'd stay for dinner. A little bird told me that you could use a cooking lesson. But if you've had enough babysitting for the day, I'll understand."

He'd given her an out before with his father, and she had to ask the burning question. "Do women usually tire of spending time with you and your father?"

"I wouldn't know. For the past few years, women haven't been a big part of my life." He dipped his head and kissed the hollow of her neck. "But I'm no saint, Talia. I don't want to mislead you. I've gone out with a few women, but, um . . ." He lifted a shoulder. "I wouldn't call them *dates*, and no other women have met him."

"Oh," she said, feeling a little uncomfortable. That shouldn't surprise her. Most of the people she knew had casual sex. But there was no denying the sting it brought hearing it from Derek. On the other hand, she much preferred his honesty to a man who would lie just to get her into bed. "Stress-relief hookups?"

"I don't know. I'd say they were more to remind myself I'm still a single guy in my late twenties even if my life isn't typical." He leaned against the counter, bringing her between his legs. "I'm not a sleazeball, Talia, but I'm not going to lie to you, even if it hurts. You mentioned having trust issues, and I want you to know that you can trust me. For you, I'm an open book."

Did he know how much of a turn-on his unrelenting honesty was? "Thank you. A cheating ex left me wary," she said softly.

"Well, I've never been a cheater, and I certainly would never cheapen our relationship in that way. My situation guides me through life, and there's no room for covering my tracks."

"Why me? Why now? Why not just try to have a one-night stand?"

His brow furrowed. "You are *not* a one-night-stand girl. You're too smart and you respect yourself too much. Hell, Talia, I respect you too much for that. And despite what I've done over the past few years, I'm not a one-night-stand type of guy. I want more out of life than meaningless hookups. Eventually, I want what my parents had. And right now"—he slid a hand to the nape of her neck, drawing her closer—"I want to kiss you until you forget everything I just said and go back to thinking about only you and me."

His lips smothered hers so exquisitely, she couldn't think at all. One hand threaded into her hair and the other slid to her ass, holding her against him from mouth to middle, and *oh*, did he feel good. Her insides flamed as their bodies took over, grinding and groping, electrifying her entire being. His whiskers abraded her skin with tantalizing prickles as he kissed the edges of her mouth and along her jaw, nipping and kissing a path down her neck. He slipped his finger into the collar of her sweater, tugging it down, stopping just short of the swell of her breast. Blood pounded through her veins as he touched his open mouth to her sensitive skin, tasting and then sucking so hard her knees nearly gave out. She stifled a moan, her gaze darting toward the living room.

He trailed kisses along her breastbone. "His chair creaks when he gets up."

"Then don't stop," she pleaded.

In the next breath, he had her against the counter, kissing her fiercely, groping her ass, and fondling her breasts. She clutched at his shoulders, bowed off the counter, trying to feel more of him.

When his mouth left hers, she arched her neck. *"Kissmekissmekissme—"*

She pushed his head lower, wanting more of the delicious sensations of his hot mouth on her skin. He lifted her sweater, revealing the blue lace bra she'd carefully chosen that morning, and made an utterly *male* sound. He kissed her above the lace, his hand wreaking havoc with her senses as he brushed his thumb over her nipple in lazy circles. Eyes closed, she pushed her hands into his back pocket, rocking against his hard heat. He sealed his mouth over her sensitive flesh and sucked so hard lust *zing*ed through her like sparks beneath her skin.

"Oh God. *Derek,*" she panted out, wanting, *needing* more.

Cool air washed over the swell of her breast as he lifted his mouth. She opened her eyes, meeting his approval-seeking gaze, and didn't hesitate as "Yes" left her lips.

Holding her gaze, he slid a finger into the cup of her bra and pulled it down, freeing her breast. And holy cow, the predatory look in his eyes was the sexiest thing she'd ever seen. He lowered his mouth, teasing her into a noodle-legged mess of desire. Her body trembled with every suck, and though she'd never before been this aggressive, this *unafraid* or turned on, she trusted him completely and guided his hand between her legs.

"Aw, fuck, Talia," he ground out.

His greedy voice sent lust coursing through her like a raging river, uncontrollable and inescapable. Their kisses turned frenzied as he shifted his body, blocking the view of her from the hallway. He adeptly unbuttoned her jeans and pushed his hand down the front at the same moment he claimed her mouth in another brutal kiss. His fingers moved swiftly to the place she needed him most, and he groaned into their kiss. That greedy noise and the feel of his hard shaft against her had her spreading her legs wider. He teased over her sex as he possessed her mouth in a kiss so deep and rough, fire sizzled in her veins. His fingers sank into her, and she gasped with pleasure. His thumb pressed on her clit, moving in a mind-numbing rhythm as his fingers found the magical spot that sent her up onto her toes. She couldn't concentrate on kissing, standing, or anything other than the pleasures radiating through her as he sent her soaring.

He swallowed her cries with more all-consuming kisses, until she collapsed in a breathless heap against him, her body jerking with aftershocks as he whispered, "Stay," in her ear.

Sometime later, after Talia agreed to stay for dinner and they both calmed enough to actually focus on something other than the passion consuming them, they watched a show with his father and then began cooking dinner. Derek couldn't stop looking at Talia. He moved closer so their arms touched as they sliced peppers, sweet potatoes, onions, and zucchini. He knew it was a lot to ask of her to accept his dancing, his father, his *life*. A shy smile lifted her lips, and in that moment he felt like she'd always been right there with him. Like she belonged there.

"You cut veggies like a pro. Are you sure you suck at cooking?" They were making herbed lamb cutlets with roasted vegetables, one of his father's favorite meals.

"I make a mean *microwave* meal." She glanced at the vegetables on his cutting board. "You cut twice as fast as I do."

"I've been doing it my whole life. You can't grow up with a chef and not learn from him. All those hours I spent at the restaurant paid off as a blessing in disguise. I can't imagine trying to order in or eating out with my father. There are too many foods we try to avoid, like processed and white foods, which aren't good for cognition, and too much agitation with crowds and unfamiliar surroundings."

"Do you cook all your father's meals?"

"Yes, except when Maria is here. It's not difficult. It just takes planning and the desire to want to eat something colorful and delicious that doesn't come from a box." He softened the tease with a kiss.

"Hey, don't dis my eating habits."

"I have no idea how you have survived this long on sugar and microwave meals, but I'd never try to get you to change, much less change what you enjoy eating."

"I never said I enjoyed them." She set down her knife and helped him put the vegetables on a large baking tray.

"Then there's hope for you yet." He kissed her again, knowing he'd never get enough. "Now we drizzle olive oil over them." He stepped behind her and placed his hand over hers, drizzling the oil with her. "I saw a flyer for a cooking class on the table by your door. Are you thinking of taking it?"

"It was part of my journey outside my comfort zone. I was considering it. Piper's been pushing me. She keeps urging me to join an outdoors club and go hiking or something like that."

He put the vegetables in the oven. "I'll teach you to cook, and I'd love to take you hiking when it's warmer. Or skiing, mountain climbing, whatever you'd like."

"Whoa, skiing? Mountain climbing? I don't even go camping anymore. Not after what happened when I was young."

He arched a brow. "Bear incident?"

"Bear?" Her eyes bloomed wide. "Another reason not to go in the woods, but no. My father took us on a family camping trip and it rained so hard our tent flooded. Five kids, two adults, and one tarp. We were two miles from our car, in the dark. It wasn't pretty."

He chuckled as she went on to describe their cold, wet night. But there was no missing the happy thread in her voice as she relayed what sounded like an adventure.

"Besides, it's not as if your life isn't busy enough already," she said as he set mint leaves and thyme on her cutting board and lamb cutlets on his.

"If you chop those up, I'll trim the fat from the lamb." When she began chopping, he said, "If you haven't guessed my selfish reasons, teaching you to cook and taking you out for a hike or whatever would give us more time together."

Her gaze flicked up to his. "Suddenly a cooking class with Chef Derek sounds perfect."

"Did you ever help your mother cook?"

"We all helped, but I always had my nose in a book, so while I helped, I never paid attention. I'm not the only one who didn't learn to cook. Piper could burn water. But Ben is an amazing cook. And I *did* learn how to make soaps and lotions from my mom. Cooking is just not my thing."

"I'd like to be your *thing*." He stole another kiss. "Your family sounds like fun, and you seem close to them. You're lucky."

"I am, but not as close as my sisters are to each other. They talk about *everything*. I'm more private."

"So, they won't hear the dirty details of our pre-dinner make-out session?"

"No!" she insisted, eyes as wide as saucers.

He chuckled and pulled her into his arms. "Good. Some things should be private."

"They wouldn't believe it if I told them anyway." She lowered her voice and said, "I'm not normally like *that*."

"You mean too sexy to resist?" He kissed her until she went soft in his arms. Man, he loved that feeling. "Trust me, babe, there's not a single moment when you're not too sexy to resist." She blushed, and he kissed her crimson cheeks. "Like now. I could carry you into my bedroom, and—"

She silenced him with her fingers over his lips. "Shh. You'll get me all hot and bothered again. I don't usually . . ."

He pressed a kiss to her fingers. "Just knowing I can turn you on with words turns *me* on." Enjoying another flash of surprise in her pretty eyes, he said, "I don't normally do or say those things, either. I have a feeling you and I are going to find we're doing a lot of things with each other that we wouldn't normally do."

CHAPTER NINE

AFTER A DELICIOUS dinner, during which Jonah complimented Derek's cooking about a dozen times, asked if he remembered when *their* mother used to cook lamb, and called him Archie twice, they sat in the living room looking over several of Jonah's notebooks and drawing journals. There were cartoons of his and Eva's wedding day, of Jonah and Derek eating apples at the top of a mountain, backpacks sitting open behind them, and of a gap-toothed young Derek with a bright blue backpack in front of Harmony Pointe Elementary School on his first day of second grade. There were drawings of meals and scenery, cars and family vacations. Jonah hadn't only captured happy memories. There were sketches of a teary-eyed, red-faced young Derek with a broken toy scattered at his feet and a watery-eyed Eva as she stood over the grave of her mother, crushing the stems of a bouquet. So many emotions jumped off each and every page, Talia thought the collection of more than three dozen notebooks and journals should be titled *Depiction of a Full Life*.

Now it was almost nine o'clock, and she relaxed on the sofa, listening to Derek play his guitar and sing "Lean on Me" in his father's bedroom. He was so caring, she wondered if he ever felt ripped off or overwhelmed. If he did, she hadn't seen it today.

She returned the drawings to the shelf and noticed the leather journal Jonah had been holding when she arrived. The journal Derek had mentioned was his. She didn't want to snoop, but she was anxious to see it. She took it to the couch and sat with it on her lap, listening to the soothing cadence of Derek's voice as he lulled his father to sleep with a song. She'd had a long talk with Fletch that morning when she'd gone to take Molly for a walk before coming to Derek's, and he'd mentioned that he'd noticed a difference in her. He'd said she seemed lighter, happier. Fletch knew her so well, he'd asked if she was frightened by not having complete control of her emotions. It was a question Ben might have asked if she'd seen him these last few days. It was frightening to feel so much so fast, especially when a good part of Derek's life was unfamiliar territory. She couldn't avoid thinking about having been hurt in the past, but that was a decade ago, and Derek had already proven to be so much better a man than most men she knew. He shouldered the weight of his family, and he had already been painfully honest about his personal life. Fletch told her what Ben had been telling her for years. *Don't let some idiot college kid ruin you for a worthy man.*

Derek's hand on her shoulder pulled her from her thoughts.

"Damn," he whispered as he sat beside her and put his hand over hers on the journal. "You've already looked at your surprise?"

"My *surprise*?"

He lifted it from her lap, unwound the leather strap that kept it closed, and opened to the first page, where cartoonish writing read *Talia's Journey Out of Comfort and Into Life.* Below, in simple script, he'd written, *As seen through the eyes of the man she almost ran over.* A cartoon of her upper body sticking out of a bottle, her waist trapped by the skinny neck, her hands pushing at the rim. Her long hair was tousled, and her eyes were wide and frightened. Raised brows brought an element of excitement to the fright looking back at her. The label on the bottle read, Comfort Zone. As with his father's drawings, only one element was colorized. Her eyes were vivid shades of brown, with flecks of gold in the shape of question marks around the pupil.

"You made this for me?" She met his gaze and saw so many emotions staring back at her, she couldn't process them all. It was good to know she wasn't alone in that whirlwind.

"This is an important journey, and I'm honored to be a part of it. I thought it might be fun to look back at it someday. You know, when we're skydiving or backpacking through Europe and your sisters are green with jealousy."

"*We're?*" she said carefully, her heart hammering hopefully.

"You didn't even blink at *skydiving*, but that beautiful brain of yours zeroed in on the more important thing I said. I really like that about you, Professor Dalton."

She took his hand and placed it over her racing heart. "It wasn't my *brain* zeroing in."

His lips came down over hers, swift and uplifting, like a summer breeze off the ocean. It was so easy to open up to him, to want more *of* him and *with* him, but she was well aware of the limitations on his time—and so was he.

He pressed a tender kiss to her lips and said, "Where's the harm in dreaming big?"

"I've only ever dreamed big when I thought about my career. I wanted to teach and become tenured. *That* seemed big to me."

"You never had dreams of a family of your own? A white picket fence?"

She swallowed hard, because that wasn't something she'd shared other than a quippy comment to her family at times. "I did, a long time ago . . ."

"The cheating ex?" His brows slanted angrily.

She nodded. "I don't dream big, and I've stayed away from guys like you, who are popular and *hot*, for a very long time."

"You think I'm *hot*?" he asked far too innocently.

She bumped him with her shoulder. "Like you don't know it."

"I only care that *you* think I'm hot. Tell me why you don't dream big anymore, because we need to fix that. You should have dreams."

"I'm starting to think maybe I should," she said, feeling the tug of hope. "Terrence, the guy who cheated on me, was popular, handsome, outgoing. Everyone adored him. We were in a study group together, and he kept flirting with me. I was surprised when he first asked me out because I'm a book girl, not a party girl."

"A gorgeous, smart, funny book girl. Don't ever demean the incredible person you are. If some asshole didn't realize that, that's on him. Not a reflection of you."

She tucked away his cherished words. It was what she'd told herself for a very long time, but somehow hearing it from Derek made it real. *Believable.* "Thank you. Anyway, what happened was horrible, and something I never want to go through again. We'd dated for a number of months. I'd help him with his classes, and we'd go out places. Sometimes I'd leave parties early because it just wasn't my thing, but he never complained. And I didn't mind that he stayed to hang out with friends. I trusted him. I thought we were good, you know? We had plans to spend part of spring break at his house and part at mine, so our families could get to know each of us better. Ben went to the same school I did, and he tried to warn me before everything went bad. He said he'd seen Terrence with another girl at a party, but when I asked Terrence about it, he denied it. I was blinded by my feelings for the guy, so I got angry with Ben. I reacted so badly. I said things to him that I still regret. I even told him to stay out of my life." She swallowed hard, ancient sadness welling up inside her. "A few weeks later, this girl confronted me after class. I'll never forget her. She had blond hair, blue eyes, a perfect figure, and she had one of those voices that's soft and makes you lean in to hear her talk. Anyway, she told me she was seeing Terrence and had been for months. She showed me pictures of the two of them. There was no denying it. When I broke it off with Terrence, I needed to understand why he'd hurt me like that, and he said I wasn't feminine enough, wasn't outgoing enough. I just wasn't *enough* for him in any way. I wondered if he'd gone out with me because I helped him with his course work, but that thought was even worse than just not being enough for him." Even after all these years, his hateful words brought the sting of tears. She refused to cry over him and blinked them away. "Ben showed up at my dorm that night because I hadn't responded to his texts."

She inhaled an unsteady breath as Derek put an arm around her, drawing her against his chest. He kissed her temple and whispered, "I'm sorry."

"I found out later that practically everyone at school who knew us was aware of his other girlfriend. I was mortified and hurt, and I never told a soul other than Ben and Fletch, and they've never told anyone. I told my family I decided the relationship was taking too much away from my studies, which they believed, because . . ." She shrugged and managed a smile. "I'm *me*, right?"

"I love who you are, Talia." He held her tighter. "What did Ben do to the guy?"

"Exactly what you would want him to, given the angry look in your eyes. Ben stormed out of my dorm and hunted Terrence down. I'm not someone who agrees with fighting, but my heart was so broken, I was glad Ben went after him. I'm ashamed to say that, because we were only kids and kids do stupid things, but still. I'd be lying if I didn't admit there was a sense of vindication in seeing Terrence's broken nose the next day."

"Sounds like Ben's a good man. I would have done much worse. And you gave up your dreams. And now you hide behind your job and probably date safe guys who aren't likely to hurt you."

How could he see her so clearly? She hadn't dated often, but when she did, she went out with guys who had what she considered safe office jobs, who didn't party or frequent bars. The problem was, while they were safe, something had always been missing. In a strange twist of fate, they were never *enough* for her. They didn't incite passion or the flutter in her chest when she saw their numbers on her phone or heard their voices, like Derek did.

She had a feeling he saw all of that, too, and didn't need her to verbalize it.

"Something like that," she admitted.

"I wish I'd known you then. I'd have kept you all to myself, so guys like him couldn't get close enough to hurt you."

"You might have been too wild for me back then."

"Ah, you like men who are strapped down by ailing parents?" he teased.

"Only *one* particular man," she said, and he kissed her again, slow and sweet. "I don't consider caring for your father as being strapped down. That would be like seeing Bridgette as strapped down because of her son. When it's family, it's not being strapped down. It's doing what's right, what your heart tells you to do. And you haven't let it keep you from living your life or having dreams. That says a lot about how resilient you are. I've been thinking about the project you're putting together with your friends."

"Speaking of my friends, they adore you. We're going skiing a week from Saturday. I'd love it if you'd join us."

"I haven't skied since I was about eight years old. My parents taught me how, but I'm really more of a lodge girl."

A wide grin appeared on his face. "Even better. I promised to help you step outside your comfort zone. This is perfect. I'll give you a refresher."

She groaned. "What if I suck? Or if I get hurt? It won't be any fun for you."

"Being with you is what makes it fun." He pressed a whisper of a kiss on her cheek, and his eyes darkened. "You won't suck . . . unless you *want* to."

She felt her cheeks burn.

"Man, I could watch you blush all day long. Don't worry. I won't let you get hurt, and I promise we'll both have fun."

She inhaled a shaky breath. "Okay. I'll try."

"Awesome. Now, what were you saying before I interrupted?"

"I'm too busy worrying about breaking my leg to remember," she teased, earning another delicious kiss. "Mm. Now I remember. We're having a birthday dinner for my mom Wednesday. I'd really like it if you'd come. You can bring your father, and I was thinking that you might want to share your idea with Ben. There's no guarantee he'll be in the mood to talk business, but it won't hurt to meet him. He knows about all sorts of businesses, and he might have some valuable advice. Besides, even though I think my family will drive you crazy—and I *know* they'll drive me batty after meeting you—I'd like for you to meet them."

"I want to get to know them," he said appreciatively. "But I'll see if Maria can stay with my father. Meeting your family all at once might be too much for him."

"Oh, right. Sorry. I should have thought of that. You don't have to change Maria's schedule."

He ran his fingers through the ends of her hair and said, "Maria's been all over me since you and I met. She won't mind. Besides, I have to work Tuesday and Friday nights and Saturday afternoon. I'll lose my mind if I don't see you in between, and I want to meet your family." He glanced at the journal and said, "How else can I know if I drew them right?"

"*Drew* them?" She anxiously flipped the page in the journal and couldn't suppress her delight at the sketch of her at the wheel of her car. She was drawn from the back, from her shoulders up. Her fingers gripped the wheel so hard he'd drawn tension lines shooting out from them. Derek leaned on the hood of her car, looking rattled, shoulders tense, hair hanging loose around his face, but in each of his vibrant blue eyes he'd drawn tiny stars forming a heart.

"Stars," she whispered with awe.

On the back of the previous page, he'd drawn all her sisters standing around a table, upon which was a phone surrounded by cupcakes and doughnuts. She couldn't stop grinning at his depiction of her family. Curvy Willow had full breasts, one hand propped on her rounded hip, while Piper was drawn petite and wielding a hammer, her mouth open wide. Bridgette's hands were splayed, rivers of worry on her brow, as if she were trying to calm the others. How could he possibly know that?

"I wanted to draw your mom, but I had no idea what she looked like."

"Her name is Roxie, and she looks like a Roxie, with thick, curly blond hair. Derek, this is incredible. I can feel the energy and can practically hear them all talking at the same time. How did you know Bridgette was a voice of reason?"

"She's a mom. She has to be." He tucked her hair behind her ear and said, "There's more."

"More?" She turned the page, excited to see her life from his perspective. He'd drawn himself in the hallway outside her classroom. He was leaning back, one ear oversized, one foot off the floor, as if he'd stopped midstride, and peered into the room with hearts in his eyes. The next page showed her standing beside the table after class, arms crossed, a serious look on her face, her foot tapping the floor. She laughed, sure she had seemed that nervous and stern.

"I must have come across like I had a stick up my butt."

"You are the most intriguing woman I know, and you do not appear to have a stick up your very fine ass. Don't apologize for being you. I happen to like you very much."

She tucked that sweetness away and turned another page. He'd drawn them sitting in the cafeteria having coffee. There was a place card in the center of the table that read *First Non-Date*. He'd drawn gears in Talia's head and had made them shades of red, as if they were churning.

She glanced at him, and he motioned for her to turn the page. She did and found the drawing his father had been looking at. She and Derek were lying in the snow side by side, hearts in their eyes, their fingers inches apart as Molly licked his face. He'd written, *Meant to Be?* with stars in the sky.

A dreamy sigh slipped out. "Derek, this is beautiful and more romantic than anything I could ever imagine. Thank you."

"I look forward to adding more to it." He set the journal on the coffee table and gathered her in his arms.

He was so close, her lips parted with anticipation.

"You deserve a world of romance, Talia, and to be surrounded by beauty." He nipped at her lower lip, and her pulse spiked. "I may not be rich," he said in a husky voice, thick with desire, "and I don't have endless hours to woo you with extravagance."

His hands moved into her hair, angling her head back so he could taste her neck. And taste he *did*, with long, slow, openmouthed kisses that made her toes curl as he lowered her to her back. *Who needs trips when your touch transports me to the most heavenly places?* His weight pressed down on her in all the best places as he lavished her with kisses. His lips brushed over her skin like whispers, and she wanted to capture every one of them.

His teeth grazed the shell of her ear, and he said, "But I'll give you every stolen second I can squeeze out of my day and sexy nights when we can sneak them in."

He drove her to the brink of madness with his magnificent mouth, kissing and licking, nipping at her lips and neck until she was barely breathing, much less thinking. His hands moved confidently, aggressively, groping her breasts and hips, making her wild with anticipation as she clawed at his arms and back, wanting so much more of him.

He pinned her in place with a seductive stare. "I want to touch you, Talia. *Taste* you. Make you lose control."

Yes, please, yes. The plea echoed in her head, but she was too lost in him to force a sound. He dragged his tongue over her lower lip, and she arched up, trying again to capture a kiss. A wicked smile appeared on his face, taunting and challenging and somehow also comforting. The safety she felt with him was beyond anything she'd ever known.

"Most importantly," he said as he caressed her cheek, "I can give you honesty. I'm a man you can trust not to hurt you."

"Yes," *finally* sailed desperately from her lips.

As if her plea severed his last restraint, Derek's mouth crashed over hers, smothering her in a penetrating kiss. Her hips bolted off the cushions, and she tugged at his shirt, bit his jaw, his lips, every nip driving his arousal higher. He devoured her with the recklessness of a man who didn't have his ailing father in the next room and knew he needed to get them behind closed doors, *stat*.

He didn't try to explain, didn't say a word as he pushed to his feet and lifted Talia into his arms. She gasped, clinging to him as he strode toward his bedroom.

"Your dad?" Talia asked in a shaky voice.

Closing his bedroom door behind them, he lowered her to her feet in the moonlit room. "There's an alarm on his door. I'll hear it if he gets up." He took her face between his hands, soaking in the sensuality brimming in her eyes. "I can't resist you, Talia, but if you need me to slow down, just tell me. I'll always listen."

Holding his steady gaze, she toed off her shoes, peeled off her sweater, and dropped it at her feet. "Your turn," she said with the sexiest smile he'd ever seen.

"Christ, baby, you're gorgeous."

He took off his shoes and tugged off his shirt, barely able to contain his desire. They came together with the urgency of a starving couple taking their last meal as he stripped off her bra, sending it floating to the floor. Her breasts pressed against his bare chest as he claimed her in another smoldering kiss that made his cock throb and his thoughts scatter. They stumbled to the bed, and he tore back the covers and came down over her as they kissed, unwilling to break their connection. It had been so long since he'd been driven by more than the need for release, he was overwhelmed by the emotions engulfing him. He wanted to take her, taste her, *memorize* every glorious inch from her fingertips to her toes, but *fuck* . . . He was desperate to bury himself deep inside her and feel her sweetness all around him.

He kissed her jaw, down her neck, slowing to slick his tongue over the rapid pulse beating there, and sealed his mouth over it, giving a single hard *suck*. A long, sensual moan streamed from her lips, spurring him on. He tasted his way down her chest, her fingernails digging into his shoulders as he teased her with slow strokes of his tongue around the taut peak of first one beautiful breast and then the other. She arched against his mouth, breathing harder as he devoured her. He lingered in the valley of her cleavage, drunk on her feminine scent, the heat of her skin, the feel of her nails digging into him. He kissed a path lower, between her ribs, his hands playing over every inch of her flesh, slowing to worship the dip at her waist and savoring the gentle swell between her hips as he worked open the button of her jeans. He lowered the zipper and hooked his fingers in the waistband. She lifted her hips, allowing him to drag the jeans lower. He took his time, kissing her thighs as he stripped the jeans down to her knees and sealed his mouth over her inner thigh, sucking hard enough to leave a mark.

"Derek," she pleaded, her hips rising off the mattress.

"Too hard?" he asked.

Her head thrashed from side to side. "I need *more*."

"I do, too, babe. I won't leave you hanging."

He slicked his tongue all the way up to the seam of her panties and then he blew on the wetness. She shuddered beneath him, clutching at the sheets as she struggled against the confines of her jeans. He placed his hands over hers, pressing them into the mattress as he sank his teeth into her panties and dragged them down her hip. She lifted and wiggled, helping him as he repeated the taunt on the other side, revealing a tuft of dark curls and leaving the thin silk just low enough to cover her entrance. He proceeded to tease all around her sex, earning one needy whimper after another. He slid his tongue over her damp curls, along the sides of her sex, inhaling her intoxicating scent. When he pushed his tongue beneath the thin material, taking his first taste of her, heat streaked to his cock, sending a surge of lust through his veins. She moaned, rocking her hips as he teased her drenched sex. He pressed his tongue over her clit, moving in a quick rhythm until she was trembling, pleading at the brink of release.

"Derek," she whispered breathily. *"Please!"*

He tore off her jeans and panties, spread her legs, and sealed his mouth over the very heart of her.

"Oh! Oh!" She grabbed his head, rocking against his mouth. "Yes! Yes!" she cried in harsh whispers. "Harder! *Oh*—"

Her eyes slammed shut, and her head thrashed as he held her at the peak, her body shuddering around his tongue. He stayed with her until the very last quiver. Then he moved swiftly up her body, rocking his hard length against her entrance, and claimed her in a rough kiss. She hesitated, and he drew back and wiped her sweetness from his face, then recaptured her glorious mouth. She was right there with him, meeting every eager stroke of his tongue with one of her own, fisting her hand in his hair, and rocking against his hard length. He longed to be inside her, to feel her come apart in his arms, but first . . .

"Open your eyes, baby." Despite her encouraging pleas, she was his careful girl. He knew they were flying at breakneck speed and he needed to be sure she wouldn't regret anything they did. He didn't want to give her any reason not to trust him, and he needed to see that trust in her eyes.

When they fluttered open, he saw the answer before he even asked the question.

"Hey, there." He brushed feathery kisses over her lips. "Just making sure we're together in this."

"As long as it doesn't end up in my journal," she said softly.

"You don't want to remember our first time together?"

"I do, but I love the journal. I might want to share it," she said cautiously.

"Okay, I promise to be *covert*," he said, knowing he'd leave this out if she hated the drawing that was already forming in his mind. He never wanted to forget his beautiful girl saying, *Your turn.*

"I trust you," she said.

Hearing those words took his breath away—and let another dose of reality in. A dose he had to share. "I want to make love to you more than I want my next breath. But we can't spend the night together. It might throw my father off if he sees you in the morning." He caressed her cheek and said, "We can wait until we have the chance to wake up in each other's arms."

"I already assumed that, and I'm still here. I don't want to wait."

"Talia . . ." His voice trailed off, because there were no more words to be said, only feelings to share, emotions to capture. He kissed her tenderly before stepping from the bed and stripping off his clothes. She watched him boldly, her cheeks pinking up as his erection sprang free.

As he reached into his drawer for a condom, she touched his hand. "Hold me first?"

It was the sweetest thing he'd ever experienced. All his protective urges surged forth as he set the condom on the bed and took her in his arms. His cock lay on her damp curls as they kissed and embraced, her softness molding to his hard frame. He didn't know how long they remained in the blissful state of unity, but it was long enough that he felt everything change, and he realized it didn't take the act of making love for them to become one.

They already were.

He drew back, brushing kisses over her lips and cheeks, and his heart came tumbling out. "Is it possible to fall for someone in a matter of days? Hours? Or am I alone in feeling like we've found something so incredible, it's surreal?"

"It's *real*," she said without hesitation, and their mouths came together, sealing their words.

He sheathed himself between ravenous kisses and aligned their bodies as he took her in his arms again, cradling, *protecting*, and giving her all of himself. They gazed into each other's eyes as their bodies came together so perfectly, he was once again swept away.

He touched his forehead to hers and said, "So real . . ."

They found their rhythm and followed it all the way to the end of the rainbow.

They lay together afterward, bodies intertwined, hands and mouths still exploring, even as they drifted in and out of sleep. When Talia moved to leave the bed, he tightened his grip and kissed her temple. "I don't want to let you go."

"I can't stay," she said, soft and sated.

For the first time since his father's diagnosis, he felt the *full* weight of his commitment and wished he weren't bound by the immense responsibilities so she could stay with him and he could wake up tomorrow and make love to her again. Have breakfast together like a normal couple.

Those thoughts were followed by a wave of guilt so big he had a hard time climbing out from under it. And then he realized he had another bomb to drop. This was his life. He forced the longing and disappointment aside, and when that didn't work, he kicked the motherfucking emotion as far away as he could.

"Babe, my dad has a doctor's appointment tomorrow. I can't come to your class. Save notes for me?"

A sweet laugh fell from her lips. "You don't have to feign interest in my class."

"I'll never feign a thing with you. I meant it." He kissed her again. "Maria's here for a few hours in the morning. I'll text, and if you're free I'll come by."

"Sounds perfect."

She touched his ring, a question hanging in her eyes.

"It was my mother's." He twisted the thick vintage-looking gold band with the engraved floral pattern and three tiny inset emeralds. "My father gave it to me after she died."

"I love that you wear it. And the bracelets?" She touched the beaded and leather bands around his wrist.

"These were my father's. I can't remember him ever *not* wearing them. Usually with Alzheimer's the oldest memories go last, but for some reason, he wanted these off one day, and he never let me put them back on."

"I like them."

"I like *you*, Tallie girl." He pressed his lips to hers, hating that he was so aware of their time together ticking by.

"Tallie girl . . . ?" she whispered.

"You mind?"

She shook her head. "I've never been anything but Talia or Tal. I like it."

"You're my Tallie girl . . ."

After some time, they reluctantly climbed from the bed. He helped her dress and tugged on his jeans. The walk to the front door felt like a walk down the plank. What kind of man made a woman leave after being so close? Another wave of guilt crashed over him.

He drew her into his arms and said, "I hate that you have to leave and that I can't drive you home and walk you to your door."

"We both knew how tonight would end."

"You're incredible. Thank you for understanding. Did you ever imagine you'd go out with a man who had a curfew?"

"To be honest, I had a hard time imagining myself going out with anyone."

"Then why me?"

She went up on her toes and touched her lips to his. "First it was your eyes, and then your honesty and humor. But your heart sealed the deal with *Team Grant*."

CHAPTER TEN

TALIA MADE THE mistake of stopping by the bakery on her way in to work Monday morning. Despite her lack of sleep, she'd felt refreshed and rejuvenated, which her sisters had immediately homed in on. She'd spent her brief visit denying that she'd been, as Piper had put it, *banged into oblivion*. Now it was midafternoon, and Talia had an hour to catch up on emails and phone calls before her next class. On her way to her office, her phone vibrated. She pulled it out, expecting to see a text from one of her sisters, who had been trying to pry the juicy details out of her all day, and hoping to get another text from Derek. He'd asked her to text when she got home last night so he wouldn't worry, and she'd happily complied, enjoying his protectiveness. But he hadn't returned her text. He'd *called* instead, saying he wanted to hear her voice one last time for the night . . . or rather, *early morning*. It was such a loving thing to do after the day and night they'd shared, she'd lain in bed afterward reveling in happiness.

She sighed at her mother's name on her screen. Her mother hadn't been at the bakery this morning, but gossip traveled faster than the speed of light around the Dalton family. She opened and read the message. *The girls said my potion worked! When can we meet this yummy creature your sisters can't stop talking about?*

She looked up from her phone and saw Ben standing outside her office. Her stomach clenched. It had been a long time since she'd been the focus of so much gossip. She put her phone in her pocket, figuring she'd reply to her mother later.

"Which one called you—the sugar pusher, the not-so-sweet mama, or the one who thinks sex is a breakfast entrée?" she asked as she walked past Ben and into her office.

Ben cracked a smile, watching her like a hawk as she set her bag on her desk. "That would be three for three, plus the petite pain in my ass."

"Aurelia? Oh, please. You guys are such good friends. You remind me of me and Fletch."

Ben's brows knitted and his jaw tensed in an expression she couldn't read, but she might have imagined it, because in the next second that look was gone.

"*Anyway*, add Mom to that list of gossipers. She came by this morning under the premise of wanting me to make sure you were in good hands, but really, I think she just wanted to drop off this." He reached into his coat pocket and set a bag on her desk. "I have no idea what's in it, but it's from Mom, which means it's scented with pheromones or something else I don't need."

"Don't you dare leave that on my desk. She sprayed my car with God knows what, and I had to leave the windows open for days just to get the smell out." She leaned her hip against the edge of the desk, both of them avoiding the bag like it was diseased. "How was your trip to the city?"

"Good. I had dinner with Aiden Aldridge to discuss a new business venture." Aiden's younger sister, Remi Divine, had costarred with Zane in a movie that was filmed in Sweetwater when Zane and Willow had first started dating.

Ben sat in one of the chairs by her desk and crossed his ankle over his knee. His dark hair and serious eyes reminded her of their father, though Ben had a snarky side she couldn't imagine her father having.

She waited for him to elaborate, and when he didn't, she said, "And . . . ?"

"I might do it. It'll mean spending a few months out in LA." He leaned back and clasped his hands behind his head.

"Zane said he grew to hate LA when he lived there."

"I'm not Zane," he said smugly.

"Hey, you should have hooked Aurelia up with Aiden. Willow said he looks like David Beckham and he's a real gentleman."

He scoffed. "Aurelia doesn't need a guy like Aiden. But he's perfect for you."

"Hm." She wondered if there was something going on between Ben and Aurelia, and then she recognized his tactic. "I expect more from you than *fishing* for info. I have no interest in Aiden Aldridge or any other man. I'm off the market. But you know that already."

They both turned at a knock on her door. She glanced over and saw Fletch walking slowly into the room. He'd been feeling better lately, and she knew he'd had a doctor's appointment this morning, but she was surprised to see him. She suddenly wondered if Fletch had told Ben about Derek, too, and if he had, if he'd told him about his dancing.

"Have room for one more, or is this a private conversation?" Fletch asked as Ben rose to greet him.

"How're you feeling, man?" Ben gave up the chair closest to the door for Fletch.

"Like a truck ran over my insides, but I'm getting there." He sat down and said, "Your sister's been walking my monster for me, which is a huge help."

"Stop calling Molly a monster," Talia said, "or I swear I'll take her home with me and you'll never see her again."

Both Ben and Fletch gave her a *yeah, right* look.

Having told them a million times she didn't have room in her life for a pet, she said, "Okay, maybe not, but she's such a good girl. She doesn't deserve to be called a monster."

Ben and Fletch rolled their eyes.

She huffed out a breath and threw up her hands. "Double-teaming me? Really? Fletch, aren't you supposed to be resting? And Ben . . . ?"

"Hey," Ben said, splaying his hands toward the ceiling. "I'm just checking up on my sister to find out the scoop on your new man."

"I couldn't stand being cooped up for another day," Fletch said.

"I guess I can understand that. What did the doctor say?" she asked.

"He said I can return to work as soon as I feel well enough," Fletch answered. "Are you okay covering for the rest of this week? I'm hoping to come back Monday."

"Yes, of course. For as long as you need me."

"Unless, of course, you need her at night, because now she's got a man in her life," Ben added.

Fletch cocked a grin. "You mean the student with the professor fantasy."

"Wait. He knows about this guy and I don't?" Ben glared at Talia.

Relief swept through her. She wanted to be the one to tell Ben about Derek's dancing. "Sort of, and he's *not* my student. He never enrolled in the class. He only went because . . ." Oh boy, her brother wasn't going to like this.

Ben narrowed his eyes.

"Because . . . ?" Fletch urged.

"Because he saw me teaching the day I nearly ran him over, and then he was interested and kept coming back."

"Interested? So he scoped you out and pretended to be your student?" Ben's voice rose, his hands clenched by his sides. "Talia, seriously?"

"That's what you homed in on?" Fletch scoffed. "I want to hear about the 'kept coming' part."

Ben glared at him. "Dude, she's my *sister*."

Fletch chuckled.

"I know what it sounds like," she admitted, pacing beside him. "I was just as skeptical. I didn't know if I should be flattered or creeped out. But he's a really good guy. He's caring for his father, who has Alzheimer's, and he's finishing his master's in health administration. He wants to open an adult day-care center for families like his who need help caring for their ill or elderly relatives but aren't ready to put them into a nursing home. And he does *not* have a professor fantasy."

"If he doesn't have a professor fantasy, that sucks for you," Fletch said. "Unless he just hasn't shared it yet."

She and Ben both glowered at him.

"I don't want to know about this dude's fantasies *or* either of yours," Ben said. "I just want to know he's not a lowlife who's going to hurt her."

"And that's why I love you," she said. "Unlike everyone else, you stay as far away from the details of my sex life as you can."

"That part of your life does not exist as far as I'm concerned." Ben held his palm up and said, "In fact, can you please refrain from using the *S* word around me?"

"Yes. Perfect," Talia said.

"I have a meeting, which is the real reason I'm on campus." Fletch pushed to his feet. "I think Ben can take over from here."

"I'll see you tonight when I come by to walk Molly," she said.

"We'll talk more then. I still want those *other* details."

"Pig," she said as Fletch left her office. She faced Ben and exhaled loudly, tired of trying to rationalize her feelings for Derek. She didn't need Ben's approval. "I asked Derek to come to Mom's birthday dinner. I want you to meet him and hear about his adult day-care idea. I thought you might be able to give him some advice. It's all very grassroots. He and his friends are saving money to get it started." She thought about telling him about how Derek was making that money and decided she wasn't quite ready to fight that uphill battle yet. It was a lot for *her* to come to grips with and she was the one falling for him. Ben would approach it as another risk calculation, and while she'd appreciate his concern, she wasn't a kid anymore. She could weigh her own risks.

"I'd be happy to. I trust your judgment with this guy, Tal. I just wish you'd met him some other way."

"You mean almost running him over isn't the ideal way to meet a mate?" she teased.

He didn't look amused.

Fletch appeared in the doorway and said in a harsh whisper, "Incoming."

He disappeared into the hall seconds before Dina Manco strolled through the doorway, all hip swagger and bouncing cleavage.

"Was that Fletch I saw heading out of here?" Her eyes locked on Ben, and her smile turned to a predacious grin. "Well, hello there, Mr. Dalton. Today *is* my lucky day."

Talia was used to Dina's overly promiscuous ways. Heck, everyone who knew her probably was, although as far as Talia knew, she'd never crossed the professional lines that could cause her to be fired.

Ben didn't move from his seat or play into her seductive game. "Dina. Nice to see you."

Dina put a hand on his shoulder, and Talia narrowed her eyes. She bit back her distaste and said, "Do you need something, Dina?"

"Oh, I *need* something, all right," Dina answered, her shameless innuendo perfectly clear.

Ben pushed to his feet and cleared his throat, locking eyes with Talia and ignoring Dina altogether. She respected the hell out of her brother and was glad he wasn't a dirtbag who would take the *man eater* up on her offer. "Talia, I'll catch you later."

"Okay," Talia said. "I appreciate you coming by to check on me."

He winked, and when he stepped behind Dina, he mouthed, *Get rid of her!*

Talia covered her laugh with a cough and walked around her desk, putting space between her and Dina. "Dina, you do realize that's my brother you keep hitting on."

Dina leaned over the desk, giving Talia an eyeful of cleavage. "There are rules about dating students, *not* about dating siblings of colleagues." She sat on the edge of Talia's desk and crossed her legs, causing her short skirt to inch up her thighs.

"What can I do for you, besides watch you drool over Ben?"

"As far as I'm concerned," Dina said as she brushed nonexistent lint from her skirt, "he's fair game. Just like *Fletch*, who I know will give in to me one day."

"You *do* like to dream," Talia said with an air of boredom. "I have work to do, so . . . ?"

"Oh, right. You know, I can't remember why I came in." She slid off the desk and wiggled her hips as she shimmied her skirt back into place. On her way to the door she said, "I guess I must have known you were stockpiling handsome men."

Talia's phone vibrated, and Derek's name flashed on the screen. She made a mental note to keep the man eater away from him, and after Dina left, she opened the text. Her heart leapt at the picture of a drawing of Derek walking into his bedroom, his long hair and broad shoulders blocking Talia from the waist down. She stood before him, her hand outstretched, eyes brimming with unmistakable passion. *How did he do that?* Her heart was drawn in 3-D, as if it were beating out of her chest, right through her sweater, and colored a pretty red. Beside her were the words, *Your turn*, surrounded by tiny red hearts.

Another text bubble popped up. *Okay?*

She typed, *I love it. It's perfect*, and as she sent the text, she thought, *Just like you.*

CHAPTER ELEVEN

DEREK FOLLOWED THE directions in Talia's text toward her office Tuesday afternoon, feeling like they'd been apart for weeks. Every step amped up his anticipation. He'd never been a needy guy, and as far as women were concerned, a text here and there had always been enough communication for him. Especially over the past few years, when he'd felt like he was on a hamster wheel, chasing the hours from caring for his father to taking classes and working. Maria was a godsend, but until Talia, he'd considered Maria's prompting to let a woman into his life a headache he didn't want to deal with. He'd never imagined finding someone who understood the responsibilities he had, much less someone smart, gorgeous, and as family oriented as he was. But then again, everything about Talia was different from the other women he knew. Hell, even the way she kissed was like nothing he'd ever experienced. She was as sweet and careful as she was eager and passionate. Why did he expect something like communication to be typical? Texts and phone calls were nowhere near enough. He wanted to look into her eyes, to share the excitement of the drawings his father had done yesterday evening. He wanted to hold her in his arms when she told him about her day, and he wanted to hear what she'd taught in the class he'd missed.

When he finally found her office, he peered into the open doorway. She was on the phone and waved him in. Hiding the flowers he'd brought behind his back, he stepped inside and closed the door, because he needed to get his lips on hers or he might die from withdrawal. She looked gorgeous in a low-cut white blouse with frills around the collar, showing just enough skin to make him want to tear that pretty blouse right off. Her slender brows arched in question as he stalked toward her. He was sure he looked as greedy as he felt, ready to collect all the kisses he'd missed.

"Dad, I really have to go," she said into the phone as Derek came around the desk and ran his fingers through her hair. Her breathing hitched. "Derek and I will see you Wednesday night. I love you."

He mouthed, *I'd love to come*, and waggled his brows, earning a flush of embarrassment as she ended the call. He pulled the bouquet from behind his back and her eyes lit up. She leapt into his arms and pressed her smiling lips to his.

"Thank you," she said breathlessly as he set her on her feet and handed her the flowers. "They're gorgeous."

"Not as gorgeous as you. How's my girl?"

She smelled the flowers. "Wondering if my father could tell I was hot and bothered by the sight of you closing my office door because of all the dirty things that went through my mind."

She licked her lips, and he backed her up against the desk. Taking the bouquet from her hands, he set it aside.

"I haven't begun to get you hot and bothered." He ran his hands up her legs and squeezed. "Do you know how bad I want to drop to my knees right now and make you feel so good you'll be floating on cloud nine for the rest of the day?"

Her breath rushed from her lungs, but her gaze darted nervously to the door.

"Tell me what dirty things went through your mind." He threaded his fingers into her hair and lowered his mouth to her neck, enjoying the fresh flush of her skin.

"Something like this . . ." She grabbed his hips and pulled him tighter against her.

Her eyes sparked with heat, but she glanced at the door again. The conflicting messages made his head spin. He tugged her lip free with his teeth, then covered her mouth with his, taking her in a slow, persuasive kiss. Her pleasure-filled noises made him hard as stone. Their kisses turned hungrier, and he couldn't resist pushing his hands beneath her skirt and gripping her outer thighs. He loved how she trembled at his touch and the way she went soft in his arms when he slowed their kisses. It was agony knowing he couldn't take this further, but he had only minutes before he needed to leave for his shift at the bar, and he knew making out in her office was *way* outside her comfort zone. But knowing she'd gone there for *him* made him all sorts of happy.

When they finally came up for air, he could barely see straight. She gazed at him through the same hazy fog, her fingers running through the ends of his hair as she said, "I thought you had to work."

"I do. I only have a few minutes." He couldn't resist kissing her again. "But I had to see you before I went. I won't get off until midnight. Is that too late to text?"

She shook her head. "Never too late."

"I had so many things I wanted to talk with you about," he said between kisses. "But now all I want to do is keep kissing you."

There was a knock on the door, and her face blanched. He gave her a chaste kiss and took a step back as she nervously stood up and smoothed her hands over her skirt.

"Thanks for making time for me. I'll text you when I get off work."

There was another knock.

"Come in," she said.

Derek hoped whoever it was wouldn't notice the flush of her cheeks like he did.

Her office door swung open, and one of Derek's favorite teachers walked in, apologizing for interrupting.

"Professor Harbin," Derek said to the stocky gray-haired man, extending his hand. "I was just on my way out."

Professor Harbin shook Derek's hand, his wise eyes moving between him and Talia. "It's good to see you, Derek. How's your father?"

"As well as can be expected. Thanks for asking." He glanced at Talia, who had somehow managed to seamlessly slip into her professorial persona.

"How do you two know each other?" Talia asked.

"Derek was my star student," Professor Harbin said with an affirmatory nod. "But if you're teaching him, then you're probably experiencing the same thing."

"I'm not teaching Derek," she said, her gaze shifting a little nervously around him.

Derek held his breath, unsure of how to handle the situation. He'd like to jump in and claim Talia, but he didn't want to say anything that could cause her trouble.

"Actually," Talia said carefully, "Derek and I are seeing each other. He's my boyfriend."

Derek tried to hide his surprise and the pride swelling inside him. He loved knowing she didn't feel a need to hide their relationship.

"Oh. Well, then, I guess you're *not* teaching him, are you?" Professor Harbin flashed an approving smile. "You can't go wrong with this young man. He's going to make a difference in people's lives."

"Thank you, Professor. And speaking of making a difference, it's time for me to go serve up some relaxation."

"Still working at the bar?" Professor Harbin asked.

"It pays the bills." He glanced at Talia and said, "I'll call you later."

Derek fended off the regulars, serving up drinks to lonely women and guys who were looking for a piece of ass. He laughed at lame jokes and nodded at all the right times. He knew how to play the game and make the tips he needed, but tonight his mind was on Talia and the way she'd owned their relationship in front of her colleague, which made it hard for him to pretend to be interested in what anyone at the bar had to say. He watched his friends Geno and Lola dancing. Lola was a tiny blonde with almost no breasts or hips, but lonely guys fed her fives and tens like she was Marilyn Monroe. She was paying her way through school by dancing. Geno was a thick-legged, barrel-chested Italian, with short, pitch-black hair, tattoos across his back, and a flirtatious personality. Women loved him regardless of whether he was dancing or bartending. After his shifts he always hung out to *grease* the crowd, and he earned even more than Derek did because of it. He gave every woman—and some of the men—the impression that one day he might go home with them, when in reality he was married with two little girls. His youngest had special needs, which was why he danced in addition to his full-time day job as a contractor. Derek had never played the game as well as Geno. He left like a bat outta hell after his shift, and when he was dancing, he imagined being nineteen years old again, partying on foreign beaches where no one knew him, when dancing hadn't been a means of income. He used to wonder what he looked like up onstage. Did customers assume he was just a dancer? Or could they see that every hip gyration, every pelvic thrust, every time he pointed at a woman was with the hopes of earning enough money to create the future he wanted for himself and his father? Nowadays he simply used that mind-numbing time to escape the stress of daily life.

"Hey, Grant." His boss, Tyler Reddington, tapped him on the shoulder, pulling him from his thoughts.

He tossed the towel he was using to wipe down the bar over his shoulder. "Yeah?"

"Geno's wife just messaged me. His daughter had a seizure and he's got to take off. Can you cover the rest of his dance shift?"

Derek ground his teeth together—at the news Geno was about to be dealt and at the idea of taking off his clothes for anyone other than

Talia. But this was his deal, and without it, Our Friends' House would never come to fruition.

Talia lay on her back in the middle of her bed looking at the drawing in which Derek had cleverly wrapped the flowers he'd given her. She'd spent the evening perusing romantic getaways on the internet for her mother's birthday and imagining what it might be like to be at them with Derek. She'd finally found one for her mother, texted all her siblings and made arrangements for her mother's gift, but her mind lingered on Derek for the rest of the night. He'd texted around eleven to say he had to work late to cover his friend's shift—*dancing*. She'd felt queasy at the thought of all those women with grabby hands and willing mouths pawing at him, but then she'd looked at the drawing and knew it wouldn't matter who wanted him, because *he* only wanted *her*. He'd drawn himself as an octopus standing behind a bar, serving drinks to big-breasted fish with puffy red lips and stars in their eyes and male sharks with sharp teeth and hungry eyes drooling over them. The octopus had a drink in each of its eight arms, a bored expression on its face, and a thought bubble over its head filled with tiny pictures of Derek and Talia. He'd drawn them kissing in her office—she loved knowing he'd hoped to do so before they actually had—lying in his bed gazing into each other's eyes, and holding hands under the table when they'd had dinner with his friends. In each drawing he had red hearts in his eyes, except the one of him standing behind the bar. In that one, his eyes were a dull blue. *The In-Between Hours* was written in curly letters along the edge of the paper, running from the bottom to the top.

She pressed the drawing to her chest, missing him more than she should after only a few hours. She'd gone to walk Molly after work, and she and Fletch had talked for a long time. He seemed genuinely happy for her, but he'd cautioned her, as any good friend would, reminding her about how she thought she'd known Terrence and he thought he'd known his ex-wife. But she knew Derek was nothing like Terrence. No man could be as unselfish as Derek *and* as selfish as a cheater. The two just didn't go together. She glanced at the gorgeous flowers beside her bed, thinking about the afternoon. She'd been nervous about mentioning her and Derek's relationship to Greg Harbin because even though Derek wasn't her student, he was a student at the school, and she didn't want to be seen as doing anything inappropriate. But all it had taken was one look at the man who had quickly become so important to her and she'd known she couldn't—*wouldn't*—deny their relationship. After Derek had left her office, Greg had raved about his drive and determination. He'd mentioned that Derek had missed classes due to his father's illness, but he'd not only followed up to make sure he had all the required materials to do well, but he'd also gone above and beyond with each of his assignments, often having intense conversations with Greg via email long after the assignments had been turned in for no reason other than sheer interest. She had the feeling her boyfriend was an academic at heart.

Her cell phone rang a little after one o'clock, and she felt herself smiling before she even saw Derek's name on the screen. "Hi."

"Hey, there." He sounded tired. "Did I wake you?"

"No. I was just admiring a blue-eyed octopus."

His low laugh rumbled through the phone.

"How was work?" she asked as she rolled onto her side and leaned on her elbow. "You sound tired."

"Work was . . . *work*. I'd much rather have been with you."

Butterflies fluttered in her belly, and she closed her eyes, picturing his face when she'd pulled him against her in her office, his full lips, the way he'd caressed her cheek. She could almost feel the sting on her scalp when his fingers threaded into her hair. "I wish you were here with me right now."

"Me too, but I need to give Maria a chance to go home. You could come to my place . . ."

She rolled onto her side, hope and desire swirling inside her. "What about your dad?"

"I was thinking . . . We'd have to get up earlier than he does, because I still think seeing you in the morning might throw him off, but I'm willing to try if you are. I don't want to wait to see you. Come over. Be with me, babe. *Please?*"

Her heart beat faster with every word he said.

"Take another step outside your comfort zone and we'll add another page to your journal."

She sat up, her pulse running rampant. "But don't you need your sleep?" *Please say no.* She didn't even know why she'd asked.

"Babe, I'll live on thoughts of sleep if it means I can be with you. Be with me tonight, Tallie. I want you in my arms. In my *bed*. I want to be buried deep inside you and kiss you until you come apart and then hold you safe and close as you doze off."

Her insides burned with desire. She wanted his mouth on her, his rough hands holding her down as he feasted and teased and took her to the moon and back.

"I will make you feel so good," he said seductively, his voice slithering through the phone like a drug lulling her in, "that next time you won't hesitate to accept."

Her eyes darted around her room as if her answer were written in the walls. But there was only one place her answer lived. She put her hand over her heart and said, "Let me pack my things."

CHAPTER TWELVE

DEREK STEPPED OUT onto the front porch as Talia pulled into the driveway, making her even more nervous. She'd never left her house in the middle of the night for sex before. *But wow, look at him.* He was all long hair and sultry eyes. His button-down shirt hung open, revealing planes of perfectly sculpted *man.*

Is this a booty call? she wondered as she stepped from her car.

Was it considered a *booty call* if they were in a relationship?

He strode toward her, and she couldn't take her eyes off the treasure trail leading down the center of his body to a patch of dark hair above the waist of his low-riding jeans. There was no hiding the fact that he wasn't wearing underwear. She grabbed her bag and practically ran into his arms, nestling against his hot, hard body like it was made just for her. He took her bag and devoured her mouth as they stumbled into the house. His skin was damp, and he smelled fresh from a shower.

"Damn, I missed you," he whispered against her lips, obliterating her worries about booty calls altogether.

She didn't care what this was called. She wanted to be there with him, for him, *beneath* him.

He took her in another toe-curling kiss, cupping her ass, lifting and pressing her against his erection. She heard a wanton sound and realized she'd made it, but there was no room for embarrassment. She didn't know changes could happen this fast, but her *heart* was in this, and when he broke their connection to close and lock the front door, the look in his eyes told her his was, too.

"You know those glasses turn me on in ways they shouldn't." He ran his fingers along her cheek. "So sexy."

"Shouldn't?"

His arm swept around her waist, and he spoke directly into her ear. "They make me have cliché fantasies about my sexy professor."

"I want to know all your fantasies." She was shocked she'd said it, but as they headed into his bedroom, she meant every word. She wanted to know his fantasies, his hopes, his fears. She wanted to know everything there was to know about him.

His mouth came aggressively down over hers, taking her in a rough, insistent kiss. He locked the door, and his gaze turned fierce. Lord help her, because she'd thought about his dirty promises on the drive over and was already wet at the mere thought of them. She'd taken her thoughts darker, fantasizing about all the things she wanted to do with him—*to* him. Things she'd never initiated before, but she couldn't hold back from wanting with Derek. Her body was vibrating with need. She *wanted* his ferocity. She wanted *everything* he had to give.

He dropped her bag and hauled her into his arms. He pushed his hands into her hair and held on tight, his eyes boring into her.

Ah, yes. The erotic sting sent scintillating shivers slicing through her.

His mouth brushed over hers. "I missed you." He nipped at her lower lip, tugging it like he'd done the other night. "I need your mouth, Tallie girl."

His mouth crashed over hers, kissing her so hungrily she went up on her toes, seeking even more. He tightened his grip on her hair, and lust seared to her core. Before she could lose her nerve, she reached for the button on his jeans and tore it open, earning another greedy noise from her man. She thrust her hand beneath the denim, her fingers circling his shaft. *Oh my goodness.* The feel of his hardness, the thrust of his hips, made her mouth water. She'd known he was bare beneath his jeans, but discovering it like this, without hesitation or urging, made it that much more enticing.

She pried her mouth from his, feeling bolder and sexier than she ever had, and said, "I need my mouth on *you.*"

She backed him up to the edge of the bed, grabbed the waist of his jeans, and *yanked* them down. His lips quirked up, those heavenly eyes stripping her bare. She put her hand on his chest and pushed, sending her willing victim to the mattress. She dragged his jeans over his bare feet and dropped them to the floor, wrestling with the troubling thought trampling through her mind.

"Um . . . are you . . . Have you . . ."

He sat up and cradled her face in his hands. "I'm clean, babe, if that's what you're wondering. You?"

She nodded.

Wickedness filled his eyes, and she pushed him to the mattress again. He was so beautiful, big and broad with a slim waist and thick, powerful thighs. His chest was covered in a dusting of dark hair, and his cock eagerly awaited her on a cloud of the same. She took a moment to admire his beautiful, athletic body as he watched her with laser focus, making her feel even more naughty. She straddled his legs, still dressed, which she did for her own sake, knowing if she were naked, she'd never get to do what she so desperately wanted.

He reached up and caressed her cheek. "Hey, baby," he said just above a whisper.

Her hair tumbled over her shoulders, brushing his chest. Heat flared in his eyes, and he shuddered beneath her. The reaction was so unexpected, so *alluring*, she swished her hair over his chest again. He sucked in a sharp breath between gritted teeth.

"You have no idea what you're doing to me," he said, and tangled his fingers in her hair.

"I have no idea what I'm doing, *period*. But I'll figure it out."

"Jesus, Talia. You're killing me. How can you be so sexy and so innocent?"

She licked her lips, watching him as she lowered her mouth and pressed a kiss between his pecs and then across his chest, slowing to tease his nipples, earning more of those tense, male, *sinful* sounds. "You've shown me that stepping out of my comfort zone is a good thing."

"Tallie." He breathed her name like a secret as she continued kissing her way south, following that treasure trail.

"Let me show you just how good."

"You don't have to do this," he said, playing with her hair as she kissed his abs.

She gazed down at the broad crown of his erection, wrapped her fingers around his shaft, and pressed a kiss to the tip. He moaned and tangled his fingers in her hair again. She ran her tongue over the head, and his hips bucked up. She'd never done this, not even with Terrence. Some part of her had always wondered if that was one reason he'd cheated, because their sex had been so vanilla. But he'd never asked for more, and she'd never wanted it. As she lowered her mouth over Derek's cock, feeding the emotions stacking up inside her, she wanted to bring him as much pleasure as he'd brought her. She felt closer to Derek in the short time they'd known each other than she had to Terrence the whole time they'd dated.

She loved him with her hands and mouth, learning what he liked by the sounds he made, the way his body moved and arched with her.

He cradled her jaw in his big hand and said, "Christ, you're amazing."

She'd always been a stellar student and an overachiever. His praise made her want to earn more gold stars. She found her rhythm, working him faster and tighter, earning one sexy noise after another. She was trembling and so turned on, she felt like one touch might make her come. She'd never realized that doing this to him would turn her on so much. She needed much, *much* more, but he was breathing hard, his fingers fisted in her hair, his jaw clenched tight, and she wasn't sure if it was okay to stop. Oh man, she should have done some research.

"Baby, baby, baby," he said in quick succession. "You've got to stop."

She released him like a hot potato. "Did I hurt you?"

"Fuck, no."

He pulled her over him and kissed her so hard and deep, his tongue probed every dip and curve of her mouth, making her want to suck his cock again. He eased his efforts, and her body mourned the loss of it.

"You were going to make me come if you kept sucking me like that. But, baby, if you keep kissing me like that, I'm going to lose it."

She loved knowing that and crawled backward toward the foot of the bed, slowing to lower her mouth over him again and suck the length of him to the back of her throat. She slicked her tongue from base to tip, lingering at the crown until *he* was shaking. Then she took him to the back of her throat again. He fisted his hands in her hair so tight, she moaned at the sting on her scalp, earning another buck of his hips. She added that little moan to her growing list of things that drove him wild, and then she did it again.

"Tallie. Stop, baby. Please? I want to be inside you."

She slowly kissed the length of his shaft, then tasted her way down his thighs and stepped off the bed.

He watched her intently, fisting his hands in the sheets, as she whipped her sweater over her head. He whistled softly, and the sexy sound gave her an idea. Her heart hammered relentlessly as she turned her back and peered over her shoulder. She trusted him to the ends of the earth. She didn't know if she'd ever get used to him dancing in front of other women, but she could at least send the message that she was trying. She swayed her hips in a little striptease as she wiggled out of her bottoms and bent to strip them off. He gripped her hips and sank his teeth into her ass cheek, sending shocks of lust zinging through her. He pushed a hand between her legs, teasing over her wetness, then swiftly pushed his fingers in deep as she straightened her spine.

"Derek," she said breathlessly.

She moved up and down, fucking his long fingers, as he drove her out of her mind, licking and biting her behind. She arched and reached for his free hand, guiding it to her breast. He groped her roughly, pinching her nipple, making her sex pulse around his fingers. He grabbed her hand and guided it to her sex, using her fingers to tease her clit. She stilled, having never done this in front of a man before. She'd already crossed about a million lines she'd never dreamed of crossing.

"It's just us, baby. Do it for me," he urged, holding her fingers to her wetness.

She closed her eyes, nervous and excited at once, knowing she'd do anything for him. His fingers stroked over that magical spot inside her as their joined hands sent her up to the edge.

"That's it, baby. You're so fucking sexy. Don't stop."

He released her hand and brought his wet fingers to her nipple at the same time he lowered his mouth to her bottom again. The combination of sensations as he tweaked her nipple—his wet mouth, sharp teeth, probing fingers, and her own hand—worked her into a frenzy. Her insides swelled and pulsed, chasing the orgasm that teased in the periphery of her senses. When he sank his teeth into her flesh and squeezed her nipple, she spiraled out of control. Her hips bucked, her sex clenched, and a long, low moan streamed from her lips. He reached up with the hand that was on her breast and put his two fingers in her mouth. She closed her lips around them, sucking as hard as she'd sucked his cock. His fingers withdrew from between her legs, and she heard him tear open the condom packet. She wanted to tell him she was on the pill. The confession was on the tip of her tongue, but she'd only gone on the pill to regulate her periods. She'd never given up that piece of herself or put that much trust in any man.

Sheathed and ready, he gripped her hips and guided her down onto his cock, sitting backward on his lap. Fireworks exploded inside her as he filled her so completely she felt every blessed inch of him, and she began to move.

He moved with her, cupping her breasts and kissing her shoulder. "You are *everything*, Talia. Everything good, everything sweet, everything I want."

His breath sailed over her skin, but it was his words that sent her heart into overdrive. "I need to see you," she pleaded.

In the next breath she was cradled beneath him, cocooned by his body, loved by his touch, and cherished by those devastating blue eyes as he whispered the words that fed her soul over and over again between frantic kisses.

"You're everything I want, Tallie. *Everything . . .*"

Then his words silenced, and their bodies took over, transporting her to a world billowing with passion. Her skin was on fire, and she felt full to near bursting as her climax engulfed her like a magnificent beast, crashing over her in thunderous waves, dragging her to the depths of pleasure as Derek swallowed her cries, surrendering to his own powerful release, and ground out her name like a prayer.

Much later, after they came down from the clouds, Talia lay wrapped in Derek's arms, her cheek on his chest as he ran his fingers through her hair, pressing kisses to her forehead between sweet whispers of adoration, each one filling an empty space inside her. She drifted off to sleep feeling safe and *whole* for the first time in her life.

The scent of Talia wound through Derek's dreams, drawing him closer to wakefulness, but he fought against it. He didn't want to leave the blissful place their bodies had taken him. He wanted to memorize every little thing about her. The feel of her hair brushing over his chest, the nervous and insanely sexy look in her eyes as she lowered her luscious mouth around his cock, and the overwhelming feeling of unity when he lay buried deep inside her. But the most trusting thing, the thing that told him she was *his*, happened afterward. When he'd gone to wash up, she'd been too sated and tired to move. She'd let him bathe her with a warm, damp cloth. It was a first for him, and he somehow knew it was a first for her, too. His urges to protect her, to care for her, to love her and be close in every way possible were stronger and more natural than anything he'd ever experienced. They hadn't had sex. They'd surpassed lovemaking. He'd only been half-right when he'd said Talia was his everything. *They* were *everything*.

Talia sighed in her sleep, snuggling against him. He blinked away the fog of sleep and pressed a kiss to her forehead. She lay on her stomach, the covers bunched around her hips. Her dark hair streamed across the pillow like silk. He gently pushed a lock away from her cheek and brushed several kisses there.

"Mm." She tipped her cheek up for another kiss.

"Morning, beautiful."

He moved over her, kissing her shoulders, the gentle curve of her spine, all the way down to her perfect ass. He ran his hands over her hips, lavishing each cheek with kisses, then trailed his tongue down the backs of her thighs. Her hips rose, and he slid his hand between her legs, finding her slick heat, which pulled a moan from his lungs. She turned beneath him, gazing up with sleepy eyes and smiling. He kissed her softly before moving lower and running his tongue in circles around her nipple, then blowing cool air over the wetness the way he'd learned she loved.

She inhaled a jagged breath. "How much time do we have?"

"Never enough," he said, and glanced at the clock. *Six thirty.* His heart sank. They had maybe an hour before his father woke up, which meant they really had about half an hour just to be safe. Rushing through their first morning together wasn't what he'd imagined, but then again, he'd take whatever they could get.

She touched his lips with her fingers and said, "Stop thinking, start kissing."

And he did. *Thoroughly.* They made love in bed, fooled around in the shower, and as they dressed for the day, he watched her step into a pair of pretty lace panties and itched to touch her again. He raked a hand through his hair, aroused again as she put on her bra and turned, giving him an eyeful of her in a matching lace bra—then stole it away when she pulled on a sweater.

He folded his arms around her as the sweater tumbled into place. "Come home with me after dinner with your parents tonight."

"You sure? What if your dad sees us and has a hard time?"

"Then we'll reconsider. I hate sneaking you in and out like this. Thank you for putting up with it."

A tease rose in her eyes as she said, "It *was* pretty hard to put up with the best sex of my life, and waking up in your arms? Well, *that's* annoying."

He pressed his lips to hers. "You know what I mean. I feel ridiculous sneaking around." Thinking of how quickly his father forgot things, and how his reactions to identical stimulants were not always the same, he said, "I'd like to think we'll figure something out, but I'm not in a position to make any promises."

"Stop worrying. I'm not a kid who doesn't understand responsibilities. Besides, this is another page for our journey book."

"*Our* book?"

"Sneaking around deserves a page, and I've been thinking, I'm probably not the only one stepping outside my comfort zone. Have you ever snuck a woman into your room before?"

"A *woman*? No. When I was sixteen, I snuck a girl in. We didn't have sex. We just kissed and I think I felt her up. The next morning I was arrogant as hell, and my father looked over the rim of his coffee cup and said, 'Next time you sneak a girl in, I'm dragging your ass to her house to tell her father why you thought it was a good idea.'"

Talia laughed. "Did you do it again?"

"Are you crazy? Nothing's scarier than a teenage girl's father." He twirled her hair around his finger and said, "But I'd gladly explain this to your father. Nothing scares me where you're concerned, Talia. Except the thought of *not* being with you."

He lowered his lips to hers, and the alarm on his father's door sounded. They both froze. Derek cursed under his breath.

"Sorry, babe. This might get uncomfortable."

"More uncomfortable than confronting a teenage girl's father?" She slipped her feet into her heels and pulled her bag over her shoulder. "I think we can handle this. You go out and distract him, and I'll slip out the front door."

"I should be shot for putting you in this position," he said as he put on his boots.

"Does that mean you don't want me to come tonight?"

"Baby, I want you to come *many* times tonight." As he expected, her cheeks flushed, making his heart squeeze. "I feel guilty, but not guilty enough to want a night without you." He took her in one last, fierce kiss and said, "Operation Distraction, here I come."

He found his father standing at the living room window in his blue pajamas. "Good morning, Pop. How'd you sleep?"

The familiar pause hung between them as Derek's father scanned his face, and Derek held his breath, wondering if he'd be *Archie* or *Derek* or if he'd frighten his father altogether. His father turned back to the window, gazing outside for what seemed like forever.

"Are you hungry?" Derek finally asked.

His father studied his face again, and Derek imagined drawing this image in a journal, showing himself suspended between darkness and light.

His father's eyes shifted over his shoulder and brightened. "Who is that?"

Derek turned, and Talia winced, mouthing, *Sorry.*

He mouthed, *It's okay*, then said, "Pop, this is my friend Talia."

She wiggled her fingers with an apology she didn't need to make showing in her eyes. "Good morning."

"Well, hello." His father walked past him and said, "Talia is a pretty name. Would you like to have breakfast with us?"

She glanced at Derek with a question in her eyes. He was so damn happy to have averted an unpleasant scene, he said, "Yes, she'd love to join us. I'll make tuxedo mochas."

"Wonderful." His father walked into the kitchen and said, "I'll cook."

Derek dropped a kiss on Talia's cheek and said, "Thank you, baby. We'll make it quick so you're not late." He hurried to his father's side. Knives and Alzheimer's were not a good combination. "We'll do it together, Pop. But how about if we get you dressed first?"

Talia set her bag in the foyer and joined them in the kitchen.

"I am dressed," his father said. He glanced at Talia. "And she looks beautiful *and* hungry. She needs applewood bacon and eggs on flatbread. Get the spinach, would you, Derek?"

It was funny how, as a kid, the way his father said his name incited different feelings. First name only was usually good. First and middle came with a scolding. But now, any time his father used his name was a gift in which he reveled.

"That sounds delicious. Can I help?" Talia asked.

"Spinach, coming up," Derek said as he grabbed the greens from the refrigerator.

"You can help shave chocolate for my boy's froufrou drink," his father said. "Then sit your pretty little behind down and let the men make the feast."

"Now that sounds like a plan." She smiled wide, her brows lifting in Derek's direction, obviously as pleased with the morning's welcome as he was.

Derek set the ingredients on the counter, put a hand on his father's shoulder, and said, "I think it's going to be a really good day."

CHAPTER THIRTEEN

LATE WEDNESDAY AFTERNOON, after Talia walked Molly and Derek put the finishing touches on his gift for her mother, he met Talia at her house with a bag of groceries. When they were cooking breakfast that morning, Talia had mentioned that her mother's favorite dish was vegetable kugel, and he'd promised to teach her how to make it. Now she sautéed leeks while he shredded vegetables.

"You make everything seem easy," she said.

"That's funny." He set down the zucchini he was shredding and moved behind her. "You make everything *hard*." He kissed her just above the neckline of her soft pink sweater. She stopped stirring as his hands came around her waist, and he said, "Uh-uh. Caramelized leeks need stirring, Tallie girl."

She sighed needily and angled her head to the side, allowing him to lavish her with openmouthed kisses.

"Is this how you teach all your girlfriends to cook?" she teased.

"I only have one girlfriend, and I actually prefer to teach her naked, but I'm afraid hot oil and bare skin don't mix well."

She leaned into him and said, "That's what cooking time is for, remember?"

He growled in her ear and nipped at her lobe, earning the sexiest little gasp. "I'm glad you remembered." When he'd promised to teach her to make the dish, he'd also promised to make the cooking time well worth her while and had proceeded to tell her about all the things he planned to do while the kugel was cooking.

After fulfilling *all* his dirty promises, they drove to Talia's childhood home, which Willow and Zane had purchased from her parents when her parents had moved to a smaller home around the corner. Derek gazed up at the sprawling white Victorian, waiting for his nerves to kick in, but all that came was the urge to claim Talia in front of her family. To let them know how special she was to him and that they didn't have to worry about him hurting her. But first . . .

He climbed from the car, feeling Talia's eyes on him as he came around to help her out. She went rigid in his arms, a bundle of nerves and unsurety, both of which he aimed to obliterate as he brushed his lips over hers. She grabbed the front of his jacket, kissing him carefully at first. He took the kiss deeper, running his hands up her back and into her hair, and he felt her tension draining from her limbs. He continued kissing her, slow and sweet, until she melted against him with a dreamy sigh. Only then did he put a whisper of space between them and gaze into her eyes.

"That has to hold me over for a very long time," he said.

"Then maybe we should do it again, just in case dinner runs late."

She didn't have to ask twice.

After several heat-thrumming kisses, he grabbed her mother's gift bag from the back of the car, and carried it, along with their covered dish, and draped his other arm around Talia.

"You didn't have to get my mother a gift. What is it?"

"You'll see," he said as they climbed the porch steps. "I bet you have a lot of good memories here."

"A lot of *loud* memories." She placed her hands on his chest, making it clear she wasn't ready to go inside yet. "Whatever you do, don't accept any lotions, oils, or any other little gifts from my mother. She swears she puts love potions in them. My family is probably going to be super annoying."

He chuckled. "Families are supposed to be annoying. It's their job to embarrass you, and I'll bet they put me through the wringer to see if I measure up for their very precious sister and daughter. I think I can handle them."

"I haven't brought a guy home for years, so they might just stare at you slack-jawed."

"Babe, do you really think they can scare me off?"

"They can scare *me* off," she said flatly.

"Then I'll have to hold on tight." He hauled her in for another kiss, balancing the dish against his hip. If her siblings were going to try to make her feel funny, he'd make sure she knew he was right there with her every step of the way and give her something much better to focus on. He heard the front door open and continued kissing her a second longer than he probably should have, but she felt too damn good to let go. And he knew she thought she didn't measure up to her sisters, and he wanted whoever answered that door to know, even sight unseen, that she blew them away—and nothing would come between them.

Three formidable men stood shoulder to shoulder, arms crossed, glowering at him with what he assumed were supposed to be threatening expressions, but the only one who pulled it off was the one on the left, the broadest of the three. He had military-short hair, granitelike features, and a glare that could cut steel. Derek recognized the dude in the middle as her brother, Ben, from the pictures he'd seen at her place. Ben was slimmer, though still muscular, had a softer face, and warm though serious brown eyes, while the third guy looked like he was going to bust into hysterics at any moment. He recognized him, too. It would be hard not to recognize Zane Walker, who'd spent years as an A-list actor.

Derek met their glares with a friendly expression. "How's it going?"

Zane straightened his spine, lifting his chin in greeting. Ben and the tough guy on the end mimicked his chin lift but didn't crack a smile.

"Good Lord," Talia said under her breath.

Ben nudged Zane with a tight expression, causing Zane to double over in laughter. *Guess he's not such a great actor after all.*

"Dude!" Ben shook his head as laughter fell from his lips.

Zane splayed his hands. "What?"

Derek stifled a laugh.

"You three are ridiculous." Talia waved at them. "Derek, meet Bodhi Booker, Bridgette's fiancé, who, believe it or not, is smiling at you right now." The edges of Bodhi's lips twitched. Talia had explained that Bodhi was a guarded guy who had seen such treacherous things when he was fighting overseas, he didn't open up easily. "My brother, Ben, and Zane Walker, Willow's husband."

"Nice to meet you," Ben said warmly. "Hurt my sister, and you'll have him to deal with." He pointed at Bodhi, who stood up straighter, puffing out his chest.

Derek was glad Talia had men looking out for her.

"Forget Bodhi." Zane chuckled. "Hurt Talia and you'll have *Piper* to deal with." He shook Derek's hand.

Bodhi *almost* cracked a smile as he outpowered Derek's friendly grip.

"Nice to meet you," Derek said as a woman who was petite as a bird with fierce eyes and straight blond hair came down the hall behind them, followed by a much curvier, friendly-looking blonde, her gaze set on Zane. He recognized Piper and Willow because they fit Talia's descriptions to a tee.

"Here we go," Talia said as Piper bullied her way around the men and set her hands on her hips, staring at Derek with a shocked, and appreciative, expression.

Willow put her hand on Zane's shoulder. "What kind of trouble are you boys causing?" She glanced at Derek and blinked several times. "Wow."

"Hey." Zane swept her into his arms, making her laugh.

"I just meant, wow, they're here," Willow said, though no one was buying it. Even Talia rolled her eyes.

"My ass, you did." Piper stepped onto the porch, shamelessly looking Derek up and down. "Where have you been Talia's whole life? And where can I get one of you?"

"Apparently in the college parking lot," Ben mumbled.

Derek chuckled.

"Okay, that's it." Talia took Derek's hand, pulling him toward the door as she said, "Derek, this is Piper. She has no filter."

"I have a filter," Piper argued. "I just choose to go *unfiltered*." Her eyes swept over Derek again. "You look familiar."

"Because he looks like that guy you liked from *Lost* that you lusted over for so long," Willow said. "Hi, Derek. I'm Willow. *Moderately* filtered."

"I've heard a lot about you all. It's nice to meet you. And, Willow, thank you for making baklava the other night. It was delicious." He held up the covered dish and said, "Wait until you see what Talia made."

"Good thing Mom cooked," Ben said as they headed toward the kitchen.

Derek glared over his shoulder. He knew Ben meant it as a joke, but he felt protective of Talia, and he wasn't going to let tonight turn into a circus at her expense. "Watch yourself," he warned. "You'll be eating those words when you taste this."

Talia squeezed his hand. The surprised and appreciative look in her eyes made the disapproving look in Ben's worthwhile. He kissed her as they entered the kitchen, where there was a flurry of activity going on. He recognized the rest of Talia's family from the pictures in her house. Her mother's blond curls billowed around her smiling face as she set a tray of meat in her husband's hands.

"You're here!" Her mother hustled across the kitchen toward them, her long colorful skirt swishing around her legs. She hugged Talia. Then she opened her arms to Derek and said, "Hi. I'm Roxie, and I'm so glad you made it." She embraced him, and as they drew apart, she touched his hair. "I brought you a bottle of my special body oil. I'll have to remember to bring you some of my lavender conditioner next time for that gorgeous head of hair."

"Mom," Talia said. "No potions, please?"

Derek chuckled, remembering her warning. "I'd love some conditioner, thank you."

"Uh-oh," her father said. "This one has no idea what he's in for."

With his button-down shirt and khakis, close-cropped salt-and-pepper hair, and serious eyes, Dan Dalton was exactly as Talia had described on the drive over, as conservative as her mother was bohemian. He reminded Derek of Talia, and Derek would put money on the fact that behind that professional facade was a man with a wild side.

"Oh, I think I do." Derek reached for Talia's hand. "I welcome your wife's secret potions where Talia's concerned. As beautiful and smart as she is, I'll bet all the single guys in town lust after her. I've got to keep ahead of the competition."

"Damn right you do," Ben said with a nod.

"My mom's potions work," Bridgette said as the most adorable brown-haired boy ran into the kitchen and nearly barreled into her. "I'm Bridgette, Bodhi's other half, and this cutie Louie's mom. It's really nice to meet you."

"More food, Mom!" Louie pleaded, arms outstretched.

Bridgette set an enormous bowl of salad in his hands. "That's it, baby. You've got it."

"Bodhi! I'm taking it into the mess hall!" Louie's eyes caught on Derek, and he stopped in his tracks, his little brows knitting. "You have long hair like my mom. Mom says little boys should have short hair so they aren't mistaken for girls. Do you get mistaken for a girl?"

"Hardly," Piper said with a snort-laugh.

Bridgette's eyes widened. "Louie, I'm sure he doesn't get mistaken for a girl. This is Derek, Talia's . . ."

"Boyfriend," Derek interjected, earning a blush from Talia. He set the kugel on the counter and bent so he was eye to eye with Louie. "Nice to meet you, Louie. I like a man who speaks his mind."

Louie beamed proudly. "When I get older, I'm going to be in the military like Bodhi was, so I gotta have short hair. But I might be a baseball player, or maybe a dog trainer. I'm good with our dog, Dahlia."

"How about if we practice your serving skills?" Roxie suggested. "Why don't you and Grandpa take the food into the dining room so we can eat?" She eyed the kugel. "May I?" She reached for the cover and peeled it off. "Oh my, this looks delicious."

Murmurs of agreement rolled through the kitchen.

"Derek's teaching me to cook," Talia said proudly, leaning into him. "It's vegetable kugel."

Her mother's gaze softened with the look he remembered seeing in his own mother's eyes when he'd played the guitar or sang for her. It was the adoring look of a mother, and he loved seeing it aimed at his girl.

"She's *letting you* teach her?" Bridgette asked and glanced at Willow, who raised her brows. "Talia is the teacher, not the student. That's . . . amazing."

An uncomfortable look washed over Talia, as if she'd been outed. He wondered about that, but before he could say anything, Willow said, "She must really trust you."

"Of course I do," Talia said.

The sound of the front door opening called everyone's attention.

"Hello?" a feminine voice rang out.

"In here, Mom!" Bodhi hollered.

A beautiful middle-aged woman with a mane of black and silver hair appeared in the entrance to the kitchen. "Hello, sweetheart." She kissed Bodhi's cheek as Louie ran into the kitchen and plastered himself around her legs.

"Grandma Alisha!" Louie took her hand and led her to Derek. "This is Derek. Don't worry. Nobody thinks he's a girl. He's Talia's *boyfriend*. Derek, this is my grandma. She speaks her mind, too. You'll like her."

Things moved quickly after that as the women ushered them into the dining room, where they feasted on brisket, potatoes, salad, homemade bread, and a handful of sides. Talia's family devoured the kugel and took full advantage of teasing him and Talia, and one another, which was a welcome change from his own quiet dinners. Even Bodhi had loosened up, gracing Derek with a genuine smile when Derek told Louie that the vegetables in the kugel were sprinkled with magic powers that he'd only have control over after he ate them. But Derek had noticed Bodhi flashing plenty of those smiles at Bridgette and Louie, and he understood that, because his best smiles were reserved for Talia.

Ben speared a forkful of kugel and said, "I still can't believe you taught my sister to cook. She's the microwave queen."

She was also the *kissing queen*, the *lovemaking queen*, and the only woman who had ever been able to make him want to try to fit more into his life. But her family didn't need to know all of that. Only Talia did, and by the loving look in her eyes, he had a feeling she already knew.

"What *else* did Derek teach you?" Bridgette waggled her brow.

Talia leaned into him again. He gazed into her eyes and said, "I think you should be asking what else she taught me. Your sister is a remarkable woman."

"If he's this good in the kitchen, I wonder how he is in the—"

"Piper!" Roxie chastised. She huffed out a breath and then turned brighter eyes on Derek and Talia. "This kugel is delicious. You two make a wonderful team."

"Hopefully in the kitchen *and* the bedroom," Piper said under her breath, ignoring her mother's warning.

Talia glared at her. "You do realize your nephew is sitting right next to you, don't you?"

"She can't see me," Louie said. "I'm invisible."

"Must be those magic vegetables," Bodhi said, and gave Derek an appreciative look.

"Apparently Derek knows all kinds of magic," Willow said. "Talia mentioned that you were taking her skiing?"

"Yes, next weekend," Derek answered.

"Ten bucks says she stays in the lodge," Piper said.

Zane gave Derek an I've-got-your-back look and said, "I'll take that bet and go double or nothing."

Everyone got in on the joke, and Talia took it all in stride, making snarky comments and rolling her eyes, but Derek vowed to give her something to come back and rave about, even if she didn't ski. Although he had a feeling there was a lot of competition in her big family and a little one-on-one attention, without the pressure of her younger siblings zooming down the slopes, might go a long way.

"How about if we take care of these dishes so we can get to birthday cake?" Ben picked up his plate, and everyone rose to help.

"Cake!" Louie hopped off his chair and yanked on Bodhi's hand. "Get up, Bodhi. The faster we clear the table, the faster we get Auntie Willow's cake."

Zane pulled Willow to her feet and into his arms, heat brimming in his eyes. "I want *all* of Auntie Willow's sweetness."

"There's so much love in this room," Roxie said dreamily as she rose to her feet. "This is the best birthday gift a mother could ask for."

"I'll say," Alisha agreed. "Nothing makes my heart happier."

Dan kissed Roxie's cheek as he guided her back down to her seat. "You two ladies sit and relax. Tonight we're spoiling Roxie, which means Alisha gets to be spoiled, too."

As Derek carried dishes into the kitchen, his mind traveled to his own parents. He wondered what they would have been like as a couple at this age if things had been different. He missed his mother every day, and as he watched Talia's parents, he realized how much he missed his father, too.

In the kitchen, Bodhi took the dishes from his hands and turned back to the sink, where he was washing pots and pans. "You okay?"

The girls carried dishes into the kitchen, laughing over a whispered conversation the guys were not privy to. Then they gathered around Roxie and Alisha at the table, looking at magazines.

"Yeah. Fine." It was interesting watching Talia with her siblings. She had a great sense of humor, and she was sexier than all of them put together. But what struck him the most was that while the others seemed to compete to be seen and heard, Talia was content in the background, observing or maybe watching *over* them.

"Chick time," Ben said as he set a platter on the counter. "They're looking at wedding shit, which is our cue to stay in here."

"My life has become one wedding decision after another," Bodhi said.

Zane carried in the last of the dishes and said, "It's estrogen overload in there. They're in full wedding mode. Willow and I did the right thing by eloping. Not only did we escape the media, but we didn't have to spend weeks worrying about wedding dresses and flowers."

"Hey," Bodhi said, "we've got the flowers covered." He looked at Derek and explained, "Bridgette and I run the flower shop in town. Did you get the lowdown on everyone?"

Derek picked up a dish towel and began drying a pot. "I think so. Talia said you do some sort of Special Forces training, Piper and her dad run a contracting business, Zane's working on getting a screenplay made into a movie, and Ben's an investor. Did I get it right?"

"Yup. Now you just need to give us the lowdown on you." Ben crossed his arms and leaned against the counter. "What *don't* we know?"

Derek chuckled at his forthright question. "Let's see. I'm pretty much an open book. I take care of my old man, who has Alzheimer's, and lost my mom when I was a teenager. I work at a bar for the flexibility in my schedule and the tips, and I'm finishing up my master's. But I doubt that's what you want to know." He set down the pot and began drying another one. "I'm totally into your sister, Ben. Talia fascinates me on every level. She's brilliant, interesting, stunningly beautiful, and she's got a soft heart. All you need to know is that I'm not a dick, and I'm not a cheater. I'm just a guy with a lot of responsibility who feels lucky to have connected with such an incredible woman."

"Well, hell, Ben," Zane said. "The guy's got game."

Bodhi turned off the water and dried his hands, exchanging an empathetic look with Ben.

"I'm sorry to hear about your parents," Ben said. "And as far as Talia goes, she deserves to be happy. I'm glad to hear you're not a prick, because I'd hate to have to beat the living shit out of you."

Derek chuckled, though he knew Ben wouldn't hesitate to try if it meant protecting his sisters.

"I lost my father when I was young," Bodhi said with a tight expression. "There's no filling that hole, is there?"

"I'm sorry to hear that. There's no filling it. It's the navigating-around-it part that sometimes makes things tough," Derek said, feeling a kinship developing. "But I've gotten used to it now."

"Roxie and Dan have been like second parents to me forever," Zane said. "They're good people." He glanced at Ben, then Bodhi, and slowly shifted his gaze back to Derek. "Well, you're with Talia now, which makes you one of us."

"There's just one more question." Bodhi crossed his arms over his chest with a serious expression.

"It's an important one." Zane mimicked Bodhi's posture.

"Vital," Ben said as he reached into a cabinet. "Whiskey or tequila?"

They all laughed, though Derek's was short-lived.

"I'm not much of a drinker," he admitted as Dan joined them in the kitchen. "Alcohol is one of the risk factors for Alzheimer's. I figure I've got enough going against me. I don't need to add anything more."

"Aw, man." Bodhi scrubbed a hand down his face. "I didn't think about that. Sorry."

"That's smart, son," Dan said. "Too many young people ignore risk factors and plow ahead like they'll go on living forever in the same manner they always have. Talia told me about your father. I can only imagine how difficult that is, much less dealing with it without family around to help. If you need anything, get caught in a bind, need a shoulder to lean on, just let us know. There are plenty of people here who would happily help you out."

"Thank you. I appreciate that." And he did, even though he knew he'd probably never take them up on it. The thought of his father getting confused and having a hard time without him or Maria there to help was overwhelming. He told them about Maria and how she'd been there to help their family with his mother and every step of the way with his father.

"Please extend the same offer to Maria," Dan said. "We all need a hand every now and again." He looked at Zane and said, "And you can never have enough family."

"Boy, that's the truth. Talia mentioned that you were thinking about opening an adult day-care center," Ben said. "I'd love to hear about it."

While they finished the dishes and cleaned the kitchen and dining room, Derek told them about his project and his plans to renovate his house to be used as the day-care center. He felt good about sharing all that he had with them. They seemed like good men. Their bond was clear and present, and they weren't afraid to talk about their emotions, which he'd found a rare trait among most men his age. He glanced into the other room. Louie sat on the floor in the living room playing with army figurines, and for the briefest of seconds, Derek allowed himself to wonder what it would be like to have a little boy or girl of his own. His gaze found Talia, sitting on the couch between her mother and Bridgette with a magazine on her lap, and that image in his mind wrapped itself around her. He was falling hard for Talia. Did she want children? Was it fair to get so involved when there was a chance his children—and he—might end up with the same fate as his father?

"Derek," Ben said, pulling him from his thoughts. "I'd love to catch up sometime to talk more about your business venture."

"I would as well," Dan said. "We can probably cut your renovation costs by a nice chunk if we do the work."

"I don't want to take advantage of my relationship with Talia in that way," Derek said uneasily.

Dan looked him in the eyes and said, "Put that pride away, son. This is what the Daltons do. We help one another. Let's talk, see if we can help make your vision become a reality without breaking the bank. You want to do something for others, and"—he glanced at Talia, a smile crawling across his lips—"you've already done something for us."

"It's better than porn," Bridgette said. The women crowded together on the couch, looking past the clean dining room to the sparkling kitchen, where the men stood by the counter, dishes drying behind them. "Alisha, you sure raised your son right."

Alisha gazed thoughtfully at her son. "I swear Bodhi practically raised himself. But I'd say your mother did a fine job with Ben and Zane, too."

Zane had gotten unlucky in the parent department. He had practically lived at the Daltons' house from the time he was around Louie's age. Talia looked at Louie playing with his toys and felt a pang of longing that she'd been noticing more often since Willow and Bridgette had found their true loves.

"Talia, your new beau is quite the charmer," her mother said. "It takes a real man to pull off that length hair and jewelry."

"He's totally not Talia's type," Piper said.

Talia glared at her. Piper didn't know the half of it. If she knew Derek danced, she'd give Talia even more shit, and Talia had no interest in dealing with that. Life was too good right now to have to explain herself or justify Derek's job to anyone.

"I don't mean it like *that*," Piper clarified. "Once he opened his mouth, it was easy to see why you two are so connected. He's a smarty-pants and a careful thinker like you, and the way he looks at you is like you're made of everything he's ever wanted. But when I first saw him? You can't deny that he's everything you've never wanted in the looks department. Long hair? Bedroom eyes? A pinkie ring and bracelets? The man looks like he should be lying on the beach wearing nothing but sunshine."

"Piper!" her mother said sharply.

"Oh, please," Piper said. "Like you can't see that?"

Talia licked her lips, imagining Derek naked. And then she realized Piper was probably doing the same thing. She turned a threatening stare on her. "Don't go there, Pipe. Not even mentally."

Piper laughed. "I'm not. It was just an observation. I mean, he's gorgeous, but he's yours, which puts him firmly in the no-strike zone." She mimed a box and put a big *X* through it. "I'm happy for you, Tal."

"Me too," Talia admitted. "And for the record, I love his hair and his jewelry. He lost his mom when he was fourteen, and the ring was hers. The bracelets are his father's." She'd already filled them in on his father's illness and what Derek's life was like.

Her mother placed her hand over Talia's. "Look at him in there with the guys."

They all looked toward the kitchen again. Talia's father had an arm slung over Derek's shoulder.

"He must be a good man to have won you over, baby girl," her mother said. "But to have won over your father? And Ben, who has looked out for you forever? That says it all."

"Okay, enough emotional talk," Piper chimed in. "Let's get this show on the road. Between wedding plans and Talia's new love life, I'm about ready to puke, which doesn't bode well for heading down to Dutch's Pub later and scoping out the unemotional men."

"You're so gross," Talia said.

"Says the girl who picked up a man in a parking lot. Hey, boys," Piper hollered. "Let's eat cake and give Mom her presents!"

Louie jumped to his feet. "Cake!"

Everyone gathered in the dining room again to sing "Happy Birthday" to Roxie. She blew out the candles, and Willow doled out slices of the scrumptious-looking chocolate cake. Talia discovered that eating cake with Derek was another thing that got her hot and bothered. While everyone chatted around them, she and Derek shared their dessert, feeding each other forkfuls of deliciousness. His *mm* sounds and the lustful look in his eyes every time he slid the fork into her mouth sent her mind reeling back to last night and the sexy loving they'd shared.

He leaned in, stealing kisses between bites, one hand resting on her thigh, blazing heat through her jeans. She was sure everyone could feel their passion igniting, but as she stole a glance around the table, she realized they were all too swept up in their own conversations to notice. Except Piper, who never missed a damn thing and was giving her an I-always-knew-you-weren't-Little-Miss-Pure look.

Oh boy.

That look should stop Talia cold, but when she gazed into Derek's eyes, she was a goner again.

By the time they finished dessert, her insides were buzzing. She wanted to drag Derek out the front door and make a beeline for her bedroom.

"Presents!" Bridgette said, starting to move toward the living room.

Derek touched Talia's hand and said, "Help me carry these into the kitchen." He handed her a plate and gathered the other dishes.

The second they were in the kitchen, he set the dishes on the counter and swept her into his arms, bringing them out of view of the living room. His mouth covered hers, sweet, hot, and insistent. Heat streaked through her, pooling deliciously in her very best spot in between.

"Your family adores you," he said in a rush. "And I adore them." His hands cruised down her body, holding her against him. "But damn, baby. There could be a million people here and *you* would be the only one I see. Your beautiful face, your happiness when you talk with your family, the way you look at Louie like you want a little boy of your own . . . I see *all* of you, Tallie girl."

She couldn't believe he'd seen so much, even her thoughts about Louie. She opened her mouth to respond, but no words came.

Louie peeked into the kitchen and said, "Auntie Piper said stop kissing so Grandma can open her presents!" He dashed toward the living room, yelling, "They weren't kissing, but he touched her butt!"

"Oh my God." Talia buried her face in Derek's chest.

He pressed his hands to her cheeks, tilting her face up, and kissed her again, grinning so wide he made her smile, too. "I've got this," he said, and tucked her against his side. They went into the living room, and he said, "You're right, Louie. I did touch Aunt Talia's butt. Do you know why?"

Louie shook his head. "I think it's what boys do when they grow up, because Bodhi's always touching Mom's butt, and Zane smacks Auntie Willow's. I even saw Grandpa touch Grandma's butt the other day, but Mom said I'm not supposed to talk about it." His hand flew over his mouth, eyes wide.

Everyone laughed.

Derek motioned for Louie to come closer. "A little bird told me that you like baseball cards."

Louie nodded vehemently, eyes wide.

Derek held out his hand, revealing a package of baseball cards, which he must have had hidden in his pocket. He lowered his voice and said, "Your auntie had these in her back pocket. I was just sneaking them out."

Talia's heart soared at his thoughtfulness and his clever save.

Louie gasped, snagging the package from Derek's hand. "Thank you!" He threw his arms around Derek's legs, hugging him tight.

Derek tousled his hair, and Talia melted a little more.

"Boy, he's good," Bridgette said softly.

Louie climbed onto Bodhi's lap, and Bodhi gave Derek one of those *guy* looks that told Talia Derek had already come into the fold of their brotherhood, which flooded her with happiness.

After that they moved to the living room again, and her mother opened her gifts. Talia sat beside Derek on the floor near Ben as her mother gushed over a clay pencil holder that Louie had made and painted for her and a pair of pearl earrings from Talia's father. She was overwhelmed at the romantic weekend getaway Talia and her siblings had given her and was excited to take advantage of the gift Alisha had given her, a day at a holistic spa.

Derek handed her mother the gift bag he'd brought. "Happy birthday, Roxie. Thank you for letting me share it with you and your family."

"Suck-up," Ben said with a feigned cough, which made everyone laugh.

Derek took his teasing in stride.

Her mother unwrapped the gift slowly, between peeks at Derek and Talia. "Oh, Derek," she said softly, and pressed a hand over her heart. She looked at Talia. "You told him about this?"

"What? I haven't seen it." Talia went up on her knees, trying to see the gift he'd kept secret.

Her mother turned the framed picture around. It was one of Derek's cartoons. He'd drawn their family huddled beneath a tarp, each of them wearing expressions of discomfort or frustration as oversized raindrops splashed in puddles all around them. The tarp was propped up with long tree branches, complete with leaves sticking out like waving hands in the wind. One side of the tarp was higher than the other, causing a stream of water to fall from the tarp and puddle on one side. Exaggerated rivers flowed from inside their tents. He'd drawn Piper and her father crouched by a small tepee of twigs and broken branches, their brows slanted in concentration as Piper rubbed two sticks together. Snakes of smoke danced from her efforts. Their mother was drawn sitting with her arms around Talia and her other sisters, amusement and love evident in her big, beautiful eyes. Talia had her nose in a book, Bridgette was leaning forward, doodling in the wet earth with a stick, and Willow was peering over Bridgette's shoulder. Ben was sticking his head out from beneath the tarp, eyes closed, mouth open, drinking the rain. In a puddle at their father's feet, Derek had drawn an oversized raindrop touching a puddle and creating an exaggerated splash of hearts arching out of the water, spelling the word *family*.

"Whoa, dude," Ben said with awe. "Did you draw that?"

Derek humbly shrugged one shoulder, nodding. "I hope I didn't overstep. Talia told me about the trip, and I couldn't stop thinking about it. I was hoping it was a fond memory and not a bad one."

Her mother's eyes dampened, and she reached for Talia's father's hand. "It's one of our favorite vacation memories. Thank you, Derek."

"That was Dad's *bonding* weekend," Piper explained. "Our punishment for having lives."

"No electronics," Talia explained. "I didn't care, but you'd think he was sending the others to jail."

Her father laughed. "It wasn't a punishment. It was a reminder about family and the value of relationships beyond cell phones and the internet."

"Well, we sure got close that weekend," Piper said.

Bridgette looked at Willow and said, "Remember how loud you shrieked when the tent started leaking?"

"Yes! And Ben ran through the puddles, splashing all of us," Willow said with a laugh.

"I remember chasing his butt around, trying to catch him." Her father laughed. "And through the whole thing, Talia sat reading, happy as a lark."

"It doesn't take much to have a happy life, does it, Tallie girl?" Derek said sweetly, and all eyes turned on them.

"Tallie girl?" Willow and Piper said in unison.

Talia felt her cheeks burn.

Derek pulled her closer, those big blue eyes holding her gaze, and said, "My girl's inner happiness can't be dampened by a little rain."

She didn't care who teased her.

She was his Tallie girl, and she hoped she would be for a very, very long time.

CHAPTER FOURTEEN

THURSDAY MORNING DIDN'T go quite as well as Wednesday morning had. Derek and Talia awoke to the alarm on his father's door at five thirty. Jonah was confused and agitated, and it took Derek a long time to settle him down. Thankfully, Talia remained calm, offering to help in any way she could, while giving his father the physical space he needed to relax, which Derek appreciated but also felt guilty about. Later in the morning, he sat in an armchair in the dining room playing his guitar, watching Talia grade papers at the table, while his father hunkered down over a notebook in which he was drawing. His father had started cartooning at the age of ten, when a neighbor who was an artist had noticed his talent and taken him under his wing. Derek was glad the disease hadn't stolen his father's artistic abilities yet. At least not all of them. Sometimes his father would be in the middle of drawing and forget what he was doing, but in the moments when his muse was present, he seemed content. Happy, even.

Talia glanced over, a pretty smile forming on her beautiful face. He blew her a kiss, thinking about the call he'd received about an hour ago, notifying him that a room had become available at the small assisted-living facility by their house. When his father was first diagnosed, he'd insisted on getting his affairs in order. If the diagnosis and the dark clouds that lay ahead weren't enough to tear Derek apart in those first few weeks, the idea of one day putting his father into an assisted-living facility, a nursing home, or hospice when necessary had nearly done him in. Derek had endured lessons in strength and fortitude he'd never imagined in those early days, and many more since. Following his father's wishes, he'd finally put Jonah on a waiting list for a room at the facility a few months ago, expecting, as they'd told him, that it could take anywhere from several months to a year or more for a room to become available. The call was anything but expected. A knot formed in Derek's chest—he was torn between wanting a chance to have a normal relationship with Talia without having to navigate his father's disease at every turn and wanting to be there to care for his father.

The sound of the front door opening pulled him back to the moment.

"Good morning, *mijo*. Good morning, Jonah," Maria called out.

Talia had Thursdays off. He was going with her to walk Molly and then they were running a few errands. Their dates were anything but spectacular, but he hoped to make it up to her sometime soon.

"We're in here, Maria," Derek said.

His father looked at Talia and said, "Eva, Maria is here."

"Yes, I hear that," Talia said, as if it were the most natural thing in the world for her to be called his mother's name.

And man, that hit him smack in the center of his heart.

Last night, after he and Talia had made love, they'd lain in bed talking about family, and he'd told her about how Maria had been like a second mother to him. He'd been thinking about mothers and families since seeing Louie, and he still didn't have an answer to his worries about ending up like his father, or if it was fair to Talia to become even more involved. But as he strummed his guitar, watching her eyes narrow as her pen moved over the paper she was grading, darkness came over him at the thought of not being with her. He had enough on his plate with the impending facility visit and the weighty decision about his father's well-being looming over him. He swallowed a dose of denial to get through one hurdle at a time.

"How is Jonah today? And how was dinner with your—" Maria's dark eyes danced with elation as they moved between her and Derek. "*Oh!* I guess dinner was *very* good."

Talia blushed, rose to her feet, and extended her hand. "Hi. I'm Talia."

Derek set his guitar down and stood, but he wasn't fast enough.

Maria already had Talia in an enthusiastic embrace. "I am so happy to meet the one who woke up my *mijo*'s heart." She touched Talia's cheek and said, "He is a good boy. Please don't hurt him."

"Maria . . ." Derek glanced at Talia, and then Maria's arms came around both of them at once and she mumbled a prayer in Spanish, as he'd often heard her do over his father. He carefully pried her arms from around them and said, "You're going to scare her off with all this mothering."

"No, she's not," Talia said sweetly. "She's your *Piper*."

Half an hour later they arrived at Fletch's house. He lived only a few blocks from Derek, in a small Cape Cod–style home.

As they walked up to the front porch, he remembered the first night he'd seen her walking Molly and said, "The night I saw you crossing the street with Molly, I thought I'd conjured your image because I'd been thinking about you so much."

"Maybe you did. Maybe I'm just a figment of your imagination."

He nipped at her neck. "You're sweet as sugar, baby. You're no figment of my imagination." He lowered his lips to hers, and she made a sexy sound that spurred him on to take the kiss deeper. Her kisses made all his worries fade away.

The sound of a throat clearing snapped him back to reality, and he reluctantly broke their connection, meeting Fletch's amused light-blue eyes. He was a handsome man, even if he was smirking at their expense.

"How was *breakfast?*" Fletch asked.

Talia rolled her eyes, pink spreading across her cheeks. "Fletch, this is Derek. Derek, Fletch."

"How's it going?" Derek shook his hand as Molly pushed her nose out the door for a pet.

"Not as good as it is for you," Fletch teased, studying Talia's face as they walked inside. "That pink stain on your cheeks is new, Tal. It looks good on you."

"Whatever," she said. "One day you might get lucky and find a woman who makes you blush."

"If you tell me Derek *blushes*, I'm going to have to rethink approving this relationship."

"Approving?" Derek gathered Talia in his arms and said, "What've you got, all of Sweetwater and Harmony Pointe watching out for you?"

"Damn right she does." Fletch cocked a brow and said, "I wasn't teasing about it looking good on you, Tal. I guess you needed a fake student in your life. What are you guys doing here, anyway? I left you a voicemail this morning letting you know I think I'm okay to walk Molly."

"But what if she pulls on the leash?" Talia asked. "Or if she gets free and you have to run after her?"

"I'll be okay, but if not, maybe I'll take a hint from you and try to run over a pretty woman, then woo her with my intelligence and amazing physique."

"Hey, don't knock it," Derek said. "The best thing that's ever happened to me was nearly getting run over."

They decided to join Fletch on the walk since they were already there. Fletch gave Derek the third degree, showing a little more grit, but Derek didn't mind. Fletch was a nice guy with a good sense of humor, and it was obvious how close he and Talia were.

After their walk, as Derek and Talia drove away from Fletch's house, she said, "Is India seeing anyone?"

He squeezed her hand. "Really? I was thinking about Piper."

"Piper would eat him alive."

Images of last night came rushing back—the two of them tangled together beneath the sheets, Talia slithering down his body and rocking his world with that wicked mouth of hers. He lifted her hand, pressed a kiss to the back of it, and said, "That's not necessarily a bad thing."

CHAPTER FIFTEEN

THE NEXT WEEK and a half flew by with a mix of laughter, late-night rendezvous, early-morning lovemaking, and a few solid doses of uncomfortable reality. Talia didn't mind the discomfort. The more time she spent with Derek and his father and the better she got to know Maria, the more adept she became at helping with and understanding Jonah's needs. That knowledge also helped her understand Derek's daily life even more clearly. He and his father had already taken root in her heart, and as their lives became more connected, she found emotions that were realer and truer than anything she'd ever known. Relationships with Derek's friends were also interwoven in this new life of hers. They'd had another potluck dinner last week at Eli's, and though Phyllis wasn't able to join them today for their ski adventure, they were taking so many pictures, she wouldn't miss a thing.

They were blessed with a perfect sunny Saturday, and thanks to a quick shopping trip with Willow and Piper last night, Talia looked amazing. Her sisters had assured her that if she looked the part of an experienced skier, she'd feel that much more confident on the slopes. They'd even watched skiing videos with her so she wouldn't be quite as nervous. Their support meant the world to her, and she was surprised how much she'd enjoyed opening up to them about her insecurities. That wasn't something she'd ever been comfortable doing before. But being around Derek and his father brought the importance of family to a new level. She'd gotten so close to her sisters lately, she'd thought about telling them about his dancing, but she didn't want to give them a reason not to like him or even to *question* his integrity. She had no idea what her family would think if they knew he took off his clothes for strangers. She was falling hard for him, but she still hadn't gone back to see him dance. It was too hard to see other women gawking at him. Even though she trusted him completely, she didn't need to have it thrown in her face.

As she and Derek waited in line for the J-bar lift with India and Eli, her love for him bloomed bigger, as if the sun fed her emotions. But it wasn't the sun, the moon, or anything else. It was her beautiful man and his loving, generous heart. She was excited to try skiing again and hoped she wouldn't make a fool of herself, but as Derek draped an arm around her and pulled her into their millionth scorching kiss of the day, she had a feeling the girls had done *too* good a job picking out her outfit, and *looking amazing* would equate to hours of weak knees.

"How's my sexy snow bunny?" he asked. "Nervous?"

"A little, but it's hard to think about that when you're standing there looking model-hot in that beanie."

"The first time I wore it with you, I ended up lying on top of you. I have high hopes." He waggled his brows and then kissed her again, slower and sweeter and hot enough to melt the slopes.

She'd been spending nights at his place, and they'd been satisfying their every desire, but it never seemed to be enough. Would she ever get used to the magnetism between them?

"Hey, kissy-face couple! Turn around and let me get a pic." India held up her phone as they both looked over their shoulders, and she took a picture. "Eli!" she called out. He stood in line in front of them, wearing the same hat he'd had on at dinner, only now it had a string tied beneath his chin. He turned for the picture, flashing a cheesy smile.

Derek pressed another kiss to Talia's cheek.

"I got that one, too!" India waved her phone.

"I want in on this action." Eli pushed his head between Derek and Talia and kissed Talia's cheek. They all laughed as India took the picture.

"Get in here, India." Derek pulled her forward as much as he could with her skis and held her phone up for a group selfie.

"I want copies," Talia said.

They took a bunch of silly pictures as they waited in line, which was a great distraction from Talia's nervousness. She and India exchanged phone numbers, and India texted her the pictures.

"We're up!" Eli said as he skied out to wait for the lift. "See you guys at the top."

Talia drew in a deep breath.

"You okay, babe?" Derek asked as Eli was swept up the hill and Talia transferred her poles to her left hand.

"Yeah, I think so." During breakfast, Derek had drawn cartoons of them skiing while he reminded her of the ins and outs of riding the lifts. She wasn't that nervous about riding the J-bar or even skiing down the bunny hill, but the bigger lifts and the more difficult slopes had her stomach in knots.

"I'll be right behind you. Remember, all you have to do is slide forward at the top. Eli will be waiting for you, and I'll be right behind you."

"Just what she needs. A freak sandwich," India teased. "You're going to kill it, Talia!"

Derek swatted Talia's butt as she skied out to wait for the lift, and India took more pictures. Talia blew Derek a kiss, and then the bar slid into place, pushing her up the hill. Eli came into view, standing at the top of the hill with his phone in one hand, either recording or taking pictures; she couldn't tell which. When she skied away from the slope, he cheered and applauded.

"You're a pro!" Eli said.

Derek and India arrived a minute later.

"Derek must have been pulling our legs about you not skiing," Eli said.

"No. He was telling you the truth. I haven't skied in forever. But this is just the kid area. It's the bigger slopes and lifts that worry me."

"I get that," India said. "It took me forever to brave the bigger slopes."

"Why do they worry you?" Eli asked. "Just tell yourself they are all bunny slopes."

"Oh, right," she said sarcastically. "A hill this size is doable. But the steeper slopes make me feel totally out of control."

"You must be an oldest child," Eli said. "How many siblings do you have?"

"How do you know I have any?"

"Because most eldest siblings need a sense of control," Eli explained. "So . . . ? How many?"

She told him about her sisters and Ben. "Once I was able to drive, I'd bring them skiing, but there were definite advantages to hanging out in the lodge."

"Hot guys," India said, and held her hand up for a high five. "I hear ya. My sister and I totally figured that out, too. All the hot guys would snowboard, then hit the lodge to warm up."

"We're breaking you of that habit today." Derek gave her a possessive—and hot as sin—stare.

She and India laughed.

"Let's go, Tallie girl," Derek said. "You set the pace, and I'll ski beside you."

True to his promise, he stayed in line with her the whole way down, even though she skied slower than nearly every kid on the slope. When she got to the bottom, India and Eli both had their phones out, taking pictures.

"What are you doing? Making a documentary?" she teased.

"Life is short," India said. "We capture the good times when we can."

Her heart squeezed at that little reminder. While she'd been enjoying the time with everyone, she'd forgotten the choreographing that had to happen in order for the others to go on outings such as this and the reality that nobody lived forever or remained the same throughout their lives. She kept that in mind as they skied the bunny hill two more times and then headed to a more difficult one. As she and Derek rode the ski lift up the mountain, the sun beat down on the glistening snow, laughter drifted up from below, and she felt a new level of appreciation for those simple things.

She took out her phone, cuddled closer to Derek, and took a selfie. She became aware of how good it felt to smile and how the man beside her kept her smiling. She turned and took a picture of India and her wild hair and Eli with that silly hat on his head on the lift behind them. Eli put his hand on India's leg, and she swatted it away.

Talia faced forward as she zipped her phone into her pocket. "What's with that hat Eli wears?"

"It was his older brother's." Derek placed his hand over hers and squeezed. "He was in the military and came home with PTSD. He committed suicide last year."

"Oh no." Her heart broke for him. "His poor family."

They rode the rest of the way up the mountain in silence, and it was probably a good thing, because Talia was so nervous about getting *off* the lift that as their turn neared, everything else fell away. Suddenly there was only the sound of blood rushing through her ears and the view of the clifflike hill they were approaching. Derek was saying something about lifting the tips of her skis, but as she fumbled with her poles, she couldn't focus on the words. She sat up straighter, watching the ground come up at her as they approached, and then she was standing and Derek was beside her, and she turned, excited to show him she'd done it! But her ski angled, catching on the other one, sending her ass over teakettle down the slope. She landed on her belly with an *ooph* as Derek tumbled down beside her. She tried to sit up, but her skis were tangled. Derek's arm came around her waist and he hauled her on top of him, out of the way of the approaching skiers.

"I'm sorry. I didn't mean to trip you!" she said, more embarrassed than hurt to have tripped him up, too.

He lay beneath her, grinning like a fool—a lovesick fool—and her heart stuttered.

"You fell on purpose?" She couldn't believe it! Why would he do that?

"Team Grant and all that," he said. Then he pressed his lips to hers, obliterating her embarrassment.

As they got to their feet, she spotted Eli and India waiting for them.

"Are you okay?" India asked as she rushed to Talia's side.

"Don't worry." Eli waved his phone. "We got it all on video. You'll be the next YouTube sensation. *Ski-Crossed Lovers!*"

Hours of friendship and laughter passed with falls and teasing taunts, making for a fun afternoon. Talia was a fine skier, even if a little nervous. There were times when they didn't say a word at the top of the mountain, and then skied down together. But other times Derek saw worries rising in her eyes or her smile trembling at the edges. He went to her then, standing close enough to demand all of her attention. In those moments, when her confidence wavered, he reminded her of who she was. Not the polished professor, but the careful woman who wanted to understand things before taking the next step. The woman who weighed her options and the risks before opening her heart to him. The woman who helped him see that he didn't have to choose between his own happiness and his father's. And then he took the time to talk through the risks and *what-ifs* that concerned her about skiing down the mountain.

He didn't push her to confront them. He simply listened and talked her through her worries. Once she felt safe and comfortable enough, they skied down. But he'd have walked down the mountain if she'd preferred.

As daylight gave way to evening, Derek looked around the dinner table in the lodge restaurant, thinking about the incredible day they'd shared. India was watching him as she whispered something to Talia. It warmed his heart to see how close the two of them had become. Across the table, Eli was scoping out a girl sitting on the other side of the room. And Derek's sweet, beautiful Tallie girl, whose cheeks were pink from a day in the sun, sat in front of the roaring fire, looking radiant as she reached for his hand under the table. He loved that she could kiss him in front of everyone and still have shy moments like these, where their connection was kept just between the two of them.

"Are you guys up for Nightingale's Wednesday night?" India asked.

Eli nodded. "Sounds good to me."

Man, Derek had been so swept up in Talia, he'd forgotten the dinner was planned for this week.

He leaned closer to Talia and said, "Nightingale's is the restaurant where my father used to work. Once a month, before they open for dinner, they host an early dinner hour for us and our parents. It's nice. I had forgotten it was this week. I'll have to get Geno to cover my shift at the bar. Can you join us?"

"You sure you don't mind?" Talia asked softly.

"Babe, there's not a single night when I don't want you with me. It would seem strange not to have you there."

"I already invited her to Phyllis's for the potluck next Sunday night." India patted her curls. "Because I'm cool like that."

"*Pushy* like that," Eli teased.

India rolled her eyes. "You like me pushy. It's who I am."

As Eli and India traded barbs, Derek said, "Pick your favorite dish for next Sunday night and we'll make it together."

She batted her long lashes, playful and sexy at once, and said, "There's no oven involved with my *favorite dish*, and I definitely don't want to share *him*."

"You're killing me, baby," he nearly growled, and kissed her until India complained and they were forced to separate.

After dinner they headed out to the parking lot. Streetlights glowed against the winter-white sky like beacons in the night. Derek was in no hurry to leave their memories behind, and he hoped Talia wasn't, either.

He drew her tighter against him. "What do you think, Tallie girl? Best day ever?"

She gazed up with the most contented expression. "There are no words . . ."

You're wrong, baby. He'd had a few very special words pecking at his heart for the past few days, and it was hell keeping them in. He leaned in for a kiss as they reached Eli's truck.

"You two are going to get lip-locked if you keep that up," India said as she pulled Talia from his arms and hugged her. "See you Wednesday?"

"Absolutely," Talia said, and then she hugged Eli. "Be careful driving."

"Of course. Have fun tonight." Eli winked at Derek.

"We always do." The bastard was going to ruin Talia's surprise if he wasn't careful. Derek reached for Talia's hand, and they headed for his car.

"Thank you for letting me tag along," Talia said when they reached his car.

"*Tag along?* Where I go, you go. That's what couples do. They go skiing and stay at lodges and take sleigh rides through the snow." He kissed her softly, and she wound her arms around his neck.

"That sounds amazing. Maybe one day Maria can stay with your dad overnight and we can do that."

He reached into his pocket and withdrew the keycard to their room in the lodge, which he'd picked up from the desk while Talia was in the ladies' room. He waved it between them. "Tonight is our night, Tallie girl. And our horse-drawn sleigh leaves in half an hour, giving us just enough time to get our things up to the room and for me to get you sufficiently hot and bothered."

"But . . ." She launched herself into his arms, and he twirled her around as they kissed. "I can't believe it." *Kiss, kiss.* "Thank you!" *Kiss, nip, kiss.* "What about your dad? Will he get upset or thrown off schedule?"

"Tonight is all *ours.* Maria's staying overnight, and she's taking him to the museum tomorrow." This was the first time he'd spend the night away from his father since he'd started taking care of him. It was a huge deal, but he'd had a long talk with Maria about it. He trusted her, and he hoped his father did okay. He and Talia deserved this night.

"I have no luggage! Not that I care, but . . ."

He chuckled and kissed her long and hard before setting her on her feet. "You have luggage, babe." He unlocked the hatchback and lifted out her bag. "I had your sisters pack for you."

"Please tell me you mean Bridgette and Willow. If Piper packed, I'll have a suitcase full of sexy lingerie and Lord knows what else."

"I'll plead the Fifth on that one—and make a mental note to have Piper pack all your bags from now on." He hoisted their bags over his shoulder and pulled her close again. "Your mother was nice enough to send along lotions and oils. I requested her most potent *love* potions."

CHAPTER SIXTEEN

THE CRISP NIGHT air stung Talia's cheeks as snowflakes fell from the sky, but she was warm and cozy, snuggled with Derek beneath heavy blankets as a beautiful chestnut horse with red ribbons braided in its mane pulled their sleigh along the snowy trail. Talia felt like they'd slipped into a world all their own, serenaded by sounds of the sleigh runners gliding swiftly through the snow and surrounded by tall pines, fluffy white snow covering their branches like mops of hair. The horse's hooves were muffled in the fresh powder, creating a soft rhythm. Derek tipped her face up and kissed her. Snowflakes melted on her eyelashes, but her hands were buffered by mittens, and her body heated as their tongues tangled and their hands began to wander. The driver seemed oblivious, though he was probably used to couples kissing and touching on the tranquil ride through paradise.

She never imagined life could be this beautiful. Not just their winter wonderland or the way Derek turned her insides to fire, but life with him, where responsibilities mattered but so did . . . *love?* She breathed a little harder with that thought as he deepened their kisses. She'd felt herself falling long before tonight, but still her pulse quickened with the realization.

Derek pulled off his gloves and caressed her cheek. "You're so beautiful, Tallie. I want to give you everything. Nights like these, days filled with laughter, friends, family. I want so much to make you happy."

"You are my happiness." It was the truth, and she felt it all the way to her bones. "I've kept myself closed off for so long, afraid to let anyone in. I have no idea how we happened, but I'm so glad we did."

"We happened the way all the best things in life happen. Our worlds collided in the parking lot, and once we found each other, we were drawn together by some inexplicable force of nature." He kissed her again, slowly and sensually. "You needed a man you could count on, someone real, who knew the value of a woman like you. And don't think I mean an accomplished woman, because that's far too simple to describe you, Talia Dalton. A *professor* is what you do, but who you are is a caring, feminine woman, as strong and determined as you are cautious. I respect and love all those parts of you. You bring light into my world, Talia, and I don't want to imagine a day when I don't wake up with you in my arms."

Her throat thickened, and at the same time, she felt like she was really breathing for the first time in years. She didn't even try to respond with words. She simply drew his mouth to hers and kissed him. She felt him smile against her lips, and then she was smiling too, inside and out. She'd watched her sisters fall in love, and as badly as she'd wanted to feel the incredible sensations they'd described, she'd never fully believed she would. And she sure as heck never expected it to feel this good.

They made out, took selfies, talked, and lay in silence, running their hands leisurely over each other's bodies on the way back to the lodge. Once they were in the elevator, Derek pinned her against the wall, hands above her head, his blue eyes burning through her like lasers.

"You're mine, baby, and I'm yours. All night, with no restrictions. No worries about anyone else needing my attention," he growled hungrily. "Tonight there's no holding back."

She couldn't stop a needy moan from escaping. His eyes flashed dark and insolent as his mouth came ravenously down over hers, kissing her like he'd been freed from years of captivity. She was right there with him, arching and moaning, biting at his lips, earning his strong, rough hands all over her body. By the time they reached their room, she was hanging on to her sanity by a thread. Derek tore their coats off, hauled her into his arms, and shoved the door closed with his hip. She pulled at his shirt as he lifted her sweater over her head, leaving her in a skintight Under Armour top.

"Boots!" fell urgently from her lips, and they both dropped to the floor, struggling to rid themselves of the confining footwear.

Four boots thumped onto the tile, and then she was in his arms again, his hot mouth caressing hers, his hands in her hair, holding, tugging, *claiming* her as they made their way toward the bed. He worked the button on her jeans free and stripped them down. His eyes locked on her Under Armour leggings.

"Baby, is this like one of those box tricks, where I have to keep taking off more layers?"

She giggled and wiggled out of her Under Armour. "Willow said to dress in layers for warmth."

"Your man says to strip naked," he said as he shucked his own clothes. "I'll keep you so fucking hot, you'll never want to wear clothes again."

"That's a big promise," she said as she tugged off her socks. "I hope you plan to fulfill it."

God, he was gorgeous, leaning one hand against the wall, those piercing blue eyes sending sinful messages, his hard length beckoning her, as he pulled off his last sock and pushed from the wall. He crooked his finger, beckoning her to him. The way he looked at her, touched her, the things he said and did, had the most empowering effect on her.

Tonight there's no holding back. She shivered as his words played in her mind. She walked slowly, trying to saunter seductively, while not focusing on the embarrassment of being on display. The wolfish look in his eyes told her she'd nailed it, and then there was no room for embarrassment. When she was within reach, he grabbed her by the hips and pulled her against him.

"Are you *doubting* my sexual abilities, Professor Dalton?" He rubbed his cock against her belly in a dizzying rhythm.

Before she could answer, he spun her around and set her down beside the bed, facing the wall. He boxed her in with his big, hot body and bit down on her shoulder just hard enough for her to feel the erotic sting of pain and pleasure *everywhere*.

He rubbed his cock against her ass and growled in the sexiest voice she'd ever heard, "I promised to never let you down, and I will never break that promise. Not in the bedroom or anywhere else." He guided her arms above her head and nudged her legs apart with his knees. "Do you trust me, Tallie girl?"

She was already so turned on, she wasn't sure her voice would work, but she wanted him to know he filled up all the empty places in her she'd never known existed and managed, "With my whole heart."

He brushed his lips along her shoulder. "You always can, beautiful." He pressed his hands over hers, flattening them against the wall. "Think you can keep those hands up there for me?"

She closed her eyes as fear of the unknown bubbled up inside her. She was so vulnerable in this position, unable to see and anticipate his next move, but her trust for him overpowered those fears. Her pulse spiked up as he gathered her hair over one shoulder and kissed his way down her spine. His lips were soft and familiar. *Safe.* His hands played over her hips as he loved her, kissing and nipping her bottom. Sharp bites of pleasure speared through her as his wicked mouth moved lower, teasing over the backs of her legs, her inner thighs. His tongue slicked over her center, and she breathed faster, her fingers curling against the wall. He spread her legs wider, tasting his way up her body. His cock pushed between her legs, resting against her needy sex. She rocked against it as he plastered his hands on her forearms, kissing her shoulder so lightly it felt like a feather dusting her skin as he thrust his hard length against her sex. His hair tickled her bottom, his solid chest pressed against her back. She tried to concentrate on one sensation, but every kiss, every thrust, every graze of his body brought shocks of pleasure. The blissful teases blended together like live wires moving over her skin. She tried to lift her hands, needing to touch him, but he pressed on her forearms, slid his big paws over her hands, and held her in place.

"Come for me."

The demand in his voice was new and *thrilling!* He was all man in bed and in life, but he'd never demanded like this. He hadn't even entered her yet, and she was on the verge of coming. She had no idea it could be so titillating to surrender complete control. But she didn't want to give it up completely. Or at least, she wanted to share in that privilege, and she gathered the courage to ask for it.

"Touch me," she said in what she hoped was a commanding voice, though it was so shaky, she was sure he heard it as a plea.

His hand slid slowly down her arm, along her shoulder, making her acutely aware of every inch of skin he touched. In her mind, she followed his fingers as they moved down her side, and *finally* his hand snaked around her belly and between her legs.

"Give me your mouth," he growled.

She tried to turn around, but he still had her pinned.

"Just your mouth," he said.

She looked over her shoulder, and his mouth came forcefully down over hers. They ate at each other's mouths as his hard length pistoned faster between her legs, and she met each thrust with one of her own, taking her higher and higher. His hand teased her most sensitive nerves in agonizingly precise and painfully *slow* strokes, bringing her to the cusp of release—and holding her there, leaving her standing on the edge of a cliff, a lifeline swinging just out of reach. Every thrust brought it closer, but not close enough. She struggled against his grip and reached between her legs, grabbing his cock. Their mouths parted as she went up on her toes, guided the broad head toward her entrance, and thrust her bottom out.

"Aw, baby," he ground out. "I need to get a condom."

In that moment, everything felt right. *Perfect. Beautiful.* "No. Don't. I want all of you, Derek. I'm on the pill, and I don't want anything between us."

"Tallie girl," rushed from his lungs, full of emotions. He touched his forehead to her shoulder, breathing harder, and pressed a kiss there. "Are you sure, baby?"

"I want to be yours and you to be mine in every way."

"I am yours, baby. Don't ever doubt that."

"I don't," she said honestly, and it was the most freeing, wonderful feeling to fully trust and to give all of herself to him.

He entered her slowly, both of them sighing at the intensity of feeling *everything*. She grabbed at the wall for fear her trembling legs would give out. His hands covered hers, and he laced their fingers together. Buried deep inside her, he pressed his cheek to hers and rocked his hips slowly, gyrating in a circular motion. She closed her eyes, reveling in the way he filled her so completely—physically and emotionally.

"Feel good, baby?" he asked.

"So good."

He showered her with kisses as he loved her tenderly, taking her to the peak of ecstasy and then easing back before sending her over the edge again so exquisitely, she cried out over and over. Every time she hit the peak, he whispered loving words in her ear. She was so lost in him, she didn't care who heard them. Pleasures tore through her like tidal waves, dragging her deeper into them, until she collapsed against him, and he gathered her in his arms and carried her to bed.

He lay next to her, and she rolled onto her side, reaching for him. "Love me again."

He turned onto his side, bringing her body flush against his. They gazed into each other's eyes as he guided her leg to his hip, running his hand down to her ankle as he rocked into her. She felt every inch of his thick length as he penetrated her.

"My sweet, careful girl." His lips covered hers in another intoxicating kiss. "Do you feel it?"

"I feel everything."

"This is who we are, Tallie. Just you and me and this amazing love between us."

CHAPTER SEVENTEEN

SUN SPILLED OVER the bed Sunday morning as Derek lay holding Talia as she slept, naked and curled on her side, one hand clutching his hip, as if she were afraid he might disappear in the night. Didn't she know how much she owned him? That she was his first thought in the morning and his last at night?

He touched his lips to her forehead, breathing her in and dreaming about what life with Talia might be like if his father were healthy. He gently pushed a lock of hair from her cheek, happy to have this time together, thinking of how often she'd blushed over the past couple weeks. He hadn't expected to fall so hard so fast, but then again, nothing in his life had gone as expected. He knew her feelings for him were just as strong. It showed in the way she looked at him, touched him, in the kindness and patience she lavished on his father. He lightly kissed her forehead, not wanting to wake her, and she murmured in her sleep, cuddling closer. He'd been pushing away some of the harsh realities of his situation, not wanting to think about or deal with them. But they were in too deep. There was no more holding back, no running from the truth without hurting Talia in the long run. It was time to share the rest of his reality with her.

"I want to go back to yesterday and experience everything all over again," she said in a groggy voice.

"Me too." He moved over her, gazing into her tired, happy eyes. "Morning, sweetness."

"Hi. Did I sleep too long? Do we need to get back?"

He loved that she even thought to ask. "No. We have time. Maria will text if she needs me."

"Then why do you look so serious?" She wound her arms around his neck.

"I can't get anything by you, can I?"

"It's the professor in me. I notice things."

He kissed her tenderly. "I notice things, too, like how you hold on to me so tight when you're sleeping, like you don't want me to get away."

"I do not," she said with a soft laugh.

"You do, babe, and I love it." He brushed his thumb over her cheek and said, "I'm falling in love with you, Talia, and I don't want to lose you, either."

"Is that why you look troubled?"

The worry in her voice tore at him. "No, and yes. I was thinking about what life would be like if I weren't caring for my father."

"Don't . . . Don't even think of that. I know you think we need to go out and do more, or have more freedom, but the truth is, I've gone out more with you in the last three weeks than I have in the last several months."

"I'm glad, baby, but this isn't about that. I need to be fair to you. There are things you need to know."

She wiggled out from beneath him and they lay facing each other as they had last night. She moved closer, resting her leg on his hip, her hand on his cheek, and said, "Okay, tell me."

"You make things seem easy."

She raised her brows with a tease in her eyes. "I thought I made them *hard*."

"You make me hard, baby, *very* hard."

She grinned. "Good, then let me make this easy on you. Whatever you have to say isn't going to change how much I love making you hard."

"I hope you're right, but I won't be upset if you're wrong, because this is some heavy stuff."

"I'm good with heavy. It's cheating I'm not okay with."

"I'll never cheat on you. I see a future for us, Tallie, and I want that with you more than anything. But there's a good chance I'll end up like my father."

"I know," she said softly, eyes serious. "I've known that since the day I met your father, when I read up on Alzheimer's."

"Then you know I could pass it down to kids."

She nodded. "They have tests . . ."

"They do. When my father was diagnosed, I thought about getting tested. But I don't want to do it. Maybe that's selfish, but I don't want to know if I have an early expiration date. I want to enjoy my life, not live it a certain way because I think it'll be cut short. I want to be happy when I'm happy and let myself be sad when I'm sad. I don't know how else to explain this, except that I don't want to view my body as a ticking time bomb, and if the test were positive, that's how I'd feel. I don't want to get angry over a disease I can't change or feel any guiltier than I already do."

"You shouldn't feel guilty. You're a good man, and you're giving your father a good life."

"Babe, this isn't about my dad. You and I are getting in so deep. I don't want you to feel stuck."

Sadness welled in her eyes and quickly morphed to determination. "I already know that it can be passed down. I told you that. And I'm with you, so that's your answer."

"Talia—"

She pressed her lips to his, silencing him. "Don't. I know what could happen, and I'm not going to walk away from the only man I've ever felt this much for because something *might* happen or because you don't want kids—"

"I *do* want children," he interrupted. "I love kids, and I want to raise another generation of Grants and tell them all about their grandparents. But unless I get tested, I won't know if I carry the mutated gene, and as I said, I'm not sure I'll ever be ready to have those tests done. I probably won't have my own biological children. I don't want to risk their lives or continue a cycle of this disease. But there are other ways to have families, and if we stay together, I want your babies, with your gorgeous eyes, your magnificent brain, and your beautiful, sweet heart."

Tears welled in those gorgeous eyes, and he held her tighter. "This is way too heavy for having known each other only a short time. I know that, but I can't stop my feelings for you, and I need to be fair."

"Do you know why I trust you so much?" She didn't wait for his answer. "Because you do the hard things, the *right* things, even when you don't want to."

"I'm not so good at it all the time. My father's been on a waiting list for the assisted-living facility for months. He insisted we take that step so the option would be open for him when the time comes that I can no longer care for him at home. We were told it could take anywhere from a few months to a year or more for an apartment to come available. But one has opened up. I'm not sold on the idea, but I'm going to check it out this Thursday."

"Would you like me to come with you?"

"This really isn't too much for you? Everything I've just shared?" Bowled over with emotions, he searched her face for a hint of it being too much, but her eyes turned sultry and she shook her head.

"I want to be there for you and with you."

"Thank you, baby. But right now"—he swept her beneath him—"I don't want to think about anything heavy. I want to make love to you." He kissed her smiling lips. "Lavish you with attention in the shower."

He laced their hands together, nudging her knees open wider as he aligned their bodies. "And then spend the morning knocking aimlessly around town. I want to buy you things you don't need, have ice cream even though it's freezing out, and pretend we haven't got a care in the world for just a little while."

She wound her arms around his neck and lifted her hips as he sank into her. "We might have to do this first part for a *very* long time."

"*Very* long."

"I think my comfort zone needs a little more stretching," she said as he kissed her neck. "I noticed a hot tub on the deck . . ."

"If perfect had a taste, it would be this." Talia scooped up the last spoonful of the mint chocolate chip and butter pecan ice-cream sundae she and Derek were sharing and held it up for him to eat.

"Perfect has a taste, and it's called Tallie Girl Dalton. I feasted on her this morning, and she should come with a warning for being so addicting."

She glanced around them in the small ice-cream shop, hoping the people at the nearby tables didn't hear him. He reached over and guided her chin back toward him and closed his lips over the spoon, his eyes darkening with desire. Forget fluttering. Her stomach did a full-on somersault. Images of those seductive eyes boring into her while they'd made love in the hot tub and gazing down at her while she'd loved him with her mouth in the shower sailed through her mind like a movie. They'd been away for only one night, and it felt like a lifetime. *The very best lifetime ever.*

"Nobody heard me, babe. I said it for your ears only." His gaze softened as he touched his cold lips to hers.

He tasted of ice cream and happiness. She loved that he knew her well enough to realize what she'd been worried about. He touched his lips to her neck, and she shivered at the tickle it sent through her.

"I love when you wear your hair up like this so I can devour your neck."

She'd thrown her hair up in a messy bun because he had been lavishing her with kisses all morning and she didn't want it to stop.

His phone vibrated, and his smile faded. He gave her a chaste kiss, then checked the message. He sighed, relief evident in the return of his smile. "It's just Ben confirming Saturday."

"Saturday?" she asked.

"He and your dad are coming by the house," he said as he typed a reply. "Ben's going to take a look at my business plan, and your dad is coming to check out the property and give me an estimate on renovations."

"That's great. I hope they can help. Do you think we should leave soon?" She wasn't anxious to leave, but they'd had such an amazing morning, she didn't want Derek to feel guilty if he wanted to get back to see his father. They'd had breakfast at the lodge, and then they'd strolled through town, holding hands and meandering through shops. They'd gone long stretches without saying a word, but the silence hadn't been uncomfortable, or even truly silent at all. Their furtive glances, the gentle squeeze of his hand, his lips brushing over hers, it was all enough. He was enough. And for the first time in forever, Talia knew she was enough, too.

"We've still got time," he said as they headed out of the ice-cream shop and into the blustery afternoon. Flurries whipped around them. "Check it out."

Derek pointed to a group of kids sledding down a hill in the park across the street. He tucked her beneath his arm as they watched a handful of kids trudging up the hill, bundled in brightly colored coats and snow pants, dragging plastic toboggans that were bigger than they were. A few feet away, two sleds flew down the hill, their passengers wide-eyed and pink cheeked. Adults helped kids at the bottom of the hill, fixing mittens and righting hats.

"Come on!" Derek dragged her down the street.

She hurried to keep pace with him. "Where are we going?"

He tugged open the door to the hardware store. "What's your favorite color?"

"Pink. Why?" she asked as he dragged her to the register.

Ten minutes later they were standing at the top of the hill with a pink toboggan among a dozen or more children and a handful of adults. A young mother wiped tears from a girl of about five who was whining about wanting to take a turn. A few feet away a boy lay on a sled. Behind him another boy, who looked to be about twelve years old, wearing a bright blue parka and hat, hollered, "Ready?"

"Ready!" the boy on his belly yelled.

The other boy got a running start and lay on top of him, sending them flying down the hill like a double-decker sandwich.

"Ready, babe?" Derek set the toboggan on the snow and guided her to a sitting position on it.

"No. I'm not ready! What about you?" she asked as he took a few steps back.

"I'll give us a push!" He ran toward her, gripped her shoulders, and pushed them over the crest of the hill. He jumped onto the toboggan behind her and *whoop*ed all the way down. She squealed with delight as they raced down the hill, snow spraying up at them, burning her cheeks.

"Look out!" Talia yelled as a little boy crossed their path.

Derek clung to her shoulders, leaning hard to the right, and they missed the boy by a few inches, tumbling over in a tangle of limbs and laughter. Those happy blue eyes locked on her, and Derek rolled them along the deep snow, covering them both with powder. She lay on top of him in a snowy heap, remembering the first walk they'd taken together, when she'd ended up in this very position, wanting to kiss him just as much as she did now.

Her hair broke free from its tether and fell like a curtain around them. "That was so fun!"

"You've come a long way, Tallie girl." He leaned up and kissed her. She tried to roll off him, but he held on tight, sweeping her beneath him, making her laugh even more.

"I have to admit," she panted out, "when you first asked me out, I wondered if I could ever be enough for a guy like you."

"You're not just enough, Tallie. You're more than enough." As he lowered his lips to hers, he said, "And I'm totally, utterly, *devastatingly* in love with loving you."

CHAPTER EIGHTEEN

DEREK HAD NEVER been one to create lists, but ever since he and Talia had come together, he'd begun mentally ticking off his favorite things. Falling asleep and waking again with Talia wrapped safely in his arms were at the top of that list. Thursday afternoon as he and Talia drove to the assisted-living center, he added *Thursdays*, Talia's day off, to the list. It didn't matter if she was grading papers, they were running errands, or they were busy with his father, Thursdays were wonderful, and he'd made sure he had Thursday evenings off as well.

Talia sat in the passenger seat looking up recipes on her phone. Every once in a while she'd ask a question about preparation or if his father liked this or that. Their lives had woven seamlessly together. He'd never imagined wanting anyone in his life on a daily basis, but he missed Talia every minute they were apart. This morning he'd been given the gift of a lifetime. His father had experienced a lucid moment, and even though Derek knew he wouldn't remember their conversation for long, he'd discussed his feelings for Talia with him. His father had looked him right in the eyes and said, *Son, if you've found the woman you want to make a life with, you must promise me not to let my disease stand in your way.* When he'd mentioned to his father that Talia had been staying at the house, his father had laughed, like in the old days, and he'd said, *You're telling me? You sure you don't want to sneak her in like you did with that little lady when you were in school?* In those few brief moments, Derek had seen a flash of who his father had once been and had also been given his blessing. He tried to hang on to those thoughts and to keep the distressing ones at bay for as long as he could.

He squeezed Talia's hand and said, "Ben called while you were in the shower."

"He did?" She tucked her phone into her pocket and angled her body toward him. Her hair was pinned up and held in place with a big clip. She pushed her glasses to the bridge of her nose, looking seriously sexy in a fluffy white sweater. She looked beautiful with the sun shining behind her and her bright eyes intent on him.

"Yeah. He and your father are coming by Saturday morning while you're shopping with the girls, remember?"

"Oh, right. I forgot. Ben's a brilliant businessman, and my father knows his stuff when it comes to renovations. You know, Ben *is* an investor. Have you thought about what it might mean for you if you got an investor instead of raising the capital with only your friends?"

"I haven't really thought about it, but if I got an investor, I probably wouldn't have to spend all my savings on the renovations."

Her face grew serious. "Would that mean you could stop dancing?"

"Tallie, I know it was a big step for you to accept my dancing." He also knew she was still afraid to come see him dance again, and that was okay. There was a difference between pushing comfort zones and respecting the needs of the woman he loved. "But I have a plan, and that plan doesn't include a life full of debt. If I want this project to come to fruition without giving up complete control, I need to stick to my plan."

"I know," she said softly. "I understand. I wasn't asking you to stop. I just wanted to see if it would make a difference."

He shrugged. "Maybe it would, but that's a stretch." He kissed the back of her hand. "They're only coming by to see the house and look over the business plan. Don't get your hopes up. I have to work until midnight Saturday. But we'll see how it goes. We can talk about it when I get home. That is, if you're still planning to come over after I get off work."

She leaned across the car and kissed him. "If you think you can get rid of me by flaunting that sexy body onstage, you've got another thing coming. Although, I'm thinking you need a couple nice tattoos that say 'Talia's' in the center of your chest and back, with arrows pointing in all directions."

He laughed. "If you're lucky, I'll let you draw it on my body tonight, and we can discuss it."

"With my mouth?" She leaned back in her seat and primly pushed her glasses up as if she hadn't just set his groin on fire and said, "That'll give you something to think about while you're dancing Saturday night."

When they arrived at the assisted-living center, those sexy thoughts peeled away like shed skin, leaving him raw and uncomfortable. He'd been there enough times to recognize the hotel-like atmosphere. The dark blue carpeting had a faint path leading from the lobby to a hallway on either side and to a wide stairwell just to the right of the desk. The air smelled a little too fresh. A picture-perfect elderly couple held hands on the diamond-patterned sofa in the lobby. The too-chipper eyes of the receptionist clearly conveyed, *Leave your relatives with us. We'll take good care of them!* Those things should be reassuring, but there was a sense of finality about moving his father here that caused a sinking feeling in Derek's gut.

Holly Carpenter, the saleswoman he'd met with months ago, extended her hand as she approached, dressed in a sharp pantsuit, her shoulder-length auburn hair perfectly coiffed. He guessed her to be in her midfifties, with kind eyes and a friendly personality that instilled trust. "Derek, it's nice to see you again."

"Thanks for making the time to show us around. This is my girl-friend, Talia Dalton. Talia, this is Holly Carpenter."

"Moral support is so important at times like these," Holly said as she shook Talia's hand. "If you'll follow me, we'll go see Mr. Grant's new accommodations. The room is in the midst of being painted and the carpeting will be replaced, but with a little vision, you can see how beautiful it will be."

Derek held tight to Talia's hand as they followed Holly down the wide hallway. It wasn't lost on him that the reason a room had opened up was that someone had either passed away, moved to the nursing home, or had gone to hospice care. As they took the elevator up to the second floor, the thought made him a little sick.

When they reached the apartment, paint fumes hung in the air. Holly talked about the facility's amenities and offered to show them around even though Derek had taken a full tour of the facility with his father when they'd first received his diagnosis and again a few months ago when, during a lucid moment, Jonah had insisted they make arrangements for him to be placed on the waiting list.

"This is really a lucky break that you got a room so quickly," Holly said as she opened the balcony door.

Derek wasn't sold on the idea, despite his father's wishes.

"There's a nice view of the grounds from this side of the building." Holly waved outside. "I know you said you have a caretaker in mind to help with your father's daily living, but as I've mentioned before, we have staff available to help with personal grooming, bathing, getting dressed. We'll make sure medications are taken on time, and of course, we handle incontinence management . . ."

She went on to point out other services, such as housekeeping and linens, and security elements throughout the building. When she began talking about game nights and trips to the library, her voice became white noise to the guilt rising up within him.

"Is there any restriction to visitors coming and going as they please?" Talia asked.

Derek was glad she thought to ask, because he was in no shape to think of the right questions.

"Visitors are welcome at any time in this wing," Holly said. "We encourage family members to visit often, and usually at the beginning they're here on an almost daily basis. But that tends to wane when they realize their loved ones are taken care of and they get busy with other parts of their lives they couldn't enjoy when they were caretaking."

Derek ground his teeth together, silently vowing to never let his father become an afterthought. "Would you mind if we spent some time alone in the apartment?"

"Not at all." Holly moved toward the door. "You know where my office is if you need me."

After Holly left, Derek stepped onto the balcony, white-knuckling the railing, and inhaled a lungful of frigid winter air.

"You okay?" Talia crossed her arms to ward off the cold.

He pulled her into his arms, struggling against the weight of this decision. The desire to have his days and nights free was as strong as the desire to continue caring for his father.

"I guess. This is what he wants. I'm just not sure it's the right time to do it." He gazed out over the snow-covered grounds, remembering the grassy expanse and beautiful gardens they'd toured when they'd first visited. "They make it seem like my father will have a normal life here, with game nights and social interactions in the dining room, but is it ever 'normal' to have people dressing him and bathing him? My father can't play games. He can't even draw all the time anymore . . ." A lump swelled in his throat.

He raked a hand through his hair and strode inside, flexing his hands to try to channel his frustrations. "I can't even picture him sitting here by himself. What would he do all day? He's not so far gone that he never recognizes his surroundings. I can't help but wonder if it would do more harm than good bringing him here now, when he'll realize he's not home. Would it be better to wait until he no longer recognizes his surroundings? Or is that too late?"

"Those are big concerns. Have you talked to his doctors?"

"Yes, but in the end it's my decision. There's no handbook for these things. His doctors provided the only guidance they could, and I have no idea if it was to cover their asses or their honest opinions, but I'd imagine it's a combination of both. When I asked how I would know it was time to put his care into someone else's hands, they said it was a familial decision based on how much a family could endure and where the patient would receive the best care. That's the problem, Tallie. I don't know if it's worse for him or better for him to be with us. Maria and I are all he has."

"And me, Derek. He has me now, too. And my family."

He turned away at the sting of tears, and she touched his back.

"Is there a reason you feel like you need to do it now? Can he stay on the list until you're sure?"

Is there a reason? Yeah, so we can try to have a normal relationship. He wasn't about to put that guilt on her.

"I don't know." He traipsed into the bedroom and tried to imagine his father waking up without him or Maria there. Would he get used to another caretaker, or would he wake up feeling like he'd been tossed aside? Like he didn't matter enough to remain in his home? Maria wanted to continue caring for him on a part-time basis even after he moved, but he'd have a new caretaker for the hours she or Derek weren't available.

Derek turned, meeting Talia's empathetic gaze. "When my father was first diagnosed, he made me promise not to give up my life to care for him. He even drew a cartoon of it, as if having it drawn by his hand would make it right, or easier."

"I don't think there's a right or wrong here." She placed her hand on his chest and said, "What does your heart tell you to do? Your father said he doesn't want you to give up your life. But isn't *he* a very big, very *important* part of your life? I don't think he'd want you to do this if *you* don't feel like it's the right time. But I've also read about how hard caretaking can be on the caregiver. The internet is loaded with information about health ramifications. If it's too hard for you, then your father would probably want you to bring him here. And no one would fault you one way or the other. But this is *your* life, Derek, as much as it's his. You can only do what feels right for *both* of you, and only you know what that is."

He embraced her, feeling like a bug trapped in a spider's web. How could he possibly know what was best for any of them?

"If he were here, he'd have doctors and nurses on call twenty-four-seven," Derek said. "Would that make it better for him? And you and I would have a chance at a normal relationship without walking on eggshells, worrying about whether my father is going to get agitated or confused. We could go on normal dates, have sex in every room of the house if we wanted to."

She laughed softly, shaking her head. "Is that what's going through your mind? Do you feel ripped off because you can't make out in every room?"

"No. But you deserve a relationship without this type of burden. Not that I think my father's a burden. He's *my* father and he's not a burden to me. But he's not your father, Tallie, and you could have any number of men with less complicated lives."

She rose onto her toes and kissed him. "You're the only man I want, and I know what being with you means, so you need to take our relationship out of this equation. You've been up front and honest since the first day we met. Well," she said with a tease in her eyes, "except for the first couple of classes you attended, but that's a different story. One of the reasons I'm with you is because you have your priorities straight. Family is important to me, and I want to be with a man who feels the same way. So please don't get confused because of our relationship. I'm with *you*, which means I'm with your father, too. If that means walking on eggshells for the next decade, I'm okay with it. Assuming we stay together, of course, but you know what I mean."

He was filled with love and gratitude. "Yeah, I know what you mean."

"Team Grant all the way," she said, loosening the knots in his gut. "And if you really want to have sex all over the house, we'll ask Maria to stay with your dad one night and do it at my place."

"How did I get lucky enough to find you?"

"It was that bull's-eye on your chest, remember?"

As his lips met hers, he realized there was nothing reassuring about placing his father's health in the hands of others, at least not yet. Not when he was already in the hands of the people who loved him most. But there was no holding back from giving the woman in his arms his whole heart, and that was the most reassuring reality of all.

CHAPTER NINETEEN

A WARM FRONT moved in, and by Saturday morning blue skies smiled down on them. Derek, Talia, and Jonah made breakfast together, as had become their morning routine. His father was having a particularly good day. He'd even remembered how to make his favorite omelets, a delicious concoction of three different cheeses and a mix of vegetables and meats. The recipe had been handed down from his great-grandmother, and Jonah had been cooking it from the time he was able to use the stove. Derek was glad for those ingrained memories and hoped his father would have them forever.

Shortly after Talia left to go shopping with the girls for Bridgette's wedding dress, Ben and Dan arrived with Louie in tow. Bodhi was off on a training mission for the week, leaving Grandpa Dan on babysitting duty.

"Thanks so much for coming out," Derek said as he hung up their coats. "I've set up everything in the dining room." He knelt before Louie and said, "How's it going, buddy? I'm glad you came to help these guys check things out."

"Mom said we needed guy time," Louie said as he pulled his Yankees cap down low on his forehead. "She said she needed to pry some stuff out of Auntie Talia. I hope they don't hurt her." He took Dan's hand, blinking wide eyes up at him. "Do you think they will, Grandpa Dan?"

Dan laughed. "Not the way you think they will, buddy." He winked at Derek and said, "It's been a long time since my girl's been this happy, and her sisters will want to get *all* the details."

"Like Mom won't?" Ben scoffed, and then a tease rose in his eyes. "They'll drive her crazy. Just make sure you're not standing in the driveway when she comes home."

They all chuckled.

"Tallie can handle it," Derek said, remembering how frazzled she'd been the morning she'd almost run him over. Something told him she was no longer someone her sisters could rattle. She'd come out of her shell, wearing sexier outfits that showed off her gorgeous figure, owning her sexuality, and doing things she said she'd avoided for a long time.

"Yes, *Tallie* can," Ben said with a smile. "The fact that she lets you call her that says everything. Ever since we were little, she'd correct us if we tried to call her anything but Talia or Tal."

"Can I watch television?" Louie asked.

"Sure, buddy." As Derek got Louie set up in the living room, he told Ben and Dan not to worry if his father called him Archie or some other name from his past. He explained that their presence might throw him off and that he tended to get confused around strangers.

"Sometimes Grandma Roxie gets confused," Louie said. "She calls my mom Talia-Piper-Willow-Whatever-the-Heck-Your-Name-Is."

They all laughed. "I'd imagine with five kids it's easy to get confused. You know, Louie, my father might even call you Derek. He might think you're me when I was younger."

Louie's face scrunched up in concentration. "What should I do if he does?"

Could he be any sweeter? "You don't have to do anything special. But it would really help if you didn't try to convince him he was wrong, because sometimes he has a hard time understanding that."

"I won't." Louie shook his head. "I hate it when people tell me I'm wrong. What's your father's name?"

"Jonah. You can call him Jonah."

"I like that name." Louie climbed onto the couch and settled in.

"Derek, whatever you need from us, just let us know. If we agitate your father, we'll leave and do this some other time," Dan assured him. "But I'd really like to meet him and tell him how fine a man he's raised."

Derek's chest tightened. "Thank you."

"Get used to it," Ben said. "You're one of us now. Like it or not, the girls will find a way to weasel themselves into Jonah's life. He'll have more people caring for him than he ever wanted. You've got to be strong enough to tell them to back off."

"I can't imagine wanting your family to back off. But it's been just me and my dad, with Maria's help, for so long, I think we'll be lucky if *he* doesn't scare them away."

"Daltons don't scare easy," Ben said as they made their way into the dining room.

Thinking of Talia's acceptance of his father and their situation, he had to agree.

As they entered the dining room, Jonah looked up from the picture he was drawing, and a warm smile lifted his lips. His baseball cap was firmly in place, and as his eyes moved between the three men, Derek hoped the introduction would go smoothly.

"Pop, this is Dan Dalton and his son, Ben." He went to his father's side and put a protective hand on his shoulder. He always felt the need to make sure his father never felt it was him against the world. *Team Grant.* "Do you remember Talia? She made breakfast with us this morning? Dan is her father, and Ben is her brother."

"Hello," Jonah said kindly, though Derek could tell he didn't remember Talia or their morning. "Why are you here?"

Not for the first time, Derek counted himself lucky. He knew of families whose loved ones had become violent or nasty as dementia stole more of their faculties. His father had not yet taken that turn, and he prayed he never would. But he'd also accepted the reality that it was a possibility he should be ready for.

"They're going to take a look at the house," Derek explained.

Dan offered a hand and a friendly smile. "Hello, Jonah."

Jonah looked at his hand as though he wasn't sure what to do with it and said, "Hello."

"You have a fine son," Dan said.

"You've met Derek?" Jonah asked. "I don't know where that boy ran off to. He's somewhere around here. Eva, too."

Ben glanced at Derek. Derek lowered his voice and said, "My mother."

Jonah turned back to his drawing.

"Why don't we go over the renovations." Derek showed them the sketches he'd drawn. "I'd like to extend the rear living space to accommodate entertaining up to fifteen people comfortably and add two additional smaller rooms for activities. It's really important that it feels like a home, not a facility." He told them about his friends who would be taking part in the endeavor, and then he gave them each a copy of his business plan.

"Ben's a shrewd businessman. You won't need my opinion," Dan said.

It hadn't taken much research to see just how successful Dan's and Ben's businesses were or to realize that Dan was being modest. He'd achieved many accolades in his academic career before retiring and was noted as one of the leading contractors in their area. But there was an even more important reason why Derek wanted his help.

"I know Ben's an expert on all things finance related, but I think a man who raised five business-minded, successful adults has a lot to offer as well. If you wouldn't mind, I'd love your opinion on my business plan, not just the renovations."

"All right, then," Dan said. "It'd be my pleasure."

Derek gave them a tour of the house, and he realized he'd never taken Talia upstairs. As they reached the third floor, a pang of longing moved through him.

"Whoa, dude," Ben said as he stepped into the finished attic, which ran the length of the house. It was long and a bit narrow, with two nice-sized nooks and a walkout on the back that led to a small veranda. "This is incredible."

"We haven't used it much in years. My mother used the nook overlooking the backyard for her office, and my father used to use the other one when he was drawing. This area here"—he waved to the main area—"used to have a couch and chairs. I played up here as a kid. When I first moved back in with my father, I thought I'd renovate it and use it as my living space, but I really need to be downstairs, closer to him."

"That makes sense, but why not freshen it up for the future?" Dan suggested. "This is a touchy subject, but one day your father may need more care than you can provide, and at that point, if you still want to live here and run the day-care facility, then you might want more privacy. It would certainly be more cost-effective to finish this space as an apartment now, rather than later."

Derek walked over to the doors that led to the deck, thinking of Talia and wondering what she would want in the future. It was easy to imagine her on the deck grading papers, warmed by the sun. Unexpected lightness flowed through him at the thought of no longer being confined to the first floor, of having the freedom to make love to her without worrying about the noise. Those fantasies were pushed aside by a wave of guilt and reality.

"I estimated the renovations would run around four hundred thousand dollars," he explained. "That didn't include this area, and I might have severely underestimated the costs. That figure is based on the information I found online of one hundred and seventy-five dollars per square foot. I've got almost half of that saved, and I think I can get a loan for the rest, but it's a stretch."

"Wait a sec," Ben said. "You're financing this whole thing yourself? Shelling out that kind of cash, and taking on a loan on top of it, is not a small undertaking."

"No. The friends I mentioned earlier are pitching in, but between the three of them, they have just under sixty thousand, which we'll need for furniture, supplies, and equipment. I know it's unusual and probably sounds like a pipe dream," Derek said. "But I've done my research, and businesses have to start somewhere. I'm willing to do whatever it takes to get this off the ground."

"I know better than to knock pipe dreams," Ben said. "Some of the most profitable companies started as pipe dreams. Are you open to an investor kicking in some capital?"

"I'm honestly not sure I want to give up that much control or run the business by someone else's standards. I'm not doing this to become rich. I'm doing it because I want to help others who are in the same situation I am."

"I get that, and it's honorable. I'd never want to hinder your vision," Ben said. "But this type of business can go belly-up if not positioned correctly so your services are reimbursable by insurance."

"Yes, I'm aware of the reimbursement guidelines. I'm open to hearing what you have to say, and I'd really like your advice and input. But above all else, it's important to me to provide the best care in a home setting. I'm not looking to have a two-hundred-resident day-care center, and I don't want the people who are taken care of, or their families, feeling like they're nothing but a number or a dollar figure."

"I understand," Ben said as his father checked out the space. "But it also might be nice for you not to have to use all your savings. I assume you'll give up working at the bar to run the facility, and you'll want to earn enough to make a living, of course."

"Yes, I'd give up bartending, but I don't need to earn a big living," Derek said. "Just enough to live comfortably and make sure my father has everything he needs." He was prepared to continue dancing for another few years in order to get the renovations paid off quickly.

"Let me read over your business plan, and I'll get back to you with my thoughts," Ben said as they headed back downstairs.

"I'll run the numbers for doing the build-out and renovations at cost," Dan said when they reached the first floor. "That should save you a bundle."

"I appreciate your offer more than you know, but I don't want to take advantage of my relationship with Talia. Please bid whatever you feel is a fair price."

Dan put a hand on Derek's shoulder and said, "Maybe you should have thought about that before going out with a Dalton. Now, I've got a date to take my grandson to the aquarium, so we'd better find him."

As if on cue, Louie's giggle floated out from the dining room. Derek rushed in and found Louie sitting on Jonah's lap. One of Jonah's notebooks from the other room lay open before them. Louie wore Jonah's baseball cap, and his own child-sized cap sat high on Jonah's head.

"This was before you were born," Jonah said to Louie. "When your mama and I first bought this house, we slept on mattresses on the floor. We barely had enough money to buy groceries, but that didn't matter, because we had each other. And we knew soon we'd have you."

"And then I was born?" Louie looked over at Derek and whispered, "He's confused, so I'm pretending."

Suddenly everything else in the room fell away, and Derek stood on unfamiliar, weak legs. Could gratitude do that to a person?

"Can Jonah come with us to the aquarium? *Please*, Grandpa?" Louie pleaded. "He loves the aquarium. He told me so."

"We don't need to impose—"

Dan silenced Derek with a firm hand on his shoulder. "If Talia's behavior this morning when she came flitting into our house like a woman in love is any indication, you and Jonah, and I assume this woman Maria she raves about, will be part of our lives for a very long time. I know you worry about your father, but you're not alone in that, son. We'll be there to help if things get difficult. And we'll bring two cars, in case you need to leave early. But it seems Louie and Jonah have connected, and I'd say that's a very good thing. We'd love to have you both join us if you can manage it."

"One, two . . ." Talia, her sisters, and Aurelia counted in unison from behind their dressing room curtains. After hours of shopping for a bridal gown and bridesmaids dresses, they'd nearly given up and were trying on the silliest dresses they could find, except Bridgette, who was trying on her millionth wedding gown.

"Three!" they hollered and burst through the curtains, arms flailing in a *ta-da* fashion.

Roxie gasped. "Oh my Lordy! I can't even . . ." She doubled over in laughter, while also trying to take pictures with her phone.

"What?" Piper wiggled her hips, sending the bells and chimes of her black tutu-style skirt into a cacophony of jingles and *clanks*, making everyone laugh.

"I think mine is definitely the *perfect* choice for Bridgette's wedding," Aurelia said as she strutted and twirled in an old-fashioned bright yellow floral gown that reached the floor, with a hoop skirt and matching bonnet.

"Frankly, my dear, I don't give a damn if you think you should wear that. The answer is *no*," Bridgette said in her best Southern voice.

Willow wiggled her shoulders in a bright pink dress that clung to her curves like a second skin and was accented with white feathers around her hips and breasts. "What do you think, ladies?" She fluffed her hair dramatically and thrust one long leg out, bent at the waist, and ran her fingertips up the length of it. "Do I look like the *perfect* slut-bunny bridesmaid or what?"

Roxie circled them, taking a video, capturing every snarky look and hysterical laugh.

"You should be kissed by someone who knows how to kiss," Aurelia said as she straightened her bonnet.

"I think Zane's got that covered," Roxie said as she ended the video. "Oh, Willow . . . Those feathers!"

Talia turned toward the mirror as her sisters teased each other and checked herself out. She'd chosen the skintight, strapless royal-blue minidress with a cleavage-baring neckline and black lace trim solely to make her sisters laugh, and she thought she'd be too embarrassed to be seen in it. But as it turned out, she wasn't the least bit embarrassed. She felt sexy in the awful dress, and that was one hundred percent because of her man, who had given her the confidence to show a more feminine, sexy side.

"I need someone who knows how to kiss," Piper said. "Aurelia, you and I are hitting Dutch's Pub tonight."

"I'm in!" Aurelia said with an exaggerated wink. "I need to find a man who acts like a gentleman in public and who's willing to do very ungentlemanly things to me in private."

I have one of those was on the tip of Talia's tongue, but she wasn't *that* into sharing.

"Benny might have issues with that," Piper said. Then she spun around and patted Talia's butt. "What has Mr. Hot as Hell done to our most prim-and-proper sister?"

Talia put her hand on her hip, jutted it out like a rebellious teenager, and brushed her fingers through her hair. "I'm thinking about pairing it with thigh-high stockings, blood-red heels, and a feather boa." *Actually, thigh-high stockings might come in handy for our office interludes.*

"Oh goodness," Roxie said with a laugh. "I think Derek has brought out a side of you that has been hiding for a very long time, and I *like* it!"

"Maybe we should start planning the sinful bartender and the sexy professor's wedding," Willow said. "I bet they have dresses for that!"

Talia's stomach fluttered at the idea of marrying Derek.

"Oh! Another picture from your father." Roxie held out her phone, showing them a picture of Louie standing in front of a big fish tank, holding Jonah's hand.

There was a collective "Aw" from the girls.

Their father had been sending pictures of Louie and Jonah all afternoon, and it warmed Talia knowing they'd embraced Derek's father just as they'd embraced Derek.

"Derek and Jonah fit right in," Bridgette said. "You know, once Louie accepts a man, there's no turning back."

There's no turning back anyway. I love them both.

Piper smoothed her hands down the black lace bodice of her dress. "That man could serve me up—"

Talia shut her down with a glare. "You really need to stop lusting over my man. I would never do that to your guy."

"I was kidding!" Piper insisted. "Besides, I don't plan on having a *guy*, as in singular. I'm not the marrying type."

"Yes you are. You just haven't met your match yet," Roxie said as she poked her head into each of the dressing areas. "Where's Bridgette?"

They traipsed through the store in their ridiculous dresses and found Bridgette standing on a platform in front of a three-way-mirror, admiring the stunning cream-colored wedding gown she wore. She looked so beautiful, she took Talia's breath away.

Bridgette ran her hand down the skirt of her A-line, princess-cut, off-the-shoulder chiffon dress and said, "What do you think?"

"Bridge, that dress . . ." Talia said. "It's perfect."

Bridgette looked down at her gown, and then at the others as they fawned over her. "I do love it. It's simple and elegant. But . . ." Tears welled in her eyes.

"What's wrong, baby girl?" Roxie asked.

Bridgette fanned her eyes, blinking repeatedly to dry her tears. "I just . . . I can't keep this a secret anymore." A smile lifted her lips, and she said, "It might not fit for the wedding. I'm pregnant!"

They all spoke at once, converging on Bridgette in a group hug.

"Oh, my sweet girl!" Roxie hugged her.

"Another baby!" Willow squealed. "I can't wait to see a little broody Bodhi or a frilly little Bridgette!"

"We'll be aunties again!" Talia exclaimed. "Bodhi must be over the moon! Does Louie know?"

"Bodhi is, of course, but Louie doesn't know. We were going to wait until I was twelve weeks, but I couldn't hold it in any longer! I'm only six weeks along." Bridgette wiped a tear from her bright, happy eyes. "It's been so hard not to tell you guys. I'm so excited, and I know Louie won't be able to stop talking about it once we tell him. We'll tell Louie when Bodhi gets back next Friday night, since our family sucks at keeping secrets."

If you only knew . . . A pang of guilt moved through Talia. Who knew she was the best secret keeper of them all?

"We have to celebrate! Let's have brunch at my house next Sunday after Bodhi's home," Willow suggested. "Talia, be sure to bring Derek and Jonah. And Maria. You said she's like a mom to Derek. I'd love to meet her."

"Oh yes," Roxie said. "We should definitely invite her."

"Thanks. I will. You'll love her." Talia knew she'd fit right in. Maria had gone with them when they'd met India, Eli, and Phyllis and their parents at Nightingale's, and they'd had a wonderful evening. Which reminded her to prepare her family for meeting Jonah.

"You guys, Derek's dad gets overwhelmed sometimes," she said. "We'll have to warn everyone to tone it down when he's there, but I really want you to meet him. He's the nicest man, even facing that horrible disease. He still remembers how to cook some of his old recipes, and we've been cooking together in the mornings. He's the one who taught Derek to draw, too, and how to play the guitar, to cook . . ." *How to love . . .* "Maybe he'll want to make a dish together to bring to brunch."

"I can't wait to meet him," her mother said. "It's obvious how special he must be to have raised Derek."

"I still can't believe Derek's got you cooking," Bridgette chimed in. "That must be love, because Microwave Girl was perfectly happy with her three-minute dinners before Mr. Blue Eyes entered the picture."

"A family of cooks," Piper said. "I need to get me one of those."

"You have one," Talia and Willow said in unison.

Piper rolled her eyes. "I meant a hot-guy family."

"Paws off mine, chickadee." Talia swatted Piper's jingly butt. "Besides, I know of another hot bartender who has the hots for you."

"*Please.*" Piper admired herself in the mirror, turning from side to side. "Harley Dutch does *not* have the hots for me. He just wants everyone to think he does so he can cock block me. That's how he gets his jollies."

Roxie put an arm around Piper and said, "You're missing the plumbing for that, darlin'."

"You know what I mean, Mom," Piper said. "I definitely need a guy who can cook. Remember when I tried to stuff the roaster chicken and couldn't get the stuffing in because I left the neck and all that gross stuff inside it?"

"She called me and said, 'I can't get it all in!'" Willow reminded them. "And I said—"

"'That's what he said!'" they all yelled in unison.

Talia couldn't remember the last time she'd had so much fun with her sisters. She waved at Piper's dress and said, "I think if you dress like that, you can pick up just about any man you want and they'd *stuff your chicken* for you. You could get a chef, a fireman, or maybe even a cock-blocking bartender."

Everyone cracked up.

"Okay, girls. Enough with that language, please. I've heard enough about *c-blocking* to last me a lifetime," their mother said as she pulled her phone from her pocket. "Oh! Another picture! Look at these gorgeous men." She held up her phone, showing them the selfie their father had taken of the five of them. Louie was looking up at Jonah, who was looking down at him with the happiest expression. Derek and Ben were making silly faces, and their father was giving Ben bunny ears.

"Oh my God. I know that guy," Aurelia said. "Wait. That's Derek? Talia's dating a *stripper?*"

Five sets of surprised eyes turned on Talia.

CHAPTER TWENTY

OH SHIT. SHIT. Shit. Shit. Talia's cheeks burned. Her gut roiled with guilt.

"Uh-oh." Aurelia's eyes widened. "You didn't *know* Derek was a stripper? I'm sorry, but he dances at Decadence, a bar in Harmony Pointe."

"He's not a stripper!" Talia turned on her heels and stormed toward the dressing room, trying to outrun the confrontation. They followed her, all talking at once, but she was too upset to hear a single word.

"Talia!" Piper snapped harshly, jerking Talia out of her own head. "If he's been lying to you, I'm going to kick his hot ass."

Oh God, what had she done? She blew through the curtain of her dressing room, and they all piled in with her.

"I thought he was a bartender," her mother said.

"Fricking liar," Willow said. "Ben and Zane will kill him."

"He didn't seem like a liar," Bridgette said.

Talia was on the verge of tears as she struggled to get out of her hideous dress. "He's not a liar!"

"So, he *is* a stripper?" her mother asked, reaching for Talia's zipper. "Let me, honey."

Talia swatted her hand away, too upset to be touched.

"Well, someone's lying." Piper crossed her arms, glaring at Aurelia. "Are you sure you saw *Derek* dancing? I knew I should have done some recon on this guy."

"Jesus! Shut up a second." Talia huffed out a shaky breath. "He's a male dancer, not a stripper, and it's just a *job*. It's not who he is."

The dressing room went dead silent.

"Is everything okay in there?" the saleswoman asked.

"Yes!" they all snapped.

Talia covered her face, mortified.

"We just need a few minutes," her mother said to the saleswoman.

No one said a word until they heard the woman walk away.

Talia yanked at her zipper until it gave, and then she peeled off the dress. "He's a dancer and a bartender," she said in a harsh whisper. "*Yes*, I knew, and *yes*, I am totally fine with it."

"Well, *fuck*." Piper tried to pace and bumped into everyone. "Damn it."

"Why didn't you tell us?" Willow asked. "We tell you *everything*."

"I'm sorry, but I'm still wrapping my head around Talia dating him," Aurelia said. "I didn't mean to out your secret, but . . . wow, Talia."

"It's not a secret," Talia insisted, shrinking against the glares of her sisters.

"You didn't tell us," Bridgette gently reminded her. "Don't you trust us?"

"I told you he worked at a bar." Talia pulled on her jeans. "It's not exactly something you just bring up out of the blue." She pulled her sweater over her head and said, "Do you think I wanted Piper running down to the bar and checking him out?"

"Why not?" Piper said angrily. "Every other chick probably is. Jesus, Talia. Are you embarrassed by his job? Because I know you're not embarrassed by his body."

"No!" She threw her arms up in the air. "It's not like I've been in this position before. It's new and different and *scary* as anything." Tears streamed down her cheeks. "What was I supposed to do, say, 'Hey, guess what? My boyfriend takes his clothes off for money'?" She threw her head back and closed her eyes, trying to stop the flow of tears. "I'm not embarrassed by what he does, and I'm definitely not embarrassed by him. He's the best man I have ever known."

"Then what the hell?" Piper demanded.

"Piper, hush!" Their mother touched Talia's arm and said, "Take a deep breath, baby."

Talia inhaled deeply, thankful for the momentary reprieve.

"Now, sweetheart, tell me why you didn't trust us with this information," her mother urged.

Sobs tumbled from Talia's lips. "God . . ."

"Honey, your sister ran off and married a musician," her mother said with a serious expression. "Piper streaked down the middle of Main Street when she was fifteen—"

"You did?" the girls asked at once.

"On a dare," Piper explained. "But I didn't know *Mom* knew about it."

"There's very little a mother doesn't know about her children's lives," her mother said.

"Except dating a stripper, apparently," Piper said under her breath.

Their mother glowered at her, then turned a softer expression to Talia. "Sweetheart, don't you know that we will love whomever you love? It wouldn't matter what they did for a living, as long as they weren't hurting someone else or doing something illegal. Derek's under a lot of pressure. He has time constraints and big dreams. I know it's hard and scary for you, and maybe we would have freaked out a little at first. But we know him now, and more importantly, *you* know him. And you're with him. That's enough for us."

Her mother's words should have eased her worries, but they also drove her guilt deeper.

"Now, I may be old," their mother said, "but please tell me the difference between stripping and dancing."

"About six inches of strategically placed material," Piper offered.

Talia glared at her. She inhaled several ragged breaths, trying to calm herself down. "He doesn't strip naked, just to a G-string," she said pathetically, as if there were much of a difference.

"And you're okay with this?" Bridgette asked carefully.

Talia looked at her sister, wearing a gorgeous wedding dress, pregnant with a new baby, and her heart ached. "Yes, I'm okay with it, and I'm sorry, Bridgette. I didn't mean to ruin your excitement over your pregnancy."

"You didn't," Aurelia said. "I did."

"No," Talia said. "I did. I should have found a way to tell everyone, but at first I had to come to grips with it myself. And then, every time I wanted to tell you guys, Piper would joke about him, or I'd worry about what you'd think. I'm sorry, but I've never loved anyone this much, and that's just it." She was breathing hard, shaking, and she didn't care. "I *love* him. I love him to the very depths of my soul. He could do just about anything and I'd learn to be okay with it. But you guys aren't me. You're *protective* of me, which I appreciate. But I didn't want to have to rationalize what he does for a living, because I don't care what he does for a living. And I don't need your approval."

Her sisters exchanged shocked expressions.

"I'm sorry," Talia said. "But I don't. I want you to love him, but I don't need you to approve of my choice. I've never met a man like Derek. He gave up everything, even his clothes," she said with a laugh-cry, "to make sure his father had whatever he could possibly need now or in the future. And he's not going to stop dancing for me, or you, or anyone else. He has a goal, and he'll do whatever it takes until that goal is met. And I respect the hell out of him for it."

"Whoa, Tal," Willow said. "Nobody said we don't like him."

"I've never seen you like this," Bridgette said. "I get it. I do. I was that way about Louie's father. I didn't tell anyone we were eloping until after we were married because I didn't care what any of you thought. That sounds horrible, but that's how much I loved him."

"Yes!" Talia said with tears in her eyes. "That's it. That's exactly it. Or part of it, at least. You have to admit, it's not even close to something I've ever had to explain before."

"You've spent your whole life worried about what everyone else thinks," Piper scoffed. "That's not living, Tal. That's *hiding*. I'm glad I don't have to kick his ass for lying to you, but I kind of want to kick yours."

Talia managed a half smile. "Please don't. I feel like I've been beaten up over this already. I hated not telling you guys. But I was afraid or . . . I don't know. I just didn't want to deal with anything bad when my life was finally so good."

Their mother wrapped her in her arms and said, "This is love, baby girl. It gnaws at all the things that have held you together, testing your strength and the resilience and loyalty of those around you." She stepped back but kept ahold of Talia's arms. "We're family, and if you know nothing else in this life, it's that even though we might not agree on everything, we love you no matter what. And as your parent, after years of protecting my kids, I had to step back when you became adults. I had to take a backseat and let each of you find your own way. The only thing that matters is that you and Derek trust and love each other. If you have those two things, then what anyone else thinks doesn't matter."

"What I think matters, because I'm usually right," Piper said.

"Hush, Pipe," Bridgette said as she put her arms around Talia. "Love is hard. Look at what Bodhi and I went through." She and Bodhi had broken up when he'd gone away on a rescue mission and she hadn't known whether he was alive or dead.

Everyone moved in for a group hug, and between Aurelia's hoop skirt, Willow's feathers, and Piper's jingly skirt, they were a noisy, sniffling mess of apologies and tears.

"I have another thing to confess," Talia said, and they all stepped back.

"Pregnant!" Piper said loudly.

"No! No, I'm not. Remember in college when I dated Terrence?"

"Of course," Willow said.

"The asshat who cheated?" Piper said.

"Oh my gosh, you *knew*?" Talia was going to kill Ben.

"I guessed," Piper said softly. "You just confirmed it."

"He cheated?" Willow reached for Talia's hand. "I'm so sorry. Why didn't you tell us?"

"Oh, baby," her mother said.

Talia lowered her gaze, old ghosts banging at the door. "I was embarrassed. He didn't just cheat. I think he might have used me to help with his grades. He had another girlfriend almost the whole time."

"That dickwad," Piper snapped.

"He was just doing what kids do," Talia said. "Or maybe he's still a jerk. I don't know or care. But I was afraid to tell you guys, because he made me feel so bad about myself. And I knew you guys were savvy enough or smart enough, or whatever, that you would never have gotten into the same situation. You would have known in your gut, but I never had that sense of self or that trust in my intuition. Until Derek." She hadn't even realized that last part until now.

They apologized and pep-talked, engulfing her in more hugs, until they began teasing her about wearing her awful dress onstage with Derek, and she knew her mother was right. They'd love and support her no matter what.

"I know this isn't the best time," Bridgette said, "but can I please go out and talk to the seamstress about getting this dress fitted? I'm truly in love with it."

Talia felt like a great weight had been eased from her shoulders. "I'm sorry. Yes, it's gorgeous. But, um . . . *fitted*? Don't you think your belly will grow in the eight weeks?"

"And your tatas. You'll have big ones by the time you get married." Piper grabbed her own boobs and said, "Almost makes me want to have a kid."

"How about getting a husband first?" Willow said as they filed out of the dressing room.

"Never mind that idea." Piper sidled up to Talia and said, "Have fun telling Dad about Derek's dancing."

"Crap," Talia grumbled as Piper went out with the others and her mother stepped beside her. "Any advice for telling Dad?"

"He's not as straitlaced as you think. This isn't his first rodeo." Her mother set her phone in Talia's hand and lowered her voice. "*Do not scroll.*"

Talia looked at her mother's phone screen and quickly read the open text message from her father. *You. Me. Naked. Tonight. No excuses. Your love machine. XOX.*

"Ew! Mom! How can I ever look at him again without thinking about *that*?" Talia shoved the phone into her mother's hand.

Her mother laughed at her discomfort. "The same way we'll all look at Derek and try not think about six inches of strategically placed material."

After shopping with the girls, Talia paced her living room, her stomach in knots over how and when she should tell her father and Ben about Derek's dancing. Worse yet, she had to tell Derek that she hadn't told them until now. The more she thought about it, the angrier she became at herself for not telling them sooner.

Her front door flew open and Piper traipsed in, wearing four-inch heels, skinny jeans, and a black leather jacket over a dark sweater. Her blond hair was pulled up in a messy bun, her eyes were heavily lined, and her lips were painted a seductive shade of red. She planted herself at the edge of the living room, arms crossed, eyes narrowed. A gallon of piss and vinegar in a pint-sized container.

"If you're here to yell at me for not telling you about Derek," Talia said firmly, "please don't. I already have a stomachache over it."

"Well, sorry about that, but I'm calling bullshit on all of it. You don't trust me, and that sucks."

"Piper . . ." She didn't want to argue anymore, even though she deserved whatever shit Piper was about to give her. "I do trust you. It was my issue, not yours."

"Yeah, maybe partly, but not totally." Piper uncrossed her arms, and her expression softened. "You're like the truth whisperer, and for you to have held back . . ." She stepped into the room and said, "I think I screwed you up. You always tell the truth no matter what, and I've been teasing you a lot about Derek. Probably too much, and it makes me sick to think that you would ever worry about me doing anything that could hurt you. You have to know I'd never in a million years make a move on your man. Not *ever*, Talia, and I'm sorry if I made you uncomfortable."

Tears threatened for the hundredth time that day. "I know you wouldn't, Pipe. Besides, it wouldn't matter what you would or wouldn't do. I trust Derek completely. He's surrounded by beautiful women throwing money at him and drooling over him every time he's at work. But I know with my whole heart that I'm the only woman he wants."

Piper shoved her hands into the front pockets of her jeans and sighed. "So, you don't hate me and think I'm a slut?"

"I could never hate you, and you're *freer* than I could ever be, but that doesn't make you a slut. It's not your fault I've been living practically like a nun for years."

"Yeah, I'm so glad he broke you out of that." Piper's lips curved up conspiratorially. "How about that lingerie I packed for your trip? Pretty sexy, huh?"

"We . . . um . . . never got to it."

Piper swatted her arm, her mouth agape. "You trampy vixen! What'd you do, go straight from the slopes to the ropes?" She waggled her brows.

"Piper! I'm not into that!"

"You're missing out, sis. A little tying up can be fun." Piper laughed and embraced her. "I love you, and I'm on your side, always. Want to hang out tonight? Aurelia couldn't make it to Dutch's after all. She had to meet Ben. He wanted to talk to her about buying the bookstore, but I think he just wants to get laid. Anyway, you and I could head over to Dutch's."

Talia still had a few hurdles of her own to get over, and now was the perfect time. "I really miss Derek. I was thinking of going to see him dance. I haven't done it since the first night he invited me."

"Oh my God, really?" Piper's eyes lit up. "I *love* strippers!"

Talia glared at her.

"*Dancers.* I meant dancers."

"Want to come with me? It's like the ultimate test, bringing one of the sexiest girls from Sweetwater to watch my boyfriend strut around onstage half-naked. If I can handle you seeing him dance, I can handle anything."

Piper's grin widened. "I just so happen to have a purse full of dollar bills."

"Why does that not surprise me?" Talia asked as she went to get her purse.

"A girl has got to be prepared." Piper eyed Talia's jeans and sweater. "Don't you want to put on something less conservative?"

"No," Talia said fiercely. "My man loves me just the way I am. And I don't care what anyone else thinks."

"You make love seem good," Piper said as they walked outside.

"Love is good, Pipe." Talia locked the door. "I hope one day you find someone who loves you for who you are, because you are definitely my coolest sister." She turned and saw Aurelia chasing Ben toward them from the parking lot. "Oh, crap."

"He is on the warpath," Piper said.

"Where are you headed?" Ben asked.

"I didn't mean to tell him!" Aurelia yelled. "It just came out!"

"What the hell, Talia?" Ben seethed. "Everyone knows about Derek's dancing but me?"

He sounded angry, but the hurt in his eyes nearly did Talia in. "I'm sorry. I was going to tell you."

"He's a stripper? And you're okay with that?" His tone was more concerned than angry or judgmental. That was Ben. He had always worried about Talia first and the details later.

"A *dancer*, and *yes*," she said firmly.

He studied her face, as if he was looking for an indication of hesitation. *Keep looking, Ben, because you aren't going to find it.*

"Then why the hell didn't you tell anyone?" He grabbed her arm and dragged her away from Piper and Aurelia. "And what does it say about how you really feel about him, having kept it from everyone?"

"It says I trust my judgment, and I don't need anyone else's approval." She wrenched her arm from his grip.

He ground his teeth together, studying her for so long it made her even more nervous.

"Fine," he finally said. "That makes sense. But why didn't you tell *me*? I thought we were closer than that. I never told a soul about what happened in college."

"We are, and I appreciate that, but I'm not a kid anymore." Her heart hurt at the thought of having broken their unspoken bond, but she'd lived beneath the safety and comfort of her brother's powerful wings for too long. "Ben, you have always been there for me. You've kept my secrets and you've made me feel safe. I appreciate that so much, and I know I'd never be who I am today without having had you behind me, protecting and encouraging me. I hope you'll be there for me in the future. But it'll be different. It *has* to be different."

He cocked his head, staring at the lake out of the corner of his eyes, his jaw muscles twitching. Her pulse was beating so fast she was shaking, but not from fear or guilt. It was from the overwhelming power that came with breaking free from living within the confines she had for so many years. And as much as she owed that strength to Ben, she owed even more of it to Derek. It was time for her to get it all out in the open.

When Ben finally met her gaze, his dark eyes softened, and he hauled her into an embrace. "Okay. You've got this, and I've got your back when you need me."

"Thank you." She sighed with relief.

When he let her go, he said, "I knew before Aurelia told me, but you can let her think she spilled the beans."

"What do you mean?"

"I was doing some due diligence on Derek tonight, thinking I might want to invest in his business. He's a smart guy, and his business plan is spot-on. He's going to be very wealthy one day, even though he doesn't want it or see it. I got the report right before Aurelia and I sat down to have a drink. I was going to talk with you tomorrow, but when she let it slip, something inside me snapped."

"That seems to be going around."

"Well, not that you asked, but his background is clean."

"*Of course* it is." She didn't like that Ben had run a background check on Derek, but when it came to investing, Ben was meticulous and scrutinizing. He crossed his t's and dotted his i's, and never made a move without doing thorough research. On that front, she'd expect nothing less from him.

"I'm sorry, Ben. I should have told you before everyone else."

"Nah. You're right. We're not kids anymore. But I still can't believe you're dating a dancer."

"Piper and I are going to see him dance. Want to come and see it for yourself?"

Ben scoffed as they walked back toward Aurelia and Piper. "Hell no. Dudes in G-strings?" He grabbed Aurelia's arm and dragged her toward his car. "Come on. We have business to take care of."

"Geez, you don't have to be so handsy." Aurelia looked over her shoulder and yelled, "Sorry, Talia!"

"What'd he say?" Piper asked as she and Talia headed for her car.

"Oh, you know Ben. Big-brother stuff."

"Want to stop by Mom and Dad's first so you can tell Dad about Derek's dancing while I'm there for backup?"

"No." Talia cringed inside, thinking about her father's text message to her mom. "I want to go see my man. No one else matters right now."

CHAPTER TWENTY-ONE

NEON LIGHTS DANCED across the stage like falling stars, slow and steady. Just when they seemed as though they'd stop, they faded away and more appeared. Derek thrust and gyrated his way through the spray of hot lights. The pungent aromas of perfume, musk, and desperation hung in the air. He sank down at the edge of the stage, staring above the heads of men and women with their arms outstretched, paying him for a few visual thrills. They tucked money into his G-string or tossed bills in his direction. He picked up a few bills scattered at his feet, closed his eyes, and pressed them to his chest, dragging them slowly down his body, thrusting to the beat of the music, until he hit his package and quickened his pelvic thrusts, earning cheers from the crowd. He pushed that money into the hip strap and tossed his hair, crossing the stage in a series of seductive moves.

The beat accelerated, and Derek whipped off his shirt, twirled it around his head as he tossed it to the crowd, earning more loud *whoops* and hollers. He dropped down to the ground, and put one hand behind his back, hammering out a series of hip thrusts. He went up on his knees, gyrating his way across the edge of the dance floor, collecting money every inch of the hip-grinding way.

He jumped up to his feet, staring above the heads of the crowd, wishing he were at home with Talia, but knowing this was what he had to do. The music sped up again, and the lights shot over the crowd, earning more cheers. Derek often focused on a picture on the walls to make it appear as if he were checking out someone in the back of the crowd, but tonight his gaze landed on a stunning woman with gorgeous dark hair, high cheekbones, and a slim, perky nose. Even in the dusky light, he knew his girl. His *careful* girl, who never came to see him dance, and yet she was there, watching him with a hungry expression, while seated with her sister.

With his eyes trained on Talia, his pulse kicked up, his every move precise and seductive, perfectly orchestrated just for *her*. She didn't look away, didn't bite that lower lip. *Holy fuck.* She pushed to her feet and strode toward the stage like she was on a mission, her pixie of a sister hurrying after her. The possessive look in her eyes was so freaking hot as she pushed her way through the crowd, up to the edge of the stage. He spun and gyrated, his eyes never leaving hers. He was going to make her proud, and if he was lucky, hot and bothered, because just the sight of her supporting him by being there made him want to carry her off to an island and love her into oblivion.

Piper shoved a handful of money into Talia's hands, and then Talia lifted those shaky hands toward him. Holy fuck, he was going to die. If ever there was a reason to dance, she was standing right there in front of him. The confidence she'd found gave way to pink cheeks as he slid down to his knees before her, legs spread wide, rocking his hips so close to her, she bit that sweet lower lip of hers. He'd go straight to hell for this, but he grabbed her face and kissed her hard. All the women squealed and cheered, offering to be next. The kiss lasted only a few seconds, but it made the whole damn night worthwhile.

Talia's eyes went wide as saucers. She grabbed Piper's arm and held out her hand. Piper gave her another handful of bills, and she waved them at him. *Oh baby, you wanna play?* He grabbed his crotch, rocking slow and purposefully. Then the music slowed, his cue that the song was almost over. He shot to his feet, moving toward the back of the stage. He pointed at Talia and mouthed, *Stay put.*

The song came to a crescendo, ending abruptly. Smoke filled the stage, and the crowd went wild. The end of his shift had finally arrived. He jumped off the stage, and the people parted like the Red Sea. With his eyes locked on Talia again, he hauled her into his arms, dancing to the regular music that kicked in after the last show. He was all too aware of everyone watching them, and he knew that though his show was over, the crowd expected more. Talia was beet-red, but she moved with him, and when she tried to hand the money back to Piper, he shook his head, took a step back, and glanced down, waggling his brows. Piper cheered her on as Talia's gaze followed his and she watched his hips pulse in slow gyrations. Talia's gaze darted around them. Yeah, it was unfair, but holy fucking hell, his girl was there, and he wanted everyone to know he was *hers.*

"Come on, baby," he urged. "Show them who I belong to."

A nervous smile lifted her lips, and the crowd went crazy as she shoved money into his G-string, and he danced just for her.

"I can't do any more! I'm shaking too much!" she hollered over the crowd, dollars falling from her fingers.

Piper tried to catch the money as it drifted to the floor.

He'd give Piper every dollar back, but first he pulled Talia into his arms and said, "I love you, Tallie girl! You're here, and you're amazing! Thank you!"

Talia looked shell-shocked, *elatedly* shell-shocked, as people cheered her on and commented about how lucky she was. They had no clue what they were talking about. Derek knew he was the lucky one. *Damn lucky.*

"Dude, that was freaking hot," Piper said.

Talia glared at Piper.

"In a very nonsexual, sister-appropriate way," Piper quickly added.

Talia hugged her. "I'm only kidding. He's crazy hot. Like, light-the-stage-on-fire hot, isn't he?" She threw her arms around his neck, pride beaming in her eyes. "And he's *mine*."

"Damn right I'm yours, baby."

Several steamy kisses later, he reluctantly went to change his clothes. When he returned, he found Talia standing alone with a big-breasted blonde who frequented the bar. She'd offered herself up on a silver platter a few times, and he'd turned her down. He didn't like her anywhere near his sweet Talia.

He slid his arm around Talia's waist as he came to her side and kissed her cheek. She stood rigidly beside him. "Hey, babe. Everything okay? Where's Piper?"

The voluptuous blonde watched them with a cold expression as she finished her drink.

"She's in the ladies' room," Talia said flatly.

"People have been spreading rumors about me for years," the blonde said. "It'll be nice to have the heat on someone else for a while." She winked at Derek and said, "Call me when you're ready to share."

"Not happening," he said, and guided Talia away from her. "What the fuck was that about?" he asked as Piper cut through the crowd.

"Nothing," Talia said, jaw tight.

"Was that the man eater?" Piper asked.

What the . . . ? "Man eater?"

"Don't ask." Talia headed for the door. "I've got to get out of here."

As they walked outside, he handed Piper an envelope. "Piper, this is for you. Thanks for bringing Talia out."

She peeked into the envelope, and her eyes widened. "I don't want your money! *She* brought *me*."

That surprised him, but he was too worried about Talia to think too much about the fact that Talia had initiated the outing. He tucked it away to revel in later.

"It's yours. You gave it to Talia." *Take the damn money so I can find out what's going on.* "Do you have a car here?"

"I do," Piper said. "Talia said she was going home with you."

Talia looked like she was ready to murder someone as they walked Piper to her car.

"Thanks, Tal. It was really great going out with you tonight." Piper embraced her. Then she gave Derek an awkward, stiff-armed *almost* hug and said, "It feels weird hugging you after seeing you in a G-string, but I'll get over it. Tal, I'll text you tomorrow."

As soon as Piper drove away, Talia said, "We have to talk."

His chest constricted. He must have embarrassed her too much with that last dance. Talia pushed her hands into her coat pockets as they headed around the building toward his car.

"Tallie, I'm sorry for coming off the stage and dancing with you like that. I was just so happy to see you there. It felt like you'd finally jumped the last hurdle and you were proud of me, and not embarrassed, or . . . Hell, I don't know what. It was just the greatest feeling, seeing you there at the front of the stage, having *your* hands on me, and I wanted everyone to know I was yours."

She didn't respond. Her eyes were trained on the pavement, shoulders rounded. He'd never seen her crawl so deep into herself. *Damn it.* He should have backed off, accepted what she'd given him, which was more than he'd ever expected, and not pushed it. When they came to his car, he embraced her.

"Babe, I'm really sorry. I will never, ever embarrass you again."

"It wasn't you."

The bite in her tone told him otherwise.

"You need to get home so Maria can leave," she reminded him. "We can talk on the way. I don't want to keep her waiting."

He ground his teeth together, knowing she was right and wishing he had a little flexibility in his schedule so he could put Talia first *all* the time. He opened her door, and when she was settled in her seat, he leaned in and took her hand in his. "I'm sorry we have to rush home."

"That has nothing to do with why I'm upset. I don't mind making concessions for your father, so please stop worrying that I do."

"Thanks, babe, but I'll always worry. It's kind of what I do."

"Well, this time you shouldn't."

Her voice still had an edge to it, one he knew meant she needed space. He just hoped the space she needed wasn't from him.

CHAPTER TWENTY-TWO

DEREK CRANKED THE engine and drove out of the parking lot, trying to figure out what the hell had gone wrong. He wanted to ask, to *push*, but pushing was probably what had gotten them into this situation, so instead he sat in miserable silence, waiting for her to explain. They drove for a few minutes in silence. The tension in the car was thicker than fog.

"It wasn't anything you did," she finally said, her tone cutting a little less deep. "It was me and that *witch* of a woman, Dina."

"*You?* Tallie, you didn't do anything wrong. There's nothing wrong with watching your boyfriend dance, for Pete's sake."

She finally lifted angry, watery eyes to him. "Not *that*. I should have given Dina hell, but I didn't. I let her threaten me, and now I have to worry about what she's going to say to my colleagues."

"Threaten you?" *What the fuck?* He wasn't going to sit by while *anyone* threatened her. "About what? What kind of threat?" He stopped at a red light. Talia looked so tortured, his protective urges surged forth. "Whatever it is, *I'll* take care of it."

She exhaled loudly. "No, you can't. She made this comment about sharing you and how she knew you'd be into it because dancers love to get down and dirty."

Motherfucker. The light turned green, and he sped through. "She's *wrong*, Talia. She's trying to get under your skin because she's propositioned me a few times and I turned her down flat. I'm not one of those guys who fucking *shares*." He reached for her hand as he turned on to his street. "Babe, I'd *never* do that. Not with you or anyone else. Ever. She probably doesn't even know who you work for, so—"

"She's my colleague at school," Talia said evenly. "People are always gossiping about her, and she's threatening to tell them that I'm dating a stripper."

He parked in front of the house. "Why would they care? And I'm not a stripper. I'm a dancer. But that shouldn't matter anyway. Can your boss fire you for dating me?"

"No! You're not my student. It shouldn't matter. But I don't want her telling everyone you're a stripper and making our relationship seem dirty and wrong."

"Then let's go talk to your boss. The two of us. We'll explain what's going on, and—"

"It doesn't work that way," she said with an exasperated sigh. "People *talk*. You can't stop them."

"Then why worry about it, Talia? I mean, I know you've been too embarrassed to come and watch me dance, but this is what I do for a living and will be for the foreseeable future. It's not going to change. Did you think people wouldn't find out?"

"No!" she said adamantly, and then in a slightly defeated voice she said, "I don't know what I thought, but I definitely don't want her making us out to be the type of couple that *would* share or that was into skanky things."

Christ, how could he not have seen this coming? He knew how private she was, and it was one of the reasons he'd been shocked to see her at the bar tonight. "Well, it clearly worries you, so let's figure out how to stop it from happening."

"We can't. I know we can't. It's just been a shitty evening all around, and I'm pissed at myself for not giving her hell when she said it. I just stood there looking at her. I couldn't believe she was there, or that she was saying it to me. I mean, she *knows* me. She knows I'd never share myself, much less share the man I love. But I was in shock, and . . ." She exhaled and looked out the window.

"Hey." He gently guided her face back toward his, slayed by the sadness in her eyes. "Babe, we'll get through this. If I have to personally meet every one of your colleagues to show them I'm not a lowlife, I'll do it."

The porch light came on, and his heart sank. *Fucking hamster wheel.*

"I have to tell you something else," she said tentatively. "But why don't we let Maria go home, and then we can talk. I don't want to hold her up."

With a hundred worries racing through his mind, he helped her from the car and embraced her. "Whatever it is, it'll be okay."

They went inside, and he hoped to hell he was right.

"Your father had a very good night, *mijo*." Maria handed him a drawing of his father and Louie standing in front of the shark tank at the aquarium. "He said that was you. Today's outing was very good for him." She pressed her hands to her chest, her expression grateful. It was the same look she had when she witnessed his father's cogent moments. "Talia, your family . . . Please thank them for me. They did a nice thing today."

"They enjoyed their time with Jonah, too," Talia said. "My sister Willow is hosting a brunch a week from Sunday. We're celebrating my sister Bridgette's pregnancy. I'd really like for you and Jonah to be there."

Relief swept through Derek. She was making future plans with his father. That had to be a good sign.

"I would love that." Maria embraced Talia, and then she touched Derek's cheek and said, "Why so serious, *mijo*? Life is good."

"I'm just tired." He glanced at Talia, wondering what else she had to talk to him about. Talia smiled sheepishly, and that sweet smile coalesced with the anguish in her eyes, tugging at his heartstrings.

"Late nights." Maria winked as she put on her coat. "Sometimes tired is a good thing."

After she left, Derek locked the door and helped Talia off with her coat before stripping out of his own. "Do you want something to eat? Drink?"

She shook her head.

He took her hand, pulling her against him. "We're not going to yell at each other, are we? Because if we are, I think we'd better talk outside."

"I'm not a yeller. Are you?" She looked a little worried.

Now he was the one shaking his head. He tipped her chin up and kissed her lips. "I can't imagine yelling at you, but I'm worried about whatever it is you have to tell me."

He took her hand and led her into the living room. He set the picture his father had drawn on the coffee table and sank down to the couch, bringing Talia down beside him. "Why was tonight so shitty?"

She fidgeted with the seam of her jeans. "I'm afraid to tell you."

"Jesus, Talia. That is *not* what a guy wants to hear." He pulled back, having no idea what to expect, because the first thing that came to mind was too ridiculous to give it any credence. What could she be afraid to tell him other than that she'd been with someone else, which wasn't even a possibility. She was too honest, too good a person to do that. "Are you afraid I'll be mad?"

"Hurt," she said, and the crack in her voice gutted him.

He crossed his arms, needing the barrier after hearing that. "Go ahead. Tell me."

She nervously chewed on her lower lip. "When we were shopping today, one of my friends, Aurelia Stark, recognized you from the club."

He didn't recognize the name, and the few women he'd hooked up with over the past couple of years didn't go to the club. "So?"

"She said you were a stripper in front of my mom and sisters, and I hadn't told them that you danced."

His gut seized. "You hadn't *told* them? All this time? I assumed they knew."

She shook her head. "They knew you worked at a bar."

"Talia . . . ?" He pushed to his feet and paced.

She went to him. "I didn't know how to tell them. I wanted to several times, but Piper kept making jokes, and I didn't want to have to deal with everyone's questions or—"

"I knew this was an issue," he interrupted. "But I didn't realize it was that *big* of an issue." He dragged a hand through his hair and stared at her. His heart felt like it was folding in on itself, crushing uncomfortably. He loved her so much he ached with it, but he couldn't be with her if she couldn't truly accept who he was.

"It's *not*," she insisted, closing the distance between them. "I told them everything, and Ben, too. And I'll tell my father tomorrow. I just . . . I've never been in this position before, and I don't care what they think. I love you, Derek, and I love your father. But for whatever reason, telling my family was hard for me."

He gritted his teeth against the burning in his gut. "Because you're ashamed of what I do?"

"No," she said harshly. "I'm not. I promise I'm not. I just didn't know what to say or how to tell them."

He glared at her, knowing by the way she was clenching her mouth that she was holding something back. "What else? Just tell me, Talia. Let's get this over with."

Her lower lip trembled again. "At the very beginning, the first time I saw you dance, I was jealous of all the women going crazy over you, and I worried that if Piper knew you danced, she'd go to the bar looking sexy and confident, and . . . *Oh my God*, this is so bad. I'm such a loser."

She sat on the couch and lowered her face to her hands. She looked up with damp eyes. "I know my faults. I know I'm not one of those girls who dresses sexy and exudes that kind of confidence. I will never be that type of person, and I know how much of a turn-on it is for guys to see those girls."

His heart was breaking, slicing right down the middle. He knew how badly she'd been hurt, and it killed him that those thoughts even went through her mind. He sat on the coffee table in front of her, and when she looked at him, the vulnerability in her eyes cut him even deeper. "And you didn't trust me enough, or know me well enough yet, to realize that I have zero interest in those types of women? No offense to your sister. She's pretty and all, but she's not you, Talia. No one is. Don't you know that by now?"

"Yes! I do. Don't you see? Not telling them wasn't about you. It was because of my insecurities at first, and then it became something else altogether. I didn't care what they thought, which, to be honest, *also* scared me. This is the first time in my life that I have ever—*ever*—put aside what anyone else might think for what *I* want. And I know I hurt you, and I know how terrible it looks that I didn't tell them." Tears slid down her cheeks. "Trust me, I *definitely* know how bad this looks. But it's not because I'm ashamed of you or what you do. You're the most admirable person I know."

"But that doesn't tell me why you didn't tell them after you knew me well enough to realize that I'd never hurt you and I'd never be interested in that kind of woman. Unless . . ." *You still don't?*

"I know," she said sadly. "I'm not sure I understand all of it, either, but I can tell you what I do know. When I got past the jealousy, I became protective of us. I didn't want to have to explain any of it to anyone because I was so happy with you. I didn't want any negativity, and that's when I realized that I didn't care what my family thought, which was scary in and of itself, but it was true. And then I guess it was just stupidity. Or maybe rebellion. I don't know. I probably should have just stood up and told them, but I didn't. I just . . ." She shrugged. "That's why I went to the bar tonight, and why I brought Piper. I wanted to prove to everyone—and probably to myself, too—that *nothing* could keep me away from you."

She wiped at her tears and said, "I never claimed to have much experience with relationships, but I did what I felt was right at the time."

He ached for both of them as he took her hand in his. "You know, I worried that my father would be too much for us, but I never gave dancing the same weight in our relationship. I probably should have. Just because it's not who *I* am doesn't mean it's not who other people see me as. Like who that blonde at the bar thinks I am. I understand that now, Talia. And I guess I thought that since you teach about the impact that societal expectations and assumptions have on people, you had this, you know? I assumed you'd tell your family and be as up front with them as I have been with you."

"I'm sorry."

"No, don't be, babe. That's *my* fault. I've got a chip on my shoulder the size of an iceberg. If people don't like who I am or what I do, then that's on them. Taking care of my father has always come first. It's always been the two of us, with Maria, of course. But it's time for me to get a grip on that, too. I want a future with *you*, and I have to think about how the things I do impact your life, not just my own."

"I don't want you to change anything—"

"I can't change things, and I won't stop doing what I have to do. But that doesn't mean I should expect you to flaunt what I do for a living. Maybe you did the right thing by waiting—until you trusted me, until your family knew I was worthy of their daughter *slash* sister."

"I'll never *not* tell anyone again," she said quickly. "It's a weird situation to explain, but I'm okay now. I know I can do it and hold my chin up high, and I want to carry some of that iceberg with you."

Her lips curved up, and the sincerity in her eyes healed the fissures inside him. He rose to his feet, bringing her up with him, and gathered her in his arms. "You want to share my iceberg?"

"Yes." She wound her arms around his neck. "But in all fairness, have you ever thought about what it would be like to tell your father, or Maria, that you were dating a woman who took off her clothes in front of strangers?"

"Do you have a secret second job I should know about?"

She shook her head. "All kidding aside, I *am* sorry. I should have told my family. I feel guilty for having kept it from them, but not so much because they need to know what's going on in my life. You've helped me become more comfortable with myself and the decisions I make that might not be what other people expect of me. Mostly I feel guilty because of how not telling them could be misconstrued into embarrassment over what you do. I am so in love with the man you are, I never want anyone to think otherwise. I love your generous heart and your confidence, and . . ." Her cheeks pinked up. "I think I've developed a thing for you in a G-string, so . . ."

"Aw, baby." He pressed his lips to hers. "How about you give me five minutes to shower off the stench of the bar and I'll give you your own private show?"

She took his hand, walking backward toward his bedroom. "I was thinking I could join you in the shower and maybe you can teach me some of your moves." She turned around and whipped off her sweater as she walked through the bedroom door. She dropped her sweater to the floor, looked over her shoulder as she stepped into the bathroom, and said, "Your turn."

CHAPTER TWENTY-THREE

TALIA AWOKE TO the sound of Derek playing his guitar. She lay on her back listening to him singing in the other room and wondered if his father had woken up agitated or if Derek had had trouble sleeping. It had been a month since she'd told her family about Derek's dancing. The next morning Derek had gone with her to tell her father, who had looked at Derek with such a serious expression, Talia had thought her father might give him hell. But he had shocked them both and said, *My grandfather used to say that you could only know what a person was truly made of when they faced the worst kind of adversity. You not only put yourself out there for the sake of your father, but you've learned from a difficult situation, and you're going to put that knowledge to good use by helping others in a big way. But, son, you've just told me that dancing is what you do, not who you are, and I beg to differ. Everything you do is part of who you are, and if I were you, I'd be damned proud of it. You're accomplishing things not many people could and putting yourself on the line to do so.*

She'd never been prouder to be her father's daughter than she was right then.

She closed her eyes, listening to Derek singing "God, Your Mama, and Me" and thinking about their lives. Derek had gotten even closer to her family, and he'd also become good friends with Fletch. Sometimes she and Derek took Jonah to the park to meet Fletch and Molly. If Jonah was having a good day, they all walked Molly together, and if not, they made the best of the time outdoors. Her mind traveled to last night, when she'd been talking to Fletch on the phone and Derek had texted from work, telling her it was a slow night and he wished she were there. Fletch had teased her about being a swoony-in-love girl, which she happily admitted to. She'd gone to see Derek at the bar a few times since the night she'd run into Dina. Each time had taken a little less courage. Her palms no longer sweat and her pulse no longer raced at the idea of watching him dance. She and Derek had decided not to play into Dina's hands and had ignored her threat. There was power in knowing who they were as a couple, and Talia reveled in the beauty of them each and every day. These days, when she went to see Derek at work, whether he was dancing or bartending, once she caught sight of him, her love for him obliterated everything other than the reason she was there—to support her man.

She rolled onto her side and found one of Derek's leather journals on his pillow. A single red rose and a handwritten note were tucked beneath the leather strap that was wound around it. She glanced at the doorway, her insides tingling at his romantic gesture. She read his loopy script.

For you, sweet girl.

She sat up with the journal in her lap and sniffed the rose, wondering what he was up to. She opened to the first page, which was filled with hearts surrounding the words *Loving Talia*. The heart dotting the *i* in her name was pink, the only color on the page.

She turned the page, surprised to find another note.

Tallie girl,
I know you asked me to keep our sexy times out of the journals, but this one is just for us, not for public consumption. More specifically, it's just for you, so you have

something to look back on when our lives get crazy and caring for my father gets overwhelming. In those times, I hope you'll turn these pages and remember we're worth celebrating . . .
—*Derek*

A lump formed in Talia's throat as she turned the page. That lump was pushed aside by a soft laugh at a drawing of their legs tangled together, the rest of their bodies cut off by the edge of the paper. The caption read, *No matter what happens, at the end of the day we'll always come together.*

Her insides fluttered as she turned the page. "Oh my God," she whispered to the empty room. The picture showed Derek lying above her on the bed, drawn from the waist up, pinning her hands to the mattress above her head, his long hair blocking their faces. The caption read, *No matter how busy our lives get, we'll always fit our workouts in.*

Her pulse quickened as she looked over the next few drawings. The first showed only their intertwined hands coming down from the top of the page. His father's bracelets puddled at his wrist, and his mother's ring was sparkling yellow. The next drawing showed them making love in the hot tub, and on the next page there was a picture of Derek standing by the bed, drawn from the back, naked, with Talia kneeling before him, her face hidden by his body. The caption read *We help each other through the hard times.*

She flipped the page and felt her cheeks burning at a drawing of them making love against the wall at the ski resort with the caption, *We'll never tire of finding new comfort zones . . .*

She pressed the journal to her chest and breathed deeply, as memories of that delicious night came rushing back, and love for her man swelled inside her. She lowered the journal and turned another page, revealing a picture of them sleeping, his body cocooning hers. Above the picture he'd written, *I will always protect you.*

A happy sigh slipped from her lips.

The next picture showed her sitting on the ceramic bench in the shower, water raining down over her. Derek knelt before her, hands on her thighs, a wicked grin on his face. The caption read, *We'll never go hungry and always eat organic* . . .

Her sex twitched at the suggestion. "Holy cow," she whispered.

She turned the page and found a picture of Derek pacing beside the bed while she slept, worry riddling his brow. She had on a pink tank top like the one she wore now. In a thought bubble above his head was a picture of a key. She quickly turned the page. In the next picture he was leaning against the doorframe with the same furrowed brow, wearing a pair of jeans and a dark T-shirt, his dazzling blue eyes beckoning her. In a thought bubble above his head was a picture of him and Talia carrying suitcases into his house.

Oh my God.

She felt his presence and glanced at the door. Her heart leapt at the sight of Derek leaning against the doorframe, wearing the same clothes as in the picture, the same furrowed expression. It was such a vulnerable, adorable look, it took a moment for her to reconcile it with the virile man before her.

"Hey, baby." He pushed from the wall and strode toward her.

"Hi," she said breathlessly as he crawled onto the bed.

He looked nervous, and her stomach tumbled. She wanted to say so much—*I love the drawings. I love you. Why do you look nervous?*—but she was afraid if she tried to speak she might choke.

"I've been up for a while." He tucked her hair behind her ear, and she caught a whiff of his cologne. "I've been thinking . . ."

She held her breath.

"You stay here every night, and have been for weeks. I don't want to have to call you to meet me after work, or worry about whether you have enough clothes here. I love you. My dad loves you. Maria loves you . . ." He took her hand in his and said, "Tallie, I want you with me every night without question, in the mornings, weekends, whenever we can be together. I don't want to waste a minute of our lives waiting for signs or social acceptances. I want you to move in with me, with us." He opened his hand, dropping a key into her palm, and curled her fingers around it. "I know it's a strange thing to ask, moving in with me and my father, and I won't blame you if you say no. You can think about it, but if nothing else, please take the key—"

Her tears sprang free, and she threw her arms around his neck. "I love you, and I love your dad. I want to be with you more than anything, and your father is part of your life, and he's become part of mine. That's a good thing, not a strange thing."

"Even if he calls you Eva? Or says you don't belong here?"

There had been a few times when Jonah thought she was a stranger and it had taken some time to calm him down, but they'd worked through it together. The three of them.

"Eva is a compliment, and . . ." She patted the journal. "When he says I don't belong here, I'll refer to this handy-dandy *love* guide. It'll be just another *hard* time to work through."

"God, I love you, baby. So, is that a yes?"

"That's a yes. A definite yes."

"Good, because if you said no, then I couldn't do this." He stepped from the bed and drew her up beside him. Then he dropped to one knee, stealing the breath from her lungs.

A wave of love swept through her so hard, she reached for his shoulder to stabilize herself.

He took her hand, gazing up at her like she was all he ever wanted, and said, "Tallie girl, you are my other half, my better half, my beloved, and I want to spend the rest of our lives exploring new comfort zones and sharing private dances."

Tears streamed down her cheeks. She wasn't sure she was even breathing as he rose to his feet.

"I want to get tested to see if I have the gene mutation, because you make me want to live forever and have our biological babies and do everything together. And if I carry the gene, we'll take another route. But for you, I want to find out. I want to make all your dreams come true, even the ones you don't realize you have yet. Will you marry me, Talia? Let me love you for the rest of our lives?"

"Yes," came out choked and teary as she threw herself into his arms. "Yes, yes, *yes!*"

"I will love you forever, baby," he said as he lowered his lips to hers, sealing his promises with a tender kiss. He took her left hand in his and slipped his mother's ring on her finger. "I'll get you your own ring if you'd like. We can design it to be whatever you want."

"You're all I want. This ring is perfect. *You're* perfect."

"We're perfect, baby," he said just as his father called out, "Archie?" He kissed her smiling lips and said, "I can't wait to marry you."

"Me too."

"Archie? Where are you?" Jonah's voice was coming closer to the bedroom.

"If I have to be Archie today," Derek said playfully, "maybe you can be Betty or Veronica." He waggled his brows.

She narrowed her eyes. "A word of caution. The day you call me someone else's name in bed is the day you see my ass walk out that door and never come back. That's a *hard* limit."

"Archie?" his father called out.

"We're up to hard limits now?" He stepped toward the door with a wolfish grin. "You really *do* want to push your boundaries. Good to know."

She threw the pillow at him as he left the room, unable to calm her full, happy heart or suppress her own naughty grin. She looked down at the ring on her finger, feeling whole and happy and knowing that after the day-care facility was open, there would probably be more people calling them by many different names. There would be interruptions and frustrations, but she also knew that at the end of the day, those people would be loved and taken care of, and she and Derek would fall into each other's arms, making it all worthwhile.

A NOTE FROM MELISSA

Spending time with the Dalton family is one of my favorite escapes, and watching Talia and Derek find their happily ever after was a joy. I often tackle heavy topics that don't usually make it into romance novels, and when I met Derek and Jonah, I knew their story had to be told. During my research it became apparent that every family's experience with Alzheimer's is different, and while it was at times heartrending, I hope you enjoyed spending time in Derek and Jonah's world.

I hope you'll also enjoy *Loving Talia*, the companion booklet to *Love Like Ours*, which depicts the images Derek and his father drew in this book along with a few bonus features.

Sign up for my newsletter to keep up-to-date with my new releases and to receive an exclusive short story (www.MelissaFoster.com/News).

If this is your first Melissa Foster book, you might enjoy the rest of my big-family romance collection, Love in Bloom. Characters from each series make appearances in future books so you never miss an engagement, wedding, or birth. A complete list of all series titles is included at the start of this book.

Happy reading!

Melissa Foster

ACKNOWLEDGMENTS

Writing a book is not a solo endeavor, and I am indebted to my fans, friends, and family, who inspire and support me on a daily basis. It would be impossible to thank all the people I met while researching early-onset Alzheimer's, but a special word of thanks goes to Professor Dale Cohen, PhD, University of North Carolina, Wilmington, and to Cyndi Oglesby Duke, both of whom fielded my endless questions at odd hours.

If you'd like sneak peeks into my writing process and to chat with me daily, please join my fan club on Facebook. We have such fun chatting about our lovable heroes and sassy heroines, and I always try to keep fans abreast of what's going on in our fictional boyfriends' worlds. You never know when you'll end up in one of my books, as several members of my fan club have already discovered (www.Facebook.com/groups/MelissaFosterFans).

Follow my Facebook fan page to keep up with sales and events (www.Facebook.com/MelissaFosterAuthor).

If this is your first Melissa Foster book, you have many fiercely loyal heroes and sassy, empowered heroines to catch up on in my Love in Bloom big-family romance collection. You can start with several free first-in-series (www.MelissaFoster.com/LIBFree).

Remember to sign up for my newsletter to keep up-to-date with new releases and special promotions and events and to receive an exclusive short story (www.MelissaFoster.com/Newsletter).

For publication schedules, series checklists, and more, please visit the special reader goodies page that I've set up for you at www.MelissaFoster.com/Reader-Goodies.

A special thank-you to editor Maria Gomez and the incredible Montlake team for bringing Talia and Derek's story to life. As always, heaps of gratitude to my editorial team and, of course, to my very own hunky hero, Les.

ABOUT THE AUTHOR

Photo © 2013 Melanie Anderson

Melissa Foster is a *New York Times* and *USA Today* bestselling and award-winning author of more than sixty-five books, including *The Real Thing* and *Only for You* in the Sugar Lake series. Her novels have been recommended by *USA Today*'s book blog, *Hagerstown* magazine, the *Patriot*, and others. She has also painted and donated several murals to the Hospital for Sick Children in Washington, DC.

She enjoys discussing her books with book clubs and reader groups, and she welcomes an invitation to your event. Visit Melissa on her website, www.MelissaFoster.com, or chat with her on Twitter @melissa_foster and on Facebook at www.facebook.com/MelissaFosterAuthor.